MW00937134

POSSESSION
AVENUES INK SERIES - BOOK 1

A.M. JOHNSON

Cover design by Mary Ruth
Cover model: Dylan Horsch
Cover photography by R. Dodson Photography
Editing and Formatting by Elaine York,
Allusion Graphics, LLC/Publishing & Book Formatting
www.allusiongraphics.com

TO THOSE WHO CAN'T STOP THE VOICES...
PAINT THEM, WRITE THEM—SET THEM FREE.

FOR SARAH S.
THANK YOU FOR GIVING DECLAN A PAINT BRUSH,
AND LET'S ALWAYS SAY CHEERS TO OUR DARK DAYS,
BECAUSE WITHOUT THEM, THE LIGHT WOULDN'T
BE AS BRIGHT.

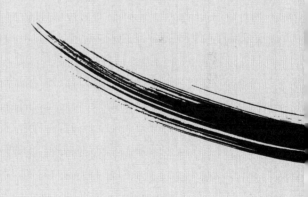

I would blow the flame out of your silver cup,
I would suck the rot from your fingernail,
I would brush your sprouting hair of the dying
light,
I would scrape the rust off your ivory bones,
I would help death escape through
the little ribs of your body,
I would alchemize the ashes of your
cradle back into wood,
I would let nothing of you go, ever...

"The Book of Nightmares"
Galway Kinnell

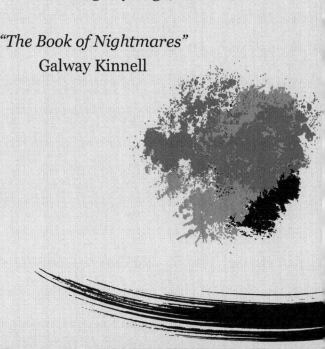

PROLOGUE

DECLAN

There are real reasons to be afraid. I learned that at a young age. I learned that no matter how hard you pray, or beg God to save you, the Devil sends demons. They whispered in my ear, they formed in my heart, and they walked this Earth as spirits—ghosts. You'd never know it if you saw one. They changed, they shifted, they burned right through you until you were ruined, until you were no longer the man you thought you once were. They scratched, and left you shaking. I'd seen it first-hand as a child, and I'd felt their presence, but it wasn't until her that these impressions took form, becoming more than just the voices in my head.

My devil... my curse... had pale blonde hair and a pair of blue eyes that captured my soul with one look. Her one kiss, I'd thought it would last a lifetime...

It wasn't until her that I really knew fear, loss, and a fathomless darkness that swallowed me whole. It wasn't until she possessed me, sank her claws into my flesh, showing me how worthless I could feel, that I found out what it felt like to be truly alone.

DECLAN

The sun had just set, and the heat was slowly evaporating from the steel of the street lamps, hovering over the surface of the concrete. Summer in the city, it was fucking exhausting. The tattoo shop's neon sign, Avenues Ink, blinked before it finally blacked out. My older brother, Liam, was still inside cleaning, counting the cash of the day, and working—always working. The bar down the street was already spilling people from its front door. It was only eleven-thirty, but the night owls and the intoxicated jocks had begun to stumble onto the streets. Drunk on easy women and smiling with vodka-tainted lips. It wasn't my scene, but the bass of Bellows always called to me. The hard thump... thump... thump... quieted the voices, if only for the evening.

A tall, thin girl in an electric-blue dress giggled as she passed me, and her eyes skimmed the muscles under my shirt. To them I seemed attractive. My blond hair and light eyes, the hours at the gym evident under the sinew, the swirl of ink on my arms, hiding away under the soft cover of cotton. I was a spectacle, and their eyes poured over me like I was a goddamn

Rembrandt; unaware of the poison that brewed deep inside the decay of my heart. The dangerous whispers that rotted my brain, and the lost soul that muddied the water blue of my eyes. Ever since her, since Paige, I'd never been the same.

She isn't coming.

The whispers inside my temples had grown louder each day. My mother called Father Hollard last week, and I'd lied to him and said I was fine. He still marked my forehead with oil and murmured some shit under his breath. I'd been forced to do several rosaries that night. It wasn't until my dad staggered in drunk, smelling of whiskey and stale tobacco that my mother gave me leave. My knees had become sore from kneeling for so long. The memory almost made me rub the now phantom pain from my knees, but I thought better of it.

The charcoal stained my fingers as I painted my last nightmare across the paper. Dark black eyes met mine from the stiff, white parchment. The building behind the specter crumbled, and one word floated in gray swirls of ink above the brick that I had drawn.

Paige.

She isn't for you.

Over and over the voice advised me.

I closed my eyes and listened to the kids mumble outside in the courtyard. I tried to discern words, and separate what was real from the hell that was leaking through my brain.

My class had about fifteen minutes left of the lunch period. I'd hoped that once I started high school I'd have learned how to hide it better, but the older I got the worse it became. I'd heard voices since I was thirteen, seen things, in life and in dreams, I was sure other kids couldn't. I'd paint them, bleed them onto paper. It was the only way the toxic thoughts were purged. My mother had said I was possessed, trapped between worlds. My older brother, Liam, said I was just fucking crazy, my father... wasn't sober enough to care. No one really paid me any mind until my younger brother, Kieran, found me with a noose around my neck. It had taken a failed attempt at death to get their attention.

Depression with psychotic features was the diagnosis.

I was psychotic.

I was rare.

I was a freak.

The warning bell sounded and I raised my eyes from the drawing on my lap. Had it really rang? Some of the kids stood and emptied their trays, but the rest still continued to eat— shoving their faces with gossip and idle bullshit. It was then the light of the sun glittered in the way it always did when it caught a glimpse of her. The facets of light shone and drew me, pulled me from my dark world of black inks and sad murals. She painted the world in color, and her pale skin was almost translucent in the mid-day sun.

She isn't real.

But she was, of that I was sure. She was lonely like me. The girls around her smiled and laughed and she'd nod her head in agreement. Her eyes gave her away, they were blank, void of real emotion, but every day, she'd gift me a glance, just one, and I'd watch the emptiness of her clear glass eyes fill with a brilliant shade of blue. She'd come alive and today was no different. The voices in my head raged, screamed, and pounded my pulse faster. They told me I wasn't good enough, told me she was a figment of my imagination, told me I'd never get the chance. They tried to force my eyes shut so I couldn't see the masterpiece in front of me. I wouldn't blink. I couldn't miss out on the moment. The moment when her lips

4

would finally separate into a small, timid smile, and those alabaster cheeks would turn a slight hue of pink.

She dropped her gaze and the girls around her giggled, never really seeing her, never really understanding how lucky they were to be near her. I kept my eyes on her as I pushed the earbuds deeper into my ears, and pressed play on my hand-me-down mp3 player. The deep bass of the beat drowned out all the voices as I flipped the paper to a blank sheet and began to draw her. I'd buy some colored pencils today, try to make the likeness of her more real. My head was down, and I was sketching her eyes—always her eyes. I hadn't been prepared.

A dark silhouette cast on the ground before me and I lifted my head. My voice caught in my throat as she smiled down on me. Her friends were walking toward the building and she pointed to her watch. I removed the earbuds.

"You'll be late," she said and the color in her eyes moved and liquefied under the rays of the sun.

I nodded.

"Don't you speak?" She laughed, it was easy, soft— perfect. "It's Declan, right?"

Was she really standing in front of me, or was this my crazy finally raising to a whole new level of fucked. I glanced behind her, and the rest of the students dumped their trays, grabbed their packs, just like every other day, but instead of watching her small frame retreat into the glass building, she stood before me.

"Come on, Paige." One of her friends lingered, waiting, looking at me with a frown.

Her eyes flicked to the paper of my art book and back at me. I'd just barely begun to outline the unearthly pair of eyes and now, seeing the real thing up close, I realized I'd never recreate them, never do them justice. I swallowed and found the courage to look at her, really look at her, each pore—each detail. The hair on the back of my neck stood as she drew her gaze from the paper and her lips tipped down.

"Those eyes look sad."

"They are." My voice was scratchy from lack of use, and her lips opened with a small smile.

"Why do you draw such sad things?" she asked as she pushed a strand of her blonde hair behind her ear. It was then I noticed her hand was shaking.

"I just draw what I see." I draw sadness, evil, hate, love... you.

Her feet fidgeted inward as her eyes sparked with questions and her brow knotted. "Don't be late. Mr. Ferris is giving a pop quiz. My friend, Lana, has him first period." She fought her nerves by biting her lip.

There were a million things I wanted to say, to ask, but I'd learned the normal social shit. "You can't just blurt what you're thinking, little bro." "Smile, Declan." "Just say hello, shake hands, and move on." "Don't stare." "Stop whispering." The words of my family embedded in my brain as I stared at the one thing I'd ever wanted, and I'd never have.

"Thanks for the heads up." It sounded normal in my head, and when her lips spread farther I chanced a smile, as well.

She nodded, and her friend called to her again, my eyes fell from hers to the paper, to the misinterpretation of her eyes. She hesitated for a moment, but once she walked away I raised my head. Her heat still hovered around me, and the smell of clean air filled my lungs.

It was just as the door to the lunch room shut that I noticed the quiet. Not one word whispered, not one sound rumbled in my thoughts. I'd taken pills for the past year, therapy, priests... but Paige... she silenced them, she brought the still, simple silence with her, and only in her absence would I feel the weight of my depression; the chatter of my demons.

She's salvation.

The bass of the club vibrated in my chest as I sipped from my glass of water. At times I wished I could drink. I wished I could lose myself in a bottle, a glass, a moment, but I'd never be like him, like my father, and the meds I took didn't mix well with alcohol. Instead, I'd sit in a dark corner and sketch, just like always, just like when I was a kid. My subjects changed. My landscapes more urban. I'd traded beauty for realism. Traded *her*, for fantasy. Traded reality for fiction. It was open mic night at Bellows. The wannabe hip-hop kings of Salt Lake made an appearance. White boys bred on wealth and luck. The sideways hats, the low-rise jeans—it was hard not to laugh. On occasion, I'd be surprised. Someone with actual talent would grace the stage, and I'd stop what I was doing, catch a glimpse of purity. Tonight the pickings were slim.

Tonight I cowered in my corner and sketched my latest dream. My work over the years had become darker. Like film noir on paper. The colors chosen were always specific, but the black ink, the slate color of my pencils, they covered the paper with smooth illusions and shadowed flickers of my thoughts.

Can't you hear them, they're whispering.

As an adult it was easier to ignore the voices and to convince the doctors that I was actually hearing shit. Eventually, I got a new label: Schizoaffective. My meds helped mostly with my depression, but tamed the beast inside my head enough to survive the day-to-day. I felt like a zombie most days, rowing through the motions of life, and I hated it. Lately though, the more I thought about Paige, the more they erupted past my walls of defense I'd spent so many years building.

I lifted my eyes and scanned the room. Two younger women were sitting at the bar. Their eyes trained on the frat boy on the stage giving some cheesy fucking rendition of

Eminem's *"Lose Yourself"*. They indeed were whispering, giggling, and smiling at each other as if they had a plan. But, there was only one of him and two of them. My lips twitched with a smirk. Sometimes being an observer wasn't half bad. The one on the right was tall and curvy with big tits, but she was trying too hard with her red lipstick, low-cut tank top, and short skirt. The other girl was soft, small, and her eyes held a certain sadness I'd seen a lot of in this place. She needed that guy on stage for her own security. Needed him to tell her she was special, to make her feel something other than just being the friend of the girl who always got everything. She'd tell herself she'd never have a chance with Captain Tool Bag on stage because she'd never be easy enough, pretty enough.

You see the world, Declan... you see it.

My throat narrowed and my jaw clenched. The voice in my head mocked me with Paige's words. I was so intent on sifting through my own thoughts that I hadn't noticed the small, shy girl noticing me. Her smile was tentative as she caught me staring. I didn't have the heart to drop my gaze, to let her know I wasn't really looking at her, that I was lost in the haze that was Declan-fucking-O'Connell. I lifted my chin at her and gave her a slight smile. I was polite, if nothing else, and I brought my attention back to the drawing. *Her* eyes always had a way of showing up in every piece of art I'd created since the day I met her. Whether it was the actual shape, or the color, or just the feeling they'd produced in my soul, they would bloom on the canvas, the paper, my flesh. My pencil stopped moving, and I turned my arm over. Scrolled in thick black ink, the words I'd heard earlier were there... *You see the world.* The O inside 'you' was in the shape of her eye. The ghostly light blue of her iris was the only color I had on my body. The rest of my ink was black or with shades of gray and white.

8

I fell into the pupil and let the power of her stare swallow me whole.

"Do you write comics?" a quiet voice trembled.

I closed my eyes briefly, just for a second, to gather myself before raising my gaze. She had a Meat is Murder t-shirt on with tight, dark blue skinny jeans. Her hair was black and shiny under the dim lights of the bar. She was shorter up close, maybe not even five feet.

"I'm a huge nerd for all things comic book-related." She bit her glossy lip at the corner and surveyed my drawing.

I'd barely started it. The alleyway was dark and shaded by nightfall. I'd depicted a looming figure in the background. A set of empty eyes peering from a window. I glanced over her shoulder; her friend had made her move with the shitty watered-down version of Marshall Mathers. He was already standing between her legs, his lips at her ear. Sometimes I wondered what it would be like to lose yourself in a stranger. The girl's smile started to fall as I brought my attention back to her. The overhead music was loud and it took me a minute to find the words.

"I'm not much of a writer," I said with little interest in the hope that she'd move along.

Her small hand rested on the table as she sat in the chair across from me.

I want to use you to make myself feel better, make my friend jealous.

I blinked and my eyes landed on her mouth. "Excuse me?"

"I said is it okay if I have a seat?" Her brows narrowed at the expression on my face.

The music, the thin layer of e-cigarette smoke, the pungent odor of vanilla all blended together and fucking confused me. Her voice was too reluctant, and I had a hard time hearing her. She was speaking now. The words flowed from rapid lips, but

9

not a sound broke through the anxious ringing in my ears. I began to tap my foot, breathing through the panic. I didn't talk to people. Just my brothers, just my clients at the tattoo shop.

"Hey, I think... yeah... you did my brother's back piece. You work at Avenues Ink, right?" The high keen of her voice broke through the barrier.

I found myself, gave her a nod and a tight smile. "I do."

Her smile broadened and the white of her teeth felt too clean for this place. "I knew I recognized you. What's your name?" She leaned in, eager for my words.

I hadn't been with anyone since Paige. Not one girl. I tried. A year after we'd split, she'd gotten married, and I figured out she would never come back. I'd seen a few chicks, but it always ended at the first kiss. My life, the love I had for her, I'd never find it again, and I fucking hated her for ruining me, for stealing my soul.

She destroyed you.

"Declan." I answered a bit too late, and I watched as the puzzlement flashed across her features.

I should have asked her what her name was, but I didn't care. She was pretty. I liked that she was an odd little thing. I liked that she kept looking down at my art pad and that her eyes glittered with excitement. I ran my hand through my hair, and her eyes trailed along my bicep.

"My name's Kate." She offered me her hand, and I stared at it as she giggled. "I don't bite."

I took her hand and the heat of it felt foreign in my grip. The bone structure too fine. A sick thought hissed through my consciousness of how easy she could break under my touch, under my body, under the weight of my sickness. Her skin felt nice below my thumb, and I wished I could shut everything out, wished I could pretend I was just some guy at a bar, and she was just mine for the night, a chance to escape. Maybe I should take it.

You'll shatter her.

"It's nice to meet you, Declan." Her eyes were a dark brown, and the lack of color made me smile. A faint rose filled her cheeks, and I wanted, just this once, the ability to feel something. To have someone.

I nodded just as her friend called to her that they were leaving. She grabbed my pencil from the table and wrote her number on the blank piece of paper next to my drawing.

"Call me." She stood and gave me a once over. Her stare lingered over the muscles in my chest as she grinned.

I didn't give her a second notice as she turned to leave. I grabbed my things, placed them in my bag, and took one last sip of water. She didn't want to know me, she didn't need to be compared to the something I'd never have again. The paper crumbled under my fist as I balled it up and threw it in the trash.

PAIGE

Taco Tuesday. Another week, another day, another tradition I didn't plan. Clark prattled on about his day, and I found myself lost in my thoughts. The only thing to pull me from my trance was the tangy smell of cilantro as it assaulted my senses. It was his favorite, and I had to make sure I always had it on hand.

"Why do you love me?" It eased past my lips like a dare.

Not really giving him eye contact, I ripped pieces of lettuce into manageable portions. The silence was a loud roar in my ears, and it took effort to even my breathing as my eyes stayed trained on the counter awaiting his answer.

"Paige? Are we doing this again?" Clark exhaled with an irritated puff, and the knife in his hand came to an abrupt stop.

I dragged my eyes to his, leaving the lettuce on the counter. His dull gray irises looked at me with disappointment. I wasn't what he thought I should be. I'd been a mirage, and I'd slowly given myself over to his needs, tried to become what he desired, but lost myself in my Stepford way of life. Paige... I was the wife with a perfect smile and the perfect hair and make-up.

The house was always clean. I went to church every Sunday. I attended, but I wasn't truthful to the Savior like I should've been. It was bland, my life, and sometimes I let myself drift into the unknown, drift into one of my internal paintings, my past sketches, wondering if I'd ever draw again. Everything in my life looked as it should. Everything in its place, but the one thing he wanted I couldn't give. I couldn't have children. I couldn't supply and replenish the Earth, his seed never took, and I never really converted. Well, that last part was what he truly thought. Even if he didn't say it, it was there, in the way he reprimanded me when I forgot to say my nightly prayers or if I didn't read the scriptures like I should.

Maybe if I had truly converted, gave myself to the Savior, I could've had a baby. It was his mantra, for the past eight years, but I'd destroyed that chance when I was eighteen, and there was no blessing the pastor could give to fix it.

"Why, Clark?" I wanted to shout it, but instead it was just a whisper.

"Do you need to call your mother?" He dropped his eyes to the cutting board continuing his work, and shook his head.

I grit my teeth and my anxiety grew as I found the strength to say what I should have said three weeks ago. "You slept with her. And you said you didn't love her, that it was a mistake. You said you loved me, but when I ask you why, you never give me a real answer."

The knife he held in his hand shook as he tried to still his anger. Clark's nostrils flared. "It *was* a mistake." He dropped the knife, and the metal clanged against the granite surface of the counter, missing the cutting board.

Clark wiped his hands on the dishrag next to the sink. He ran his fingers through his jet black hair and exhaled. His broad shoulders relaxed as his eyes met my now tear-filled gaze. He hesitated, and his lips parted then closed into a thin line.

"Why do you love me?" I asked again, my voice tremored as he moved toward me.

His cool fingers gripped my chin. "I don't." His tone was just as empty as those steel eyes.

I swallowed down my sob.

"But we're married, for better or for worse, in God's eyes, you're mine, and even if I don't love you, you're my wife, and you'll do what you can to change my feelings." He gave me a soft smile, dropping his tight grip on my chin, and the acid bubbled up my throat. The air in my lungs seized. I closed my eyes to control my panic. He'd been cold, but never this cold.

I'd asked for it.

The scraping of the knife was the only sound in the kitchen, as Clark started prepping for dinner again, and I finally opened my eyes. I watched in silence. Clark had never been what I'd pictured for myself. He was handsome, strong, had a great job at his father's practice as a physician's assistant. His father was my father's partner at Canyon Internal Medicine Clinic. Our marriage? That had been chosen by our parents. My life had fallen apart just after high school, and being with Clark, joining Midway Heights Christian Church of the Savior, had been my only salvation. Together for nine years, married for eight, he'd saved me from my past, my damnation. My parents and I had decided to join his father's church and they were faithful followers. The church was a mix of popular Christian beliefs. It pulled from all Christian-based faiths. His father was the founder of the first Utah branch and, after what I'd done, after Declan, *my heart skipped at the thought of his name,* I needed something, anything to pull me from Hell. I'd been just as faithful as my mom and dad had been, gave myself to my husband in every way I could. I had tried, but the more I asked questions, and the more I sought out answers, all I found were closed doors.

"Paige." He finished chopping and scooped the cilantro into the bowl I'd gotten out of the cupboard earlier. "Hand me those tomatoes." His smile was tight, and I realized he was going to push what he'd said under the rug, like he always did.

The heat in my cheeks drifted to the tips of my ears. My anger bloomed through my chest and it made it impossible to stop my hands from shaking as I grabbed the tomatoes and placed them on the cutting board. He'd cheated. He'd had sex with the church nursery advisor. He'd had an affair for months. I'd always suspected he'd cared for Cheryl, but I'd only caught him because he'd been distracted and messaged me a salacious text instead of her. When I confronted him, he didn't deny it, he said he had needs, and that I hadn't been the wife I should've been. I'd gone to the pastor, spoke with him, and he'd told Clark's father. We'd both—*both*—had to serve penance. Clark, for his infidelity, and me because I'd led him astray. That was the day I knew I wasn't meant for this faith. I wasn't a true follower of the Savior, because my God, my Christ, the Creator I prayed to every night, would have never punished me for the sins of my husband. My Savior already knew my crime, and I'd never wash it away, never pray it away, I'd never be clean of it. My Savior had already doled out my sentence.

I sucked in a ragged breath gaining every last bit of courage I had. "I want a divorce."

His eyes narrowed. "What?"

"I want a divorce," I spoke just above a whisper.

"No." He gripped the dishrag in his hand and twisted his fingers through it. The red juice of the tomatoes stained the bleached white fabric.

"You don't love me," I tried.

He stood still. Calculating. Clark's eyes looked past me, through me, measuring every sin I'd committed, every piece of ammunition he could use to wound me. "I don't."

"Then let me leave," I pleaded.

He shook his head. "You belong to me, we were married before God."

"Clark, you were unfaithful... before God." My tone held all the acid that churned in my gut.

"You're a murderer." The words slithered over his lips.

It wasn't a surprise he'd call me that, it was what kept me. It was the truth that bound me to him, to God, to my inability to have children. I'd never be free of my sin, no matter what punishments life held, but I was tired, tired of living through a suffocating death.

"I am." I ran my sweaty hands down my light tan, linen pants once, and then again, as I tried to iron out the wrinkles from the day, a habit I'd acquired. "But, I've paid the price. I'm paying it every day, while you get to do whatever the hell you want."

He growled, "Don't swear in this home."

"This isn't a home, it's a *prison*." I raised my voice and my heart hammered, and my pulse was like a drum in my chest, but I felt it. I felt something.

His movement was quick, and I hadn't a chance to react as he gripped his hands around my arms. "You'll get nothing. You. Are. Nothing."

The words should have sliced me open, bled me dry, but I'd known his truths for years.

"I know." My voice cracked as he shoved me away and tears singed my cheeks.

His chest was heaving with suppressed rage, and for the first time in nine years, I felt actual fear. He didn't want me, he wanted something to control, someone to berate, someone to put down to make himself feel better.

"I wanted a family. I wanted a woman who could actually be a wife. You should have stayed with that crazy piece of

16

trash." He smirked, sharpening his verbal knife. "But, he didn't want you either not after—"

"Stop it." My voice was cold, dead, and terrified. "*Stop it, Clark.*"

His smile dissipated and his mask of indifference fell into place. "Get out."

The tree-lined street was still lit by the setting sun, and the neighborhood kids giggled and shrieked as they weaved their bikes through the looming old tree trunks. My car idled as I checked the address on the curb. This was it, I had nowhere else to go, and when I'd dialed Lana's old number I'd suspected that it would've been disconnected, but it hadn't. I didn't grab a stitch of clothing from my closet, just my purse, keys, phone, and I'd left. *I left.* I couldn't go to my parents, they'd talk me into staying with Clark. They had so much tied up in his family, in the church, they'd never let me leave.

Lana's place was a cute, little, red brick house, with a heavy looking wood and stained-glass front door. The street was quaint, and I wondered if she lived here with her own family or if she lived here alone. I hadn't seen my once-best-friend since my wedding day. My past life was completely prohibited, and because she was my one and only link to my life before Clark, before the church, she was cut out.

I turned off the engine and stepped from the car into an oven. This summer was the hottest I could remember, and as I moved toward her front door, tendrils of heat curled around my bare ankles. The front door opened before I even had the chance to make it to the porch.

"Well, shit, if it isn't little Mrs. Holy Roller... in the fucking flesh." Lana's smile broke across her face.

My eyes dropped to the ground at the sound of the harsh words. My body stopped automatically, and my anxiety grew.

"Paige?" Lana was close, close enough to hug, but my breathing became shallow as her familiar scent filled my lungs. The words, the heat, everything burst all at once, and a sob wracked from my lips.

"What did he do to you?" she asked as she wrapped her arms around me. My knees wobbled. The stress of my life weighed down upon me in that one second and I almost couldn't stand. Lana's arms tightened around my body, my own arms fixed at my sides.

"I don't know who I am anymore." It was the only thing I could say, it was the only truth I had.

"I know who you are, I always have." She squeezed me tighter as if she was struggling to hold all my broken pieces together.

The moment I was through her front door it all came crashing down. Her house was filled with warmth, color, clutter—life. Books spilled from her shelves, her couches were hand-me-downs from her grandmother. I'd recognize those sofas anywhere. Lana had been adopted by her grandmother because her parents were always in and out of jail for drugs. Before my parents turned into self-righteous zealots, they'd once loved Lana, like their own.

"How is your grandmother?" I asked as I set down my bag on her scratched up coffee table.

"Dead as a doornail, the old bat finally croaked." She smiled at my wide eyes. "It's okay, I use humor to suppress my deep-seated sadness. I'm truly a dark spirit."

I was afraid to smile, but the corners of my lips had other thoughts, and a slow grin spread across my face.

"And, there she is, folks. Paige Simon, welcome to my humble abode." Lana's smile stretched wider. "I'm glad you called me, I've missed you. I just made some tea, do you want a cup?"

I was about to shake my head, I wasn't allowed to have tea, but I paused. I'd left him, them—everything. "Yes, that would be really nice, thank you."

"I'll get it, have a seat. Relax, the Inquisition starts soon." She nodded toward the couch and I complied.

The place was small. Just a kitchen to the right with a breakfast bar that opened into the living room, and down the hall a few rooms, maybe. "This place is—"

"A tiny, little rabbit hole." She laughed as she grabbed cups from the cabinet and poured the tea. She didn't take long, no cream, no sugar, no fuss, as she sat down next to me. The steam smelled like spiced oranges, and I immediately felt relaxed. "This house... it's good for now. Blow on it, Paige, it's hot..." I did as I was told then took a small sip as she continued, "But yeah, I bought it after my grandmother died a few years ago."

"I'm sorry."

"It's life, she was old. She lived a good life, besides, it made it really difficult to bring men home when you live with a ninety year old." Her lips turned up at the corners.

"Never married?" I asked over the rim of my mug, and she rolled her eyes.

"Hell, no. I'm working on my doctoral thesis, I don't have time for men." She smirked. "Well, at least not for the long haul. I like dating professors, it's a sickness." She laughed again and pulled her straight and shiny, chin-length, dark chocolate hair behind her ears. Her green eyes searched mine and her brows knotted. Her jovial expression turned serious. "Did he hurt you?"

My hands trembled as I placed my mug on the coffee table. "No," I said. "And, yes. He had an affair."

I spent the next hour cataloging the last eight years of my life. The emotional abuse, the constant ridicule. I told her all of it. How we couldn't have children, how I'd lost myself in religion, lost myself in a marriage, an ownership... anything, *anything* to help me forget my unforgivable crime. I'd done everything I could do to save myself, save my life after I'd taken one. I was so close to death, so close to ending it all after I'd left Declan. *His name*, twice now I'd let it slip through. It stirred something inside of me, the sleeping monster's eyes opened, and I asked, "Do you ever see him?"

"Who?" Lana glanced over my features. The fear must have drained my cheeks because she whispered, "Declan?"

I nodded.

"On occasion." Her eyes wouldn't meet mine.

"How... how is he?" It was a stupid question. I had no right to know, and when Lana let her gaze meet mine, I wished I'd never asked.

"I heard it was rough for him, Paige, I mean... I've only seen him a few times, at this place called Bellows. I go there sometimes with friends from school. He looks... good," she added with a chipper beat. "But, if I'm being honest, how you left things, I'm not sure someone like him could recover from that."

Lana always wanted to be a social worker, help kids like her, but she always said the system was broken, and she'd have to figure out a way to fix it. Child psych, it was her thing.

"I know." The guilt ate holes in my stomach every day. "Where's the restroom?"

"Down the hall. Second door on the left. You alright?"

I didn't smile, but I nodded. I was grateful for the short distance and the plush bathroom floor rug as I kneeled and emptied bile from my throat into the toilet. Cold sweat beaded on my forehead as I wiped my mouth with a piece of toilet paper and threw it in the trash. I took several shaky breaths as I bowed down and started to pray. The hushed words rushed from my lips as I let myself remember, remember him—remember Declan.

I mumbled, "Heavenly Father, please forgive me, forgive my sin, forgive my sin, forgive my sin, please help me, help me... help him, please... please... please—" my voice broke, and I rocked back and forth as I brought my right hand to my womb. "I'm sorry. I'm so sorry."

DECLAN

Black, white, black, white, bright blinding flashes flickered through the open blinds. It wasn't the train rumbling past that had woke me. The grating sound of steel on steel was a welcomed friend. It created certainty when I couldn't decipher between dreams and realities. Sweaty, naked, wet sheets, clammy skin, each breath I took was a desperate choke of air. Gray sheets, black blanket, large, framed murals, art, my art, I was in my room. I lifted my hands to my face and rubbed my eyes as I sat up. My fingers raked through my hair. It had been a dream that pulled me from peace. An idyllic morbid fantasy. I pulled the sheets back and sat at the edge of the bed, watching the flashes of light, letting myself remember, letting the voices eat me alive.

She's gone.

You ruined it, you let her go.

She's dead to you.

Forget her.

"No," I said to the void in a tight whisper.

Forgive her.

Hate her.

Love her.

Gone.

Useless. Useless. Useless.

The train had finally passed, but the pounding in my head remained. I shut my eyes tight and pressed the heel of my palm into my temple. When I opened my eyes again, I was knelt down on the carpet, still naked; my canvas laid out before me. My hands were covered in whorls of color, and my fingers gripped a paint brush. I glanced at the red numbers on the clock. It was just past two in the morning. I shook my head. Time, time... I continued to lose it. I continued to fall into black holes. It didn't matter how many fucking pills I popped, I belonged to the abyss, and no chemical on Earth would drag me from its depths. These... blank moments were few and far between, but lately, I welcomed them.

The smell of paint saturated the air. I didn't remember getting out of bed, I sure as hell didn't remember creating this. I took in the painting in front of me. It was the brightest thing I'd painted since Paige. Since the after that had swallowed me whole. The buttery yellow glow of clear Christmas lights spilled across the canvas, two twisted figures, one black and one gray, embraced. A bulky pine tree lit with tiny balls of ghostly light sat in the corner. It wasn't an exact rendering, the color was off, it was truth mixed with a false understanding, but if I stared at it long enough... I could almost taste her.

It was the dream I'd had. The one that had woken me, the one that chilled my skin with beaded sweat, the one that now came to life with oil and pigment. But the memory, that real thing, it played behind my eyes.

Red, green, white, and blue... the spectrum bounced off the white walls of the dimly lit and narrow hallway. Her smile pulled her cheeks into dimples, and I leaned in as she rested her back against the surface of the wall. Her hand trembled as she pulled the soft strands of her blonde hair behind her ear. I breathed her in. She smelled like rain, like comfort, like warm hues of light. My eager inexperienced lips found hers. The taste of candy canes spilled over my tongue, and her quiet sigh fueled my wavering control. We were too young to feel like this. I was too young to believe in forever and always. My mouth with hers forever. My hand fisted in her hair always. This rare moment... it felt as if I'd never wake up.

The pressure built as her arms wrapped around my neck, pulling our bodies together. Her breasts flush against my chest. Her kiss stopped the voices completely, stopped the sound... stopped time.

The loud laughter from the kitchen startled her and she pulled away. Paige's lips spread so slowly into the sexiest grin I was sure I'd ever see.

"Merry Christmas, Declan."

Her voice was velvet, gold, bright savage colors against my wet lips. She kissed me again, a lazy tease, before hiding her face in my neck with a giggle.

"Merry Christmas."

I was fourteen when I kissed Paige in the hallway of her childhood home. We'd only been together a month. It was the beginning of everything. The beginning of something I thought would save me from myself, from the demons that possessed me. Little had I known, four years later Paige would destroy everything.

A pornographic, female moan ripped me from sleep. A loud bang, a grunt, and another moan, another breathless sigh. *Shit.* The sun was up and baking the open paints I'd left out overnight on the floor. I got out of bed abruptly, grabbed my sweats and slipped them on. I quickly picked up a few bottles of paint and closed the lids, setting them on my work table. *Shit.* I tried not to look at the painting I'd created last night. I tried to push back the memory I'd had, and the time I'd lost, but it was pointless. The scene I'd masterfully placed on display spit curses at me.

Tear it up. Cut it up, Declan.
Destroy it.

I didn't let my eyes linger as I stepped over the canvas. I rummaged through my dresser drawer and grabbed the first t-shirt I could find. The sounds of my brother, Liam, fucking some chick just a wall away was starting to piss me off.

You're jealous.
Listen. Listen. Listen.
You'll never have it, never feel it.

I mumbled the lyrics of my favorite band, *Brand New,* in an attempt to ignore the antagonistic hiss of voices playing through my head. I slipped my phone and earbuds off the top of the dresser. I turned on some music and placed the white buds in my ears. The deep bass, the angry rhythm, I closed my eyes and drowned it all out. The painting, last night... forgotten. My bathroom wasn't connected to my room, unfortunately, so I skipped my normal morning routine in effort to give my brother some privacy. My pills were in the kitchen anyway, I could shower later. There was a small part of me that wanted to make as much noise as possible, let Liam know I was awake, but I wouldn't do that... not to him. He'd given up so much for me, for our family, he deserved a piece of ass every now and then.

I snuck out to the kitchen, quietly passing his door. The oblivion the music provided was a nice veil. The hallway led to a large industrial space. The kitchen opened to the living room. Metal beams and supports ran the length of the entire apartment just below the ceiling. The floors were a dark brown wood, and the only delineating line between the kitchen and living area was the beige, oversized throw rug. The apartment was cold with its metal beams, black furniture, and my dark, fucking thoughts that hung from the brick walls in frames. The wood floors and the tan rug were the only warm tones Liam had allowed during the renovation. The floor of the kitchen was cold against my feet as I poured cereal into a bowl. The stainless steel fridge door was heavy, the industrial feel flowed, even in the kitchen. I grabbed the milk and shut the fridge with as much ease as possible.

After our drunk of a father passed away six years ago, Liam took the small amount of money he'd been saving, got a loan, bought Avenues Ink from his boss and renovated the apartment just above the tattoo shop. Our dad had been diagnosed with cirrhosis a few years before he died, but still he'd chosen to drink himself to death rather than provide for his family. He'd had to quit his job at the oil refinery and had lived off his vet benefits. Our mother had never worked, she'd been a stay-at-home mom all our lives. Liam had taken it upon himself, as the eldest son, to drop out of school at the age of sixteen to help supplement our father's income. He'd gotten a job here, at Avenues, cleaning and running the front desk, but always watching, and he'd learned fast. His talent had always rivaled mine when it came to art, but he didn't have voices holding him back, so he'd fucking flourished. Just after he'd turned eighteen, he'd become one of the best artist's at the shop.

He'd been working there for eight years when Pop had died. He'd been saving, running our house, paying the medical bills, Liam was the man of the house. He was there for me when I'd tried to kill myself. He was the one who finally took the initiative to get me the help I needed. If it wasn't for him, if left to the devices of my overly Catholic mother and drunk father, I would've never made it past thirteen. I swallowed down my first bite of cereal, and it was dry as it scratched my throat. I owed Liam everything.

I carried my bowl to the granite breakfast bar and sat down on a stool. It wasn't until after our dad died that Liam finally felt safe enough to move out. Being home, all the memories, fed the monster, so I moved out with him. Kieran, my baby brother, was still studying theology when we'd left and it had been agreed upon that he'd stay and take care of Mom. We all had taken care of Mom, we still did. Avenues Ink became a family business, the original owner wasn't the best businessman and had almost lost the place. If it hadn't been for Liam, this tiny little empire would have crumbled. Avenues was now one of the most thriving ink shops in Salt Lake City. The original owner retired, bowed out, and we took over. Liam and I were the top artists out of our small staff, and Kieran had put his hopes of becoming a priest on hold to help us run the books. Eventually, he gave up the dream, and worked with us full-time.

A movement in my peripheral vision caused my thoughts to pause. The minute I lifted my eyes from the bowl, I wished I hadn't. Liam was half naked with just boxer briefs on as he entered the kitchen with the girl, the porn star, scuttling behind him. I removed one ear bud as I watched Tana, one of our regular customers, squirm under my glare. My brother ran his hand through his dark hair; he looked more like our Pop than any of us did and he hated it. Liam's arms, legs, his chest, neck, and hands were his pallet of color, his disguise. His entire body was covered in ink. He looked just like the owner of an ink shop should; muscles, gages in his ears, piercings in his nose, his right brow decorated with a barbell, and enough tattoos to cover who he really was, who he really despised.

"Hey, Declan." Tana's spritely voice was sweet and it bugged me.

I nodded.

"Don't be a fucking bastard." Liam narrowed his eyes. "You know Tana, where're your manners." He barely concealed his smirk.

"I didn't sleep great." I stood, walked to the sink, and dumped my full bowl of cereal down the drain, running the water to wash it away.

Tana whispered something, at least I think it was her. I shut off the water and turned to look at them, to make sure, and caught her kissing Liam on the mouth. It was weird to watch. I'd seen him with quite a few women over the years, but Tana reminded me too much of Kelly and, as she pulled away, I saw the slight wince in his eyes. The tiny regret Tana pretended not to notice.

She lifted her heavily tattooed arms and pulled her curly, dull brown hair into a ponytail as she smiled up at my brother. "See you this Saturday?"

He took a deep breath. "I'll text you." The dismissal caused her fake smile to wane.

"Okay." She had enough self-respect not to lean in for another kiss before she turned to leave. She grabbed her bag off the back of the couch before disappearing out the front door.

Liam and I watched her go in silence. Once the door shut, I removed the other bud from my ear and turned off my phone before placing it back into my pocket.

"She reminds me of Kelly," I said.

"Fuck off." He clenched his jaw.

"I'm serious. She looks—"

"I don't see it," he lied and swallowed down the lump of truth.

I afforded him the fiction. "Maybe I'm just seeing shit again."

His lips twitched. "It wouldn't be the first time, Dex."

He helped himself to the box of Cap'n Crunch I'd left on the counter.

"I'm going to shower before I head down to open the shop." He wasn't my keeper, technically anymore, but old habits die hard.

"Did you take your meds?" he asked, not looking up from his breakfast.

"I will."

"Don't forget, Dex, last month—"

"I won't."

Last month I'd tried to wean myself off, I was tired of not feeling, of being a zombie. The voices fucked with me, but they gave me life, too. They bit and gnashed at my heart, but the side effect was art, images, and color. They told me I was alive, despite the lies that nourished me, and filled my gut with rot... I was alive.

"The med change, it's helping, right, better balance?" He locked his dark eyes on mine.

I nodded. "I'm still wading through shit, but it's better than being a robot."

He gave me a small smile.

"The women? Does it help?" I risked asking, but seeing that small smile, it gave me fucking hope... for him... for me.

The muscle in his jaw pulsed as he raised his chin. "They fucking left us, Dex, nothing we can do about it but move the hell on. Paige stole your spirit, and Kelly, she... she left, Declan. What I had to offer wasn't enough for her, it's time I take care of myself... you know?"

I did.

Being alone, for so long, was beginning to feel too good. The vacant feeling inside my chest cheered too much at the dark and dank corners of my existence. When Paige left, she left me gaping, bleeding. The nails of her fingers still ripped and tore through my heart. She was the very specter that still sliced and clawed her way into my soul. Maybe it was time to wash myself clean of her curse.

"A woman gave me her number the other night." I glanced at him with little interest, my usual mask.

Liam's spoon dropped from his hand and clanged into the bowl. "And?" His lips curved up at the corners.

"I threw it out." I dropped my eyes as his smile fell.

"Fuck," he muttered under his breath.

"But, it was the first time, Liam, that I wish I hadn't."

DECLAN

Marking another human being, gifting them a rainbow of well-orchestrated pigments and lines, creating that perfect picture, the quote they'd always wanted, it was an art. More people than not had tattoos these days. Shops were popping up left and right around the valley. The religious subculture of the city waned under a kaleidoscope of color, of individuality. Today, I held my machine instead of my brush, my canvas—flesh. The girl laid out on the padded table had her shirt off, her ribcage poking out on either side. At times, it felt as if I could see through skin, straight to the bone, a flash of reality. I'd blink my eyes and the gruesome vision would disappear. It happened three times today. This girl was too thin.

You allowed it.
You took a life once.
Look at her bones, Declan.

My hand paused. My eyes slammed shut but the girl's intake of breath brought me back to clearer thoughts.

"Almost finished," I muttered as I wiped away the excess ink and blood from the small of her back.

A butterfly. I wondered if she'd picked it because she wanted to be reborn. This girl with her waif body, spindly arms, and limp hair. She was young, maybe just moved from the nest, just weaned from the milk of her mother's love. A symbol of resurrection, change, a new beginning.

I finished up the last few shades of purple, filling in all the vibrant life I could into this girl's hope for peace. After I was finished, she listened carefully, her eyes locked on mine as I explained the aftercare. She admired the reflection of her first tattoo through the small mirror in her hand. She smiled over her shoulder as she turned trying to get a better look.

"It's perfect," she said with an excited gleam in her eyes, she'd be back for more.

I repeated the instructions again as I smeared a salve over the ink and then covered it.

She rambled about how her friends were going to be jealous, and then she disappointed me when she mentioned she'd picked the butterfly from the book because it looked cool. I should've fucking known, it was a tramp stamp, after all. I walked her to the front and gave Kieran my bill so he could ring her up.

"One hour?" He glanced down at the invoice and then back up at me. "She was back there for at least two." He raised his left eyebrow.

The girl smiled as I spoke, "It's her first."

It was all the explanation he needed. It was my thing. Discounting the first tatt always brought them back, it bought loyalty where loyalty was rare.

"Thank you, again. It's really pretty."

"Send your friends," I said with a genuine smile right before she walked out of the front door.

Inside the shop it was easy to pretend like I was normal. I could be anybody. To that girl, the girl with the cool butterfly, the girl who hadn't known she'd picked a symbol that was just as powerful as it was beautiful, to her I was just the guy who'd popped her ink cherry. I could hide the voices behind a smile and my love for art. I could hide the loneliness while I helped my brothers build an empire. But mostly, I could hide my fear... my fear of firsts. First glances, first touches, first kisses, first... Paige had been the one I experienced everything with, and occasionally, when I was out in the real world, it was hard not to compare. I kept myself busy, I breathed in, and I breathed out. I lived, but sometimes, sometimes all I wanted to do was remember.

"Declan?" Kieran's deep, usually easy voice held a note of worry.

"Yeah?" I swallowed and ran my eyes down the appointment log on his desk.

"You're done for the day, unless you want to stay and take some walk-ins?" Kieran's eyes were blue like mine, we had our mother's azure irises while Liam bore the dark tones of our father. I was the only blond. My mother had said it was a fluke, but I'd known I was different, even from the point of conception. She'd sung the praises, all my life, of great aunts who lived in Killarney with blonde hair and blue eyes, and how lucky I'd been to be born with so much light. God had blessed her with a baby who was bright like the sun. It wasn't until I was twelve that she'd realized my life had become a perpetual night.

"Did you hear me?" He chuckled.

"No." I shook my head and pinched the bridge of my nose.

"I said stay, take a few walk-ins, then when we close up we can all go to Bellows." He slapped my shoulder as he stood.

"I'll be in the back if you need me," I said.

"Seriously." He lowered his voice to a low hum, almost matching the buzz of the tattoo machines. "Liam said the med change has been good?"

I allowed my shoulders to sag. He worried too much. He'd been the one to find me hanging by a sheet from my closet door. Liam had cut me down, but it was Kieran who'd picked up on my silence, my moods. He was the first to ask me what the voices said. The older he got, the more fixated he'd been on becoming a priest. A part of me questioned if that was my fault. I wondered if he wanted to exorcise the voices, help the damned, and keep the link he had between those who suffered and those who needed help.

"All is well in the world, Father." I smirked.

He punched me in the shoulder. "Fucking smart ass."

"Whoa, they teach you that language in seminary?" My smile faded as his jaw clenched. He'd never made it to seminary. He'd gotten his degree and that's as far as he got. My mother wasn't capable of living on her own, so Kieran had put his life on hold for her. "Sorry." My shame brought my eyes to the floor. Both of my brothers had sacrificed so much, for her, for me. "I'm an asshole."

"At least you're truthful." The smile was evident in his tone as I raised my eyes back to his.

"I'll be in the back."

Liam was busy working on an intricate back piece and raised his chin to me as I walked by. Ronnie was picking at her talon-like fingernails as I passed her station. Kemper, as always, during down time, was sniffing around, flirting, trying hopelessly to get her attention. If he actually looked beyond her tits and pretty face he'd realize she liked girls just as much as he did. The shop was organic. It lived off the creative blood of our staff, it swallowed and breathed, it fought to survive, and Liam... Liam was the heart of this place, and as I walked past each of the stations with their tall mirrors, clean, white floors, red leather tables, and black shelves, I smiled. My therapist had been telling me for years to stop harboring shit, to see things for what they were and, since my psychiatrist lowered my doses, I've been able to see so much more.

The cocktail I'd been taking had made me feel like a walking corpse. But at my last visit, the doctor lowered my dose of risperidone and finally stopped the clozapine. The new script for escitalopram was really starting to help with my depression and, the longer I was on it, the easier it became to deal with the memories of Paige, of everything we'd been through. Or so I'd hoped. I'd let the painting from the other night sit on my floor for a few days, avoiding, evading the fact I'd painted something so joyful, so full of happiness, and I hadn't even remembered doing it. It wasn't until two days ago that I'd finally framed it, and this morning, when I woke up and looked at it, it hurt a little less than the day before.

The break room was small, with only enough room for a black futon, side table, and a fridge. I opened the refrigerator and grabbed a bottle of water before I sat down. I twisted the cap and the cold water slid down my dry throat. Licking my lips, I placed the bottle on the table, and then leaned my head back into the soft cushion. I'd been thinking about Paige a lot lately, and maybe it wasn't a bad thing.

She left you.

You hurt her.

You let her do it.

I took my phone from my pocket and opened up the music files. I pressed the shuffle button, and when the first few notes played through the speaker, my pulse nearly stopped. It was the song I'd been listening to that day in ninth grade, when I'd gotten kicked out of class for mumbling. I hadn't even realized I was doing it, always trying to subtly quell the nagging taunts my brain kept on repeat. The teacher had flipped, called me out in front of everyone, and then told me to spend the remainder of the period in the hall. I'd been sitting on the cold linoleum, with my back against the lockers listening to music, as I'd worked my latest creation across the thick brown paper that covered my textbook when Paige, for the first time, had looked at me... with more than just a morbid curiosity.

I'd had real conversations with her before that day. She'd remind me about tests, we'd steal glances across the cafeteria, the courtyard, the classroom, but that day—it'd been the day she'd said *yes*.

The Roots played with a caramel beat in my ear as I shaded the cheekbones and oval features of the girl on the corner of the cover. It was a rendition of her. Paige Simon. She was elegant: a fine line of curves, blonde hair that I was sure smelled like honey and sunshine, blue eyes that were ghostly, clear and soulful, but only for me. Only in those moments when she'd let herself see me.

She doesn't see you.

I had to be more careful, I couldn't get in trouble again, and I couldn't add anymore shit to Liam's plate. A pair of black Converse appeared against the beige floor, and I looked up. The tip of my pencil stilled. Her cherry lips were glossy as she spoke with a smile.

"I'm sorry?" I removed my headphones.

Her laugh was soft and warm and pink. "I asked if you wanted company. Mr. Ferris is a jerk." She sat down before I could answer, and the smell of powder, cotton, and soap surrounded me.

She was wearing dark blue jeans and a light green shirt. The porcelain surface of her skin was creamy and, as she scooted closer to me, her arm brushed mine, and a shock ran up my spine.

"I lied and said I had to use the restroom, we only have like fifteen minutes left anyway." *She moved a piece of hair*

36

behind her ear, and then leaned in even closer; her eyes falling to the cover of my book. "You're really talented, Declan."

My fourteen-year-old hormones were raging, my fucked-up, crazy mind was spinning. I was sure this was a hallucination. I'd only had a few visual ones before, but this was all too real.

"It's customary to just say thank you," she said. Her smile was smart, soft, and it lit her eyes as I laughed.

"Thank you."

"Can I tell you a secret?" Her eyes widened as she moved in, closing the electrically charged space between our arms. Her skin was touching my skin again. My heat was absorbing her heat. My throat went dry, and my heart thrummed behind my chest. "I like to draw, too. I have so many sketch pads at home, hidden in my closet, and someday…" Her voice was conspiratorial as she turned to look at me, she was close enough I felt her minty breath brush across the skin of my cheek. "I want to learn how to paint the things I see."

I was captivated, my entire body was relaxed as I fell into her gaze. "Why is that a secret?"

"I'm supposed to learn how to play the piano, take anatomy, and become a doctor." She rolled her eyes and leaned back, resting her head against the lockers, granting me a moment to catch my breath.

"You're fourteen." I chuckled.

"Do your parents plan out your life, too?" she asked. Her brows furrowed with an honest interest.

"My father can barely plan his own life beyond which bottle of whiskey he should open."

The truth of my statement didn't faze her. "And your mother?"

"She just hopes I make it out of high school." My lips pulled into a sideways smile, and she shook her head with another full-bodied laugh. "What do you like to draw?" I asked.

"I like to create worlds, I like to make this boring little planet something more... surreal. I might have an obsession with Dali. We went to Florida last summer, and while we were there we visited the Dali Museum. I now find myself drawn to weird art and men with mustaches." She shrugged, her face deadpan as if this was a normal thing to say.

"Mustaches?" I unconsciously lifted my fingers to my upper lip.

Her serious face broke into a smile that stretched almost past her ears. "You'd look good with a mustache." She bit her lip suppressing a laugh and knocked her shoulder with mine. It was playful, flirty, and I suddenly had the urge to brush my knuckles across her bottom lip, her cheek, her stomach...

She pities you.

"What's your favorite thing to draw?" she asked, giving me full eye contact.

You.

"It depends. I love graphic novels. My brothers' and I, we've always been into comics. My older brother works at a tattoo shop. He's better than me... at drawing." And most things.

"I doubt that." She crossed her feet and stretched her legs out into the hallway. "I wish I had half your talent."

"You should show me something of yours sometime." It was risky, but the way her arm still rested against mine, how her smile was shy, and her cheeks were heated with blush, I figured I'd throw myself on the grenade. "I could teach you some stuff, if you want?"

Her blue eyes deepened and filled with hope, anticipation, and something I'd later learn was longing... lust.

"Really?" She shoved my shoulder again with hers. It was light, cute, and I wanted her to say yes more than I wanted anything, more than I wanted the voices to stop.

I nodded.

"Okay." Her lashes fanned down and dusted along the rising, rose color of her cheeks. "I'd really like that."

The quiet was comfortable between us as we sat arm to arm, thigh to thigh, shoulder to shoulder in the hallway. Not a whisper in my head, or an inkling of self-doubt. Just me and her and the most tempting thing of all... possibility.

PAIGE

Alarm clocks, overly excited chatter, car horns, sidewalk patrons shouting, cash registers dinging, door chimes, customers complaining, these had become the sounds of my life. The sounds of my future. But, in the dark, in the night—silence. Silence so still it suffocated me. It drowned me. Clark used to talk in his sleep. He'd moan, or make some illogical statements. Our backyard sprinklers would spray the windows in timed perfection. Here, in Lana's house this morning, as I got ready for work, all I could hear were my own thoughts, and my worries ate me alive from the inside out. Where did I go from here?

It had been exactly one month since I'd left Clark. My parents were refusing to accept it. I hadn't braved a visit to them yet, and they weren't too pleased that I was staying with Lana. My new address, though, magically never came up in conversation, leading me to believe they probably didn't really care how I was, that I wasn't with Clark was more of their pressing concern. My mom tried to coddle me, told me to "take my time." My father had said, "He'll take you back, let him give you another chance." That phone call, as productive as it was, had been the last time I'd chosen to call my parents. I'd visit them when I was ready, once my divorce was final. Clark had acquired an attorney, and he called me yesterday to inform me that the paperwork would take a little longer than expected. Lana was not impressed and gave me the number to one of her friends from school with a wife who was a divorce attorney. Apparently, this friend was the only professor she hadn't slept with.

The weight of the attorney's business card was heavy in my hand as I sat on my bed. I stared at the artful lettering, the sleek black design, and my stomach knotted. I already owed Lana so much. She'd gone and gathered my clothes from Clark and gave me a place to sleep each night. She hadn't wanted to charge me rent but I'd insisted, even if I couldn't really afford it. I had acquired a job at a small art store downtown and it paid very little, but I had to start somewhere. I had a high school diploma and a love for Surrealism. In the real world, that equated to starving artist, at best. There was no way I would be able to afford an attorney. I exhaled a long breath, stood, and placed the card on my night stand. My room was small, the bed, hardly full sized, and the large, dark black dresser took up most of the free space. The mirror above it ridiculed me. My eyes were so tired, the blue color of my irises barely visible anymore. My heart ached. Declan had always told me that my eyes would come alive when I looked at him.

My dead eyes closed as I remembered the first day I'd seen him, shutting out my now haggard appearance in the mirror, focusing on a better time. It was my first year in high school, and I remembered how he'd sat across the courtyard from where I'd been sitting with Lana and a few friends for lunch. I'd thought he'd looked too masculine to be in ninth grade. He'd seemed quiet, beautiful with lean muscles, and a jawline too strong for a teenage boy. I'd watched him for weeks before I'd finally gotten the courage to speak to him. It'd been just like every other day with our stolen glances, but his light eyes stayed on mine longer than they ever had before.

The vivid memory caused my eyes to open, and I watched my reflection in the glass. My cheeks turned pink, and the heat in my chest burned through the skin as I recalled that day. The day I took unsteady steps toward where he'd sat. The day his deep voice filled my head with cotton. The day I saw my eyes in the drawing on his lap.

I brought my hand to my heart and rubbed my palm along my sternum until it hurt. The pain had never faded, but thinking about him, about us, made it almost impossible to breathe. The stark white walls of my room and bedding felt too cold. It felt as if I was in some type of sterile purgatory, and even if I was grateful for the roof over my head, the soft pillows to have nightmares on, I wanted to make it my own. And as I watched the color, the memory, drain from my cheeks, I decided I'd stop letting men control my life. But my soul, it no longer belonged to me. I'd given it to the Devil the day I'd killed my baby, our child—Declan's heart.

"So what are you saying?" Chandler watched me with a smirk, and I narrowed my eyes.

"I'm saying I'm married," I spoke softly, my eyes cast down. Chandler's eyes scanned my body, as if there was something to like, to desire. I was a waste of what I'd once been, and I certainly didn't deserve the looks he'd been giving me since I started at The Gallery.

"But you're separated? Available?" His husky voice held humor, and I raised my gaze to his.

I shook my head with a small smile. "You're determined, I'll give you that much." I leaned down and grabbed a box of supplies from where I stood behind the counter and placed it onto the work surface. "Hand me that box cutter, please?" I asked as I pointed to his pile of boxes in the aisle.

He grabbed the red knife from the top box and brought it over to the register. "That's not a no." He was hopeful.

"Chandler, I'm flattered, but I'm barely remembering what it feels like to be human. I'm not ready to date. Not to mention the fact that it would still be considered infidelity." I took the box cutter from his hand and opened the blade. It cut through the packing tape like butter, and when the box opened, I couldn't help my grin. Paints. Every possible color in oil and acrylic.

"That's the first big smile I've seen on you." His grin mirrored mine and, as much as it felt good to let a little joy shine, I let my smile fall.

"Well, it's been known to happen from time to time." I gave him a stern look. "I'm serious. I'm not ready."

He exhaled. "Okay."

My eyebrows raised. That was too easy. He'd been hitting on me for two weeks, since my first day. "Okay?"

He nodded and turned back to his pile of boxes. "I've gotta haul these back to the studio, just leave those paints for tomorrow. Can you help me carry some of these?"

"Sure." I lifted the box from the counter and placed it back on the ground.

"One of our regulars is coming tomorrow. He booked the studio last week. I'll show you how to set everything up." Chandler's smile was repentant. Maybe he really would back off.

The boxes were heavy and it only took us three trips to get everything back to the studio. The Gallery was an art supply store and had a huge open space in the back that the owner rented out to the local artists to use. It was perfect for large canvases, and a lot of the local, urban artists rented the place out by the hour. Sometimes we'd even sell the artwork here at the store if that's what the client wanted. This place was perfect. It had everything I'd ever dreamed of, and I couldn't wait to test out the studio one day for myself.

I helped Chandler carry a huge canvas to the center of the back wall. It was sixty inches wide by thirty-six inches tall. My excitement spread across my skin in the form of goose bumps. My eyes danced across the blank canvas as I imagined what the artist would spill onto its surfaces tomorrow. I was dying to see the sprawling art, to breathe in the beauty, to see color, alive, and swirled with a talented hand. See life brought to the dull, white rectangle.

"There's that smile again. You keep it up, I'll have no other choice than to ask you out every time I see you." Chandler grinned and I laughed.

I laughed and the sound of it echoed in the empty space. It sounded foreign, as if the music of it didn't belong to me, as if I hadn't laughed in months. I hadn't, not freely, not with actual mirth.

"Thanks," I said.

Chandler quirked his left eyebrow. "For what?"

"For... for making me laugh, I guess," I stuttered. I wasn't sure how I should explain to the guy I worked with that my life had been soundless, boring, not even worthy of gray paint, and the fact that he made me laugh, even if the moment was small, I was grateful for it.

"Well, if laughter is the way to go... then—"

I giggled. "It was a thank you. Not an invitation."

He ran his hand through his coffee brown hair. His smile

was pulled wide. In an easier time I might've thought him handsome. "Can't blame a guy for trying."

His advances were mostly in jest, so I didn't let it bother me. If anything, it was a comfortable routine, and routine was all I had known for the past nine years that I'd been with Clark. Chandler walked me through the list of what the customer had ordered for the next day. He showed me where to find the palette, the brushes, the supplies, even spray paint. By the time we were finished setting up, the store had been closed for over an hour. It was just past eight and I was tired and a smidge starving. Chandler walked me to my car, and it wasn't until I was tucked inside that he finally felt it was safe to leave. He was a genuine kind of guy, maybe I could set him up with Lana. She needed to stop with the professor thing. I shook my head and puffed out an exacerbated laugh. I reached into my purse, found my keys, started the engine, and turned the A/C on full blast. The heat of the day was thick within the small confines of my car.

My phone vibrated on the passenger seat and, when I opened the lock screen, I saw I had a couple of texts from Lana.

Lana: There's a package here for you, I'm putting it on your bed. I think it's from Clark.

My heart leapt into my throat. I hated that he knew where I was, but maybe the papers had been finalized already? I scrolled down to her next text from an hour ago.

Lana: I'm on my way home from class, going to grab a pizza. Want?

Me: Sorry running late, save me a slice.

My thumb hit the send button, and I didn't bother waiting for a response. I pulled out of the parking lot and headed home. Headed to the mysterious, possibly life-changing package waiting for me.

The house smelled like basil and tomato sauce as I walked in through the front door, laying my bag and keys on the small foyer table. Lana was sitting on the couch with her legs crossed underneath her. A pizza box was sitting open and half empty on the coffee table. The television was on and from what it looked like she was watching porn. Her eyes were fixed on the couple practically conceiving on the screen as she sipped deeply from her bottle of beer.

"Grab a plate, there's beer in the fridge," she said as she lowered the bottle from her lips.

"What the heck are you watching?" I asked as I quickly hurried past the television to the kitchen.

"*Vampire Diaries.*" Her expression fell as if to say I should've known this.

"It looks like a porno," I said as I grabbed a plate and bypassed the beer for a soda. I hadn't had a drop of alcohol since... since I couldn't even remember. Probably high school. I never drank. Not even before I'd joined the church. Declan's father had been an alcoholic, so I... we avoided it, and once I became a member, it was prohibited.

"It's primetime TV, you Puritan," she scoffed and moved over a little so I could sit down.

"This is on primetime television?" I asked in horror.

"Well, this isn't, *this* is *Netflix*, you know Internet, streaming... but yeah, I think this year is the final season for the network show." She leaned over, grabbed another piece of pizza and looked at my Coke with a scowl. "This weekend, we're going to Bellows, and I'm breaking your vow of alcohol celibacy... or whatever you call it. We will drink, be merry, and get laid. Preferably by males of the largest persuasion." She waggled her eyebrows and I rolled my eyes.

"I'm not big on alcohol, I wasn't even a drinker with–"

"Declan. I know. But you're past that, right? Declan? Clark? You gotta move on, Paige." Her tone was soft, sad, and begged for me to accept my fate, my future.

I took a bite of my pizza so I didn't have to answer. Even though I was slowly figuring out who I'd become over these past nine years, I was past Clark. I wasn't even sure I had ever loved him, but, Declan, he was the marrow of my existence. Every moment of my life, since that day at lunch, he'd always been the one. But, I'd tainted it. The pizza turned to dust in my mouth, and I swallowed a big gulp of soda to try and wash down the acrid taste.

"I'm not very hungry." I sat my plate onto the coffee table and stood.

"I'm sorry. Just sit, eat. Watch hot vampires with me." Lana's green eyes glittered and for a second I thought she looked tearful. "I'm sorry, really." She waved out her manicured hand at my empty seat.

"I know." I rubbed my hands down the front of my jeans then pushed my hair behind my ears. The nervous tension in the room reeked. "I should look at what Clark sent me. Save me a slice. I'll be right back."

I didn't give her time to protest before I rounded the coffee table and headed back to my room. The bright white of my comforter was interrupted with a small sized cardboard box. Clark's address, my address, my old life was on the label. I searched my dresser for something to open it with, and I found my nail clippers. The small, attached metal file ripped through the packing tape with little struggle. My breathing was uneven as I lifted the flaps and removed the butcher paper from the top.

My heart fell into my stomach.

He did this on purpose.

Sitting on top of a shoe box, my memory box, the only item I'd kept of my relationship with Declan once I married, was a piece of paper. I'd kept the box hidden in our closet, and when I'd left in a hurry I hadn't had the time to grab it. Clark had opened it. He'd found the only piece of concrete evidence of my damnation, and placed it front and center. I lifted the piece of paper and it shook in my grip as I read the business name on the letterhead in a whisper, "Women's Wellness Center." The date stamped below, August Thirteenth. My signature was at the bottom, my payment agreement, my deal with the Devil. Big, wet drops of water plopped onto the paper. Tears. I hadn't even realized I was crying. I dropped the paper to the bed and lifted the shoe box from the package.

The lid was brittle from years of being opened, years of me rifling through a time I'd never get back. My skin crawled as I thought about how Clark would have touched everything in here to find that paper. It had been at the bottom. His fingerprints fouled the history I had never wanted him to see. My breath caught as I looked through the mementos and found the only picture I had of Declan. I raised it from the box with trembling fingers. He was wearing a tight, white shirt and worn jeans. He was covered in paint. His head tipped down, his hand running through his hair, his smile lopsided as he avoided the lens. He was just seventeen years old, but he looked every bit of a man. I let out a staggered breath and brought the picture to my chest as my knees sank to the floor in grief. My forehead rested against the edge of the bed, my shoulders shook with suppressed sobs, and my heart broke all over again, like it did every time I let myself see what I had destroyed.

DECLAN

"Tell me again," she whispered. Her head rested on my chest and, even though I couldn't see her face, I could hear her smile.

"You make me better... and I love you." The palm of her hand splayed across my bare stomach and the muscles twitched.

"I love you, too." She turned her head and the tip of her nose grazed my skin. She inhaled and my lips spread into an involuntary grin. "So much."

The sound of my arguing brothers barging through the front door made me jump, and Paige's body stiffened as I pulled her closer.

"They won't come in here, will they?" she asked, her voice strangled with worry.

"Nah, they know you're here."

She pushed away from me and raised up onto her elbow so quickly she almost seemed inhuman. She smacked my chest and I laughed. "What do you mean? Oh, my gosh."

She tried to pull the blanket over her naked breasts, but

I pulled it back down and let my eyes run along her skin until she blushed. I played with a piece of her hair before I gently placed it behind her ear.

"They knew you were coming over tonight, not that we... this..." I lifted my hand and cupped her cheek. "...is between you and me." She closed her eyes and leaned into my touch as I sat up. My lips pressed softly against the lid of each of her eyes and, as I pulled away, they fluttered open.

"I know how close you guys are, you trust them with everything, and I figured you'd—"

"Paige, two years ago you sat next to me on that fucking hallway floor and opened up my world. You gifted me back my sanity, and today..." I wanted to kiss her. To create that electrical, expectant pulse again. I wanted to hear her breathe deeply, sigh, and to recreate the moment when we... our bodies finally aligned. Recreate the moment she took every piece of me and turned it inside out, and I exploded into more than just a sixteen-year-old boy. "Today... you gave me you."

"You already had me, Declan." Her lips parted into a shy smile.

"You gifted me your body. Those idiots out there, yeah, I trust them, but with you... our trust, it's different, you have faith in me when no one else does."

She leaned her forehead against mine and raised her hands to my face. She exhaled and her warm breath tickled my cheeks. She smelled like mint and soap, and when she brought her mouth to mine, I groaned. The world outside my bedroom door didn't exist as she sat astride me, filling herself with more than just my body. She filled her lungs with my heartbeat and tasted my soul with her sweet tongue. It didn't matter how loud Liam was shouting at my drunk father just a few doors down. Our breathing, hurried puffs of sex and desire, clouded the room, and all I could hear was what I was feeling. Heated skin, silky against my chest, the building fire in my stomach burned low as I gripped her hips.

She is meant for you.

She is yours.

The needle dug too deep and my eyes opened. "Shit."

"Buck the fuck up, Dex. I'm almost done. I saved the worst part for last. It always hurts like hell on the ribcage." Liam shook his head with a grin. "You know this."

I decided to get the quote by Galway Kinnell, *"Never mind. The self is the least of it. Let our scars fall in love.",* tattooed on my left ribcage. *The Book of Nightmares* had always been a book I could relate to, the crazy as hell imagery he'd created seemed to fit my warped brain. I never thought too much of myself. Paige had been the only one to build me up, but she'd also left me scarred and wounded, so the quote, it fit.

"You going to Bellows tonight?" Liam wiped at my skin and it stung.

"Yeah, but I have a studio session I booked for tomorrow, so I won't be around long. Tana going with you?"

His eyes darkened with regret. "Maybe. I don't know. I told her I needed space."

"She's never going to fill the void. You should cut her loose." I watched his jaw tick, and I gave him a minute to calm down before I spoke again, "It's not that bad being alone."

"Speak for yourself. I think at this point you'd be a better priest than Kieran," he joked but I could hear the worry laced within the words. He rolled his stool back to admire his work.

"I'm feeling better, Liam. You don't need to worry about me."

He placed his machine down on the worktop. "When was the last time you got laid, little brother?"

Paige. It was always Paige. My silence was answer enough.

"That's what I thought. You don't date, you don't fuck, and it's making you crazy." He stood, removed his gloves and threw them with force into the trash.

"I'm feeling—"

"Better, yeah, I heard you the first time." He grabbed the ointment and threw it at me. I caught it and he shook his head. "You have to try. Just try, Dex."

He was right.

Who will want you?

I closed my eyes briefly, willing away that nagging voice.

"I will."

Liam stared at me for a few seconds and then nodded. "Alright, then. Let's get this place cleaned up. Kieran left thirty minutes ago. He texted and said he saved us a table."

I opened the tube and spread the salve on my skin before I stood to look at it in the mirror. My flesh was red and angry around the thick, dark letters. It looked badass, though, and I allowed myself to smile.

"You going to help me clean or stare at your ugly mug all night?" Liam's smirk made me laugh.

"Grab my shirt, dick."

Both of my brothers were drunk. I nursed my bottle of water as I watched them prowl around the bar. Tana sat in the corner eyeing Liam with a sour expression as he whispered into some slutty looking girl's ear. This wasn't an O'Connell norm. My brothers didn't get wasted, and seeing Liam whore himself around, in front of his current girl, it was pissing me off. Kieran was just on the other side of the bar. His smile was fake, and his jaw pulsed as he talked with a few guys I recognized. He'd gone to school with them and, if I remembered correctly, they were assholes. My eyes scanned the group to see if anything seemed off and it was then I spotted her. The girl from the other night. Kate. She stood next to one of the guys, and I swallowed when her dark brown eyes spotted me, too.

Shit.

I dropped my stare back down to my sketch pad. I chanced a glance up again and she was no longer standing by the guys, but I noticed my brother, Kieran, seemed more at ease. I checked on Liam again and my eyes narrowed. He was standing between the stranger's legs with his mouth on her neck. He stepped away from her and took her hand in his. He looked over his shoulder and gave me a knowing nod. He was leaving with her, and didn't give a shit about the wake he would leave with Tana who sat alone in the corner. If this was him moving on, I didn't want any part of it.

"Hey, you." The voice was familiar.

I turned my head as Liam left through the front door. "Kate, right?"

Her smile was simple. The pink shade of her lips reminded me of the sunset as they pulled up into a dimple. I made myself notice her details. I'd promised to try and she was attractive. I liked that she wore old band t-shirts. Tonight it was a black Joy Division tee. It tented over her tiny frame. She took the seat across from me.

"You remembered." Her voice was full of hope.

"I did."

She smiled again, this time it was flirty and it made me uncomfortable. "Drawing?" she stated the obvious and let her eyes fall to my work.

Kate's black hair was pulled into a loose bun. Stray strands fell every which way, and it reminded me of how Paige's hair had looked when she would paint. It wasn't a thought I wanted to have, but the longer I looked, the more I wished her black hair blonde. Kieran's eyes met mine from across the room. His jaw was pulsing again. For a minute, I thought he wanted to leave. The look he gave me almost pleaded, for what I wasn't sure. He scanned the room to where Liam had been and then shook his head before resuming his conversation. His posture no longer easy, but steel straight.

Kate's admiration of my work was short lived as she noticed my attention was not fixed on her, but on someone behind her. She looked over her shoulder and then back at me. "I went to school with those guys."

"Kieran's my little brother."

"Oh, yeah? I can see a resemblance." She smiled. "Kieran hates those guys, not sure why he's chatting them up. I used to date the idiot with the fauxhawk." She rolled her eyes and laughed.

I shrugged. The silence fell between us too easily, and I hoped she would recognize it, but instead she watched me with a quiet effort.

"Look, you didn't call, but you have this whole silent is sexy thing, artist bad boy vibe. I like it."

My chuckle rumbled in my chest. "Silent is sexy?" I raised my eyebrows.

"Mm-hmm." She nodded and another dimple popped in her other cheek.

"But I didn't call."

"Why is that?" she asked and her grin wavered.

She isn't her.

You had your chance and you lost it.

"I'm not really—"

"Available?"

I nodded. "Not really."

54

"Ex-girlfriend?" Her brows furrowed.

My jaw clenched.

"Bingo."

"Kate—"

She held up her hands as she stood. She leaned over and whispered into my ear. "Friends. Friends call friends all the time." She pecked me on the cheek quickly and pulled away. I could smell the scent of liquid courage on her breath.

"They do," I said and forced myself to hand her my pencil. Maybe this time I would actually call her.

She scribbled numbers, almost illegible onto the bar napkin before she walked away and, if I hadn't been paying close attention, I would have almost missed the slight wobble in her gait. She was drunk. Before I could think much more about it, Kieran stepped into my line of sight.

"You done, can we leave now?" He was angry.

"Sure. You okay?"

"Just fucking peachy. Let's go."

The next morning Liam was sporting a huge chip on his shoulder and a nasty hangover. The woman from the bar hadn't been there when I had left this morning. I'd been in a hurry to avoid the conversation we'd inevitably have to have about why he'd drank so much. But, I pushed away the previous night's events so I could concentrate on the painting in front of me. I'd been at the studio for a couple hours, and I was lost inside the canvas. Chandler had stopped in a few times, asking me if I wanted something to drink. He'd told me that another associate would be coming in soon and he would be leaving, so if I needed anything I could ask her. I didn't pay him much attention as I swirled two giant blue orbs in the center of the white. The purples, oranges, and pinks blended behind them. They formed the ovals surrounding those haunting eyes, the same pair I loved to torture myself with. It was a mix of sunset and Paige. I hadn't been able to get the color of Kate's lips out of my head, not because I wanted them or her, but because the color pushed me to look harder, to see another female in the light of beauty beyond Paige.

My mouth was dry and my gut was empty. The growl almost echoed throughout the work space. I covered my palette with clear plastic wrap and headed to the bathroom to wash my hands. The bathroom was located in the back of the studio, down a hallway that led to an emergency exit. The water here never really got hot enough, and I had to scrub my hands almost raw to get most of the paint off. When I got home I would use turpentine under my nails and on the rest of the leftover paint. Earlier, I'd asked Chandler to book out the studio for me for the next couple of weeks. I was enjoying myself and, as I took in my paint-splattered appearance, my white shirt covered in blots of color, my lips spread into a grin. I hadn't been lying to Liam. I really did feel better.

I dried off my hands and headed back to grab my bag. The music I had on played off the acoustics in the large space and it sounded fucking amazing. My mood was high, and I was so entranced I almost tripped over my own feet. In the entryway to the studio, I kneeled down and quickly tied my loose lace. A quiet gasp startled me and I raised my head. All the air in my lungs evaporated. The room was too bright, I was seeing shit. I focused my eyes on the apparition in front of me.

Paige?

I stood slowly, afraid of myself, afraid of the thin, blonde girl standing with her back to me in front of the canvas. Her head tilted back gazing at the giant pair of eyes looking back at her. She had to be a hallucination. But still, I moved with measured steps as my pulse pounded. Her hair was longer than I remembered, her waist leaner, her arms too thin. I imagined her face with fangs, and her nails as talons, and I was afraid that she would turn and look at me before I got within a safe distance. She looked too real to have been conjured up by my sick imagination.

Touch her.

Without thinking, I reached my hand out and took a lock of her hair between my thumb and finger. She gasped again, but this time with fear as she whirled around, her hair ripped from my easy grip.

"Declan?" she nearly shouted. The hand she brought to her mouth trembled, and her wide, empty eyes filled with that pretty shade of blue I knew all too well.

PAIGE

Stagnant. I felt utterly wrung out. The bags under my eyes were circled with what looked like bruises. My nightmares kept me tossing and turning for the majority of the night, and though I was grateful Chandler let me take the morning off, I was sure he'd have me make it up to him somehow. I exhaled a noisy breath at the thought. I'd spent most of the previous night remembering after sifting through the box Clark had sent me. Forgotten dreams, forgotten songs—a forgotten life. I'd spent so much time focusing on how we, Declan and I, had ended that I'd let the treasures fade. I paid for it by letting myself look through those small memories. My eyes fell to my fingertips, and I could still feel the soft shred of cotton I'd saved from one of his old t-shirts. Keeping the whole thing, I would've never been able to hide it, so I'd cut a piece off and put it in the box. After I'd fallen asleep last night, I'd been haunted over and over again. It had been the same dream no matter how many times I'd woken up, each time I fell back to sleep, the last days of us, of him, played viciously through my head.

I rubbed my arms as a sudden cloak of cold covered my skin. My eyes welled with tears, but I quickly wiped them away. Declan was a constant ebb and flow. Clark had tried to wash him away, tried to bleach my colorful mind clean. The church kept me down with tales of sin and used my crimes, my own fears, against me. I'd become overly exhausted, always hungry, but not able to eat much. I was falling apart.

At least today I had some luck on my side, The Gallery was empty except for the artist in the back. His music breathed through the walls of the store and it was the only thing holding me together. I loved this album and I'd used to paint to it. I turned and stared at the studio door. Chandler had said only to disturb him if I thought it necessary. I was curious. It wouldn't be so terrible if I wanted to see what the guy was working on. I loved art and I missed it. I'd take a quick look, possibly offer him some water. Maybe he needed more paint. Besides, it would be a nice distraction from reality. My stomach flipped and I bit my lip. It was settled. I'd let myself have a peek.

My hands were clammy as I moved toward the door, and I rubbed them on my jeans, feeling more nervous than I'd felt in a long time. I'd been sheltered by my husband's perversions of God, being immersed in this world of art again, as much as its beauty swallowed me whole, it scared the heck out of me, too. Because all I'd had before was art and Declan, and what if I'd forgotten how to create? What if Clark, the church, had sucked every last bit of who I was from my veins? I'd never have Declan again, but I still had hope in the smell of paint, and the feel of a brush in my hand. After what I'd done, I wasn't sure that I deserved hope, but as my fingers touched the cool metal knob of the studio door, hope bloomed inside me like a sterling rose.

The dream-like quality of the music fed my heartbeat as the door opened. I took a few timid steps and realized no one was there. The place was empty. The lights were on and there was a stool holding a palette filled with paints, but it was covered, as if he'd finished. Maybe I missed him leave while I was counting out the register with Chandler. I noticed an iPhone plugged into the stereo, and wondered why he hadn't shut off the music. The door shut loudly behind me and I jumped.

A nervous giggle erupted and I shook my head. "Hello?"

Nothing.

My feet felt weighted as I took a few more steps, and once my eyes landed on the canvas, my chest tightened with each erratic beat of my heart. Gorgeous swaths of color filled my vision. Purples and oranges mixed to create a stunning sunset effect behind a pair of blue eyes. I stepped closer to the painting as the hair on the back of my neck stood, and goose bumps pricked at my skin. The sensation in my fingertips tingled as the familiar color, set, and brush strokes stared back at me from the canvas.

A whispered gasp spilled from my lips. Those were my eyes. *Was it possible?* I was about to take a step back, take a better look when I felt something touch my hair. My scream caught in my throat as I spun to see what or who had touched me. My eyes widened and the strangled scream came out as a loud, breathy gasp.

"Declan?" My voice sounded fake, like I hadn't been the one to say the word. Like looking at him, in the flesh, was just a dream. I was stuck in a dream. My hand shook as I brought it to my lips.

He just stared at me in horror. His light blue eyes filled with insecurity, as if he wasn't sure I was really there. His shoulders were too broad, much broader than I remembered. He had a full, but trimmed beard. The dark blond color of it was appealing. He looked like a stranger, but the confused, sad sheen of his eyes made me ache to touch him, to soothe him.

I took another step forward and he backed away. The movement bringing everything into pristine clarity.

"No." His deep voice stabbed me. I'd lost the quality of it years ago and hearing it almost brought me to my knees. "How—"

He closed his eyes briefly and his jaw clenched before the full bore of his hatred hit me in the chest.

This wasn't the Declan I knew. The Declan I knew was a boy on the cusp of manhood. His eyes had been kind, his body had been strong, but lean. His facial features had still held the softness of youth. This Declan... he was a man. Etched and stark. His body was built and full of cut muscle. His arms were covered in full sleeves of tattoos and they flexed nervously under his paint-splattered, white t-shirt. He was worn, weary and absolutely beautiful. My stomach knotted as the silence grew. His eyes scanned my body and I wondered what he was thinking. There was no happiness on his lips, no joy in those crystalline eyes.

"How did you know I was here?" He shook his head again, his eyes closed, and he brought the heel of both of his palms to his temples.

"I-I work here." My stutter caused his eyes to flick open and lock with mine. His arms now hung at his sides, his hands balled into fists.

Declan's lips moved, but nothing came out, no words and no sound. My heart hammered as I watched the man transform into the boy I had loved, that I still loved. He was sifting through that noise in his head and every nerve ending in my body wanted to reach out to him like I used to. It was what I'd always done. The urge to console him won over self-preservation. My hand touched the twitching muscle of his bicep and it was surprisingly soft. His eyes darted to where my fingers rested. My blank skin against his ink. It didn't match... not anymore.

He shrugged away from my touch. "Don't fucking touch me."

The threat in his voice gripped my spine and I stumbled backward. "I'm sorry." The terror in my tone registered and his eyes softened.

How did I proceed? What could I say? The last time I'd seen Declan was a week after we'd both decided to abort our pregnancy. He never wanted to do it, it was against everything he'd believed. He would have married me, he would have lost himself inside of some crappy job, given up everything he'd ever wanted to support us just like his father had for his mother. I was young, scared, and his dad had turned into a drunk.

It didn't help that my parents had started attending that damn church and had told me to leave Declan several times. They'd begun to plant seeds of doubt even back then, and when it looked as if I wouldn't comply, they'd threatened me, told me I'd have nothing if I stayed with him. And when I found out I was pregnant, instead of celebration, all I felt was agony. My parents would have sent me away if I'd chosen to keep the baby, and I would've never seen Declan again. At the time, terminating the pregnancy, it felt like the only option.

Declan hadn't originally said it, but he'd hated me for asking him to agree to it, hated me for making him take me to the clinic, and hated me for actually killing our child. It had taken exactly seven days for our entire world to end. Declan had never looked at me the same, and that last night we were together... everything we'd loved about each other had been laid to ruin. As I gazed at him now, anger rolling off his shoulders, with each rapid breath I knew, he still hadn't forgiven me. He still hated me and had every right to. I was a murderer, and I'd killed everything.

"I'm sorry," I repeated and the tension in his shoulders eased as tears poured from my eyes.

He swore under his breath and turned toward the stereo. For a moment, I wanted to bolt. Leave the studio and the store behind. I wanted to run and jump in my car. Flee, get as many miles between me and my past as possible. Instead, I stood still. Trapped by his smell and how it mixed with each unsteady breath I took. I missed it. I missed him, and how *he* used to make me feel. There were so many things I wanted to tell him, that he should know, but the room went silent and he pocketed his phone. He turned and made a move to come forward but stopped. Nine years was an eternity compared to the fifty feet between us now, but as his eyes clouded over, I felt him slip into the darker side of never again.

"Declan, I don't know what to say." My voice cracked and he stepped backward.

"There's nothing you can say, Paige." He winced at the sound of my name just before he turned and disappeared into the back hall.

The blaring, overhead alarm went off. The emergency exit door had been opened and a hard sob burst from my chest.

He was gone.

DECLAN

L *iar*
  Her palm singed against my ink-stained skin.
  "Don't fucking touch me."
Touch me.
She deceived you.
You're weak.

The room was a fucking vacuum as the roar in my head raged. My heart pounded, ripped, and almost tore through my chest. I couldn't breathe. Her eyes. Those goddamn eyes brimmed with fear when I raised my voice, but her hands felt like fire and, having her skin on mine again, it was agony and glory all at once.

"I—I'm sorry." Her voice shook.

My fury poured down my spine in crashing waves. Paige tried to shrink down inside herself, and the silence grew like an infection, the decayed air smelled like rust between us.

"I'm sorry," Paige spoke again, her tone soft, mournful... ethereal.

My shoulders fell and the tight muscles in my jaw relaxed. The fury transformed into murky gray hues of sorrow. My war between hate and love, certainty, and the consequence of her, drummed deeply in my chest. My hand twitched. Her skin was just a breath away, and I had longed to remember the texture. I swore under my breath and turned. I had to put some distance between us before I did something I'd regret. I switched off the stereo, grabbed my phone, and turned to face the executioner. From this distance I could pretend she was just another delusion, another wraith I'd summoned to taunt and tease me. My feet moved toward her, involuntarily, my body seeking out its other half, but it took everything I had left inside of my shell of a soul to stop myself from moving closer to her. If I got too close I would surely burn.

"Declan, I don't know what to say."

It was the rejection I'd expected and the pain of it sent me reeling. I hadn't even realized I'd allowed any hope to seep through.

"There's nothing you can say, Paige." The truth sliced me open and the pain of it woke me from my dream. Paige Simon was a fucking ghost. Everything good about us died the day our baby did.

The waiting room was sterile white. Magazines sat on the tables scattered throughout the room, with moms and babies on their covers as a giant 'fuck you' to those who were here to end life instead of nurture it. This was the last place I wanted to be. Paige's cold hand was in mine, her face was stark as she stared forward. She wouldn't, couldn't look at me. I should've begged her not to do this, took her to the courthouse and married her the day she told me she was pregnant. She'd said she was only seven weeks along, and I'd told her maybe if we gave it time she'd change her mind. But she'd been

petrified. Terrified of the future I'd offered her. She'd told me her parents would have never allowed it, and that if we kept the baby they'd send her away, and losing her... it wasn't a possibility I wanted to entertain. What we were about to do, this choice, I'd been raised to believe it was the worst kind of sin, and if my parents ever found out, Liam... Kieran... I'd beg for Hell. But, part of me understood, we were too young, and when I married Paige I wanted it to be because she wanted to, not because we had to.

She'll never marry you.

I closed my eyes. The stress of the past week had slowly dismantled my progress. Since I'd been with Paige the past four years, my meds, therapy, it all really worked. She was a constant in my life, and even though my doctor said it was my medication compliance, it was Paige who kept the voices at bay entirely.

"Are you okay?" she asked and I opened my eyes.

I shook my head. "No."

"Me either." Her eyes were void of the color I loved.

"We could leave. We don't—"

"Paige Simon," a nurse wearing light blue scrubs called her name.

Our hands were linked as we stood, and I was just about to follow her when she shook her head. "I'll have them come get you when I'm in recovery."

"I want to be there for you."

Her eyes filled with tears. "Please, I can't... I won't... I need to do this on my own."

My eyes blurred as she dropped my hand. The separation, I felt it in my gut, the hollow emptiness made me sick as I thought about how she would soon feel that emptiness too, if she wasn't already. The nurse glared at us. We were holding up her day. Maybe she wanted to go to lunch, maybe she was judging us, or maybe she was just tired of waiting on kids who were making decisions too big to bear.

"I love you," she whispered and leaned up on her toes to kiss me on the cheek. The desolation in my stomach grew.

"I love you, Paige."

I hadn't realized back then that "I love you" really meant goodbye. The sickly sweet, brown liquor coated my throat and tongue as I sat on my bedroom floor and swallowed deeply from the bottle. I'd stolen some of my brother's whiskey and locked myself in my room. I'd lost time again, intoxicated and hazed from the day and the Jack. How long had I been home? This was foolish, immature, and reckless, but I was done denying myself a moment to fade... crash, and I wanted to be devoured by the pain. The *Christmas Kiss* was hanging on my wall. I'd framed and placed it next to the painting I'd done of Paige's eyes a few years back. Her eyes the day of the procedure had been especially void of color, and I wanted to paint them as a memorial.

I kept my gaze trained on the *Christmas Kiss* as I stood and let the resentment spark the fuel of the alcohol. The music blared angrily from the speakers of my computer and the sound of it was the only thing muting the voices. They were mocking me, they rejoiced in my faults and, the more I drained the bottle, the worse they became. Disgust, hatred for myself, for her, for every-fucking-thing fisted my hand around the neck of the bottle. I wanted to break it, shatter it, and when it didn't fold beneath my grip, I threw it. The bottle smashed against the wall, against the painting of Paige's eyes. The liquid trickled down creating an illusion of tears and my eyes stung with my own.

"Declan!"

I slammed my eyes shut willing the voice away.

"Declan, open the door!"

My bedroom door handle started to rattle, and a pounding noise caused me to open my eyes. The door seemed to bow inward, and a spike of adrenaline ran through my veins.

"Open. The. Damn. Door."

Liam.

"Declan! Please. Please, God don't—" his panicked voice rose above the music and the door strained on its hinges as he fought against it from the other side.

I moved to unlock it, but before I had a chance, splinters of wood scattered to the floor from the door jam. The handle dangled, broken and useless. I stumbled backward and the noise in my brain began to hammer around my temples. Liam's eyes were wide as they fell to the floor. The room reeked of alcohol.

"Why the hell didn't you answer me? I thought... I thought—"

"I was dead?" The words were flat.

Liam's eyes found mine. His jaw ticked with suppressed emotion, and he swallowed before he spoke. "Are you fucking drunk?"

"I might have had a little."

He moved past me and turned down the music. "Talk to me, Dex, what the fuck?"

"There's nothing to say." It was basically what I'd said to her and it still held true.

His jaw clenched even tighter and he gripped my shoulder. "Talk to me, because this shit..." He waved to the shattered remains of his Jack Daniel's. "Is not okay."

"I saw her." The lump in my throat was like glass.

"Paige?" he asked with an irritated patience.

I nodded.

"I thought you said the meds were working?"

"I really saw her, at The Gallery," I said, stepping back from his touch.

"The Gallery?" He was skeptical.

"Yes, that's what I just said. She works there, I guess." I turned away from him and grabbed the small garbage can by my desk as the realization of my truth filled his eyes.

I carefully picked up the shards and placed them in the can. I'd deal with the ruined painting later. Liam's eyes followed every movement waiting for me to dissolve, but I wouldn't, not in front of him, not when he was barely escaping his own chaos.

"So? What happened?"

"Nothing... we saw each other, it hurt like hell, and I left."

He avoided my lack of details and I was grateful, the details were mine... private.

"You should've called me, you shouldn't be drinking."

"Just like you shouldn't?" I threw the last chunk of glass hard into the trash can before I set it down.

He raised his eyebrows. "I barely—"

"You were wasted last night, and I know you brought that chick home, too."

"This isn't about me, Dex. You can't drink when you're taking those meds, it's not safe, and you can't let that fucking bitch do this to you."

I shoved him hard in the chest. "Don't ever—"

"What? Call it as I see it? She left, Declan, she's gone, and I'm tired of watching you die over some bitch who chose to leave without telling you why or where she went."

Each muscle in my body ached as I held back my rage. "You don't know what you're talking about."

Liam's palms planted on my chest as he pushed me backward. "Then fucking tell me, tell me how you can still defend that—"

All the pent-up aggression connected with his jaw in the form of my fist. Liam took the hit with hardly a misstep. "You don't know everything!" I let my voice raise, let the growl out, let myself free, let myself feel the throbbing in my knuckles as I sank to the floor. It was better than feeling nothing.

"Then tell me."

I'd never told anyone about how Paige and I really ended things. I'd never confessed my sins. They didn't belong solely to me and talking about it would've been a betrayal to her. Liam's eyes met mine with an understanding as he sat down next to me on the floor without a word, waiting for me to make the next move. It was like I was a teenager all over again, but now, Liam was the only person I could talk to about the sickness inside me. We sat in the stillness for a while before I gathered the courage to speak.

"Paige was pregnant." I kept my eyes forward and traced the quickly dried rivers of bourbon along the wall. Anything to keep myself from seeing the disappointment in his features. "I'd always wanted to marry her, Liam. You know that. But, she was terrified, terrified of having a life with me... I think... I think she thought getting rid of it was her only option. She talked herself into it, told me her parents would never let us be together and then afterward it was..." I let my head fall into my hands. "It was different. She wasn't the same, and neither was I." I raised my head.

"Declan—"

His eyes held pity that I didn't deserve.

"It was *our* choice, don't fucking look at me like that." I stood abruptly and the alcohol buzzed in my head like a bee. "I'm just as guilty as she is."

"Guilty?" he asked as he stood. "Declan you were frightened kids." He was incredulous.

I shrugged. "It doesn't matter, what's done is done, and she left, and I think this is my punishment, being without her, it's my cross to bear."

He narrowed his eyes. "You sound like Mom."

70

"Maybe she's right, maybe we should all go to church more, look at Kieran, he's happy." I exhaled a breath, picked up my phone from my dresser and put it in my pocket.

Liam chuckled. "I wouldn't be too sure of that, this whole family is screwed."

The thorn in my heart twisted. Paige and I, we'd made a choice and we could have suffered through the loss together, healed, and moved on, but the night she left, she'd made sure I wouldn't follow.

"I couldn't have married you, Declan. We'd end up just like your mom and dad. You would've had to get a job working minimum wage. There would be bills, and mouths to feed. You would've thrown away everything that is beautiful about who you are until you drowned your regrets in a bottle and ended up hating me for trapping you into a marriage that was doomed from the start."

I was no better than my father to her.

You're disposable.

"I'm exhausted, Liam." The bone-tired words spilled from my mouth.

"I wish you would've told me, you shouldn't have had to go through that all on your own. I could have helped you through everything. All this time, Declan... you need to move on, this shit... it's unhealthy."

"And banging random chicks is healthy?" My eyes slid to the napkin with Kate's number sitting on my night stand.

He shook his head and followed my gaze. "No, Dex, it's not, but it sure as shit feels better than being alone." He gripped my shoulder again. "You were doing better, don't let this set you back."

This.

She's so close.

Her.

She's waiting.

Paige.

"I think it might be too late." I ran my hands through my hair and watched him as he walked over to my nightstand and picked up the napkin.

"Is it?" He walked past me and handed me the napkin. "I'm heading out, Kieran wants to go to Bellows again. I think the whole priesthood thing, or lack thereof, is getting to him. You coming?"

I read the phone number in my hand over and over again. The whiskey pumped through my rushing pulse.

"Yeah, let me just clean up this mess real quick."

Feels better than being alone.

"One hour... take a shower, and tomorrow you're helping me fix this damn door."

Once he left my room, I pulled my phone from my pocket and opened the lock screen. The Jack made me bolder than I was really feeling, or maybe I was just giving into the fatigue of loving someone who couldn't love me back.

Me: *This is Declan, want to meet at Bellows tonight?*

My stomach churned as I awaited a response. Something told me it would've been smarter to just stay home and pass out on whatever else Liam had in the kitchen, but I didn't have a chance to back out.

Kate: *I'm already here. See you soon.*

DECLAN

Stress. It built like a boiling tea kettle in my chest as I walked through the doors of Bellows. The bass thumped and the room smelled of stale beer, perfume, and desperation. The tables were full, and I kept my eyes down as I followed behind Liam. My palms were sweating and, for a split second, I hoped that maybe Kate had decided not to wait here for me and had gone home. Liam stopped abruptly and I raised my gaze. She was sitting at the bar. Kate's black hair was shiny and straight and the shots I'd taken while Liam showered fed my swarming buzz.

Liam's knowing eyes fell across my face and he swallowed. "Maybe." He paused and shook his head. "I don't know, Dex, maybe—"

"I'm okay." I attempted to lift the corners of my mouth.

Kate's eyes slid across the room and her lips parted with a smile once she found me. She was wearing all black, her dress was short, exposing ghostly white legs. The dark fabric made the tone of her skin stand out, and I wished for her skinny jeans and old band t-shirts. My anxiety was about to trickle over the

73

surface as Kate confidently pushed her hair over her shoulder and stepped off the bar stool.

"Hey." Kieran's hand clapped down on my shoulder.

"Declan's meeting a chick tonight." Liam sounded proud and it should have made me feel better, but I knew he was infusing the lie into his voice to help me. He knew me better than anyone, and he saw terror written all over my face the minute we stepped foot into the bar.

"Who?" Kieran's smile spread across his face.

"Hey, Declan." Kate's voice was sultry under the silhouette of alcohol. It poured like silk between us. The dim light of the room set the mood, purposefully nursing the notions of anticipation, sex, and need. And maybe it was just the whiskey, but it put me at ease.

"Hi," I said and gave her the best smile I had. Her face lit up and the glossy shimmer of her lips drew my attention. She was beautiful. The easy line of her nose, the rise of her cheekbones, her small stature, and full breasts, I should be pleased, but instead I suddenly felt nauseous.

"If you need us, we'll be in the back playing pool." Liam gave me a nod.

Kieran lingered, his eyes fixed on Kate, and they narrowed into a hard glare. She was facing me so she'd missed the look, but it bothered me and my sick stomach churned.

"Come on, little brother," Liam spoke, and Kieran took a step backward; his brows furrowed as his eyes met mine with questions just before he turned and walked toward the back room with Liam.

Was he disappointed in me?

Of course he is.

She's not her.

The air in the room was hot and thick, and maybe it was panic or maybe I was being a pussy, either way, I needed a moment to breathe. "Let's go outside for a minute?"

74

I was without the shield of my sketch pad and even the hard bass wasn't silencing the doubt or the voices tonight.

"Okay." She smiled at me and, before I had a chance to walk toward the front, she grabbed my hand and laced her fingers through mine. Her skin was sweaty and foreign. She smiled up at me and a slight quiver of her bottom lip made me feel better. Maybe I wasn't the only nervous one.

I exhaled as I led us through the crowd. She tightened her grip, and it felt good to have someone hold onto me again. The night air was dry and warm as I opened the door to Bellows. It washed over me and cleansed my worried thoughts, if only for the moment.

She followed next to me, hand in hand, her purse over her shoulder, the strap positioned between her breasts as we walked a few more steps into the night. The heat of the sidewalk burned beneath us, and I almost felt like a man again as my eyes fell to our clasped hands. I stopped mid-step and sucked in a ragged breath.

She giggled. "Are you nervous or something?"

My smile was genuine as I let the Jack Daniel's encourage me to speak the truth. "Yes."

She hiccupped and I laughed. "Sorry, I might've had a few drinks before you got here. A little liquid courage never hurt, right?" She quirked her perfectly sculpted black brow.

I shrugged. "I normally don't drink, but I did tonight and I'm feeling—"

"Sick?" she guessed.

I nodded.

"I could tell. You went pale when I walked up to you." She bit her lip. "Are you feeling better with the fresh air?"

It was still too warm at night, and the oven we were standing in was only mildly helping. "I think it's the heat that's getting to me," I admitted.

The thin, white fabric of my cotton V-neck was damp with sweat.

"I'm parked just behind Bellows, we could sit and talk? I have this wonderful thing called air conditioning." She smirked. "Come on."

She dropped my hand as she led the way. My heart pounded as I followed her. I silently wished for the bottle of Jack, for my sketch pad, something... anything to distract or hide behind. I didn't talk.

"This is me." She pulled a remote key out of her purse and the headlights of a red SUV blinked.

Kate walked to the driver side and got into the car. The engine started and I stared at the tinted windows.

She's not her

"That's the point," I said to no one in particular and opened the passenger side door. Acoustic guitars and faint female vocals greeted me as I sat in the passenger seat. No bass. No hard lyrics. Nothing to disguise what I really was, nothing to keep the Devil fed. The voices in my head celebrated. I swallowed as I situated myself into the leather seat. She was parked in the almost vacant parking lot behind Bellows that was reserved for the businesses next door. The cool air of her A/C calmed my nerves, and I leaned back resting my head onto the plush seat.

We didn't talk at first and just listened to the music. After a while, my voices grew bored of mocking me, and I was able to relax and actually enjoy the sound of my own breathing, of hers, nervous with anticipation.

"Do you like working with your brothers?" Kate's voice was small as she turned and faced me, her head still resting on the seat. Her mouth pulled into a grin as I met her stare.

"Sometimes." I chuckled and I almost didn't recognize it. The words felt fuzzy and I licked my lips. Kate's eyes fell to my mouth and my pulse quickened.

"I work retail over at The Gateway Mall. Very respectable place called Victoria's Secret, you might have heard of it?" Her lips pulled wide into a warm smile.

"A job is a job."

It was her turn to lick her lips and I briefly wondered what she would taste like. *Would the gloss of her lips be sticky on mine, was it flavored?*

She laughed and turned her head forward to look out the windshield. I thought we were going back to the silent waiting game, but instead she spoke softly about the little incidentals of her life. She started off telling me about her love for comic book movie remakes and bad Chinese food. She told me about the time a customer's husband propositioned her in the dressing room. She told me how she hated living alone, and how she thought for sure she'd be in L.A. by now, acting, doing something more than wasting away in her one-room apartment. She told me about high school, how she had been a cheerleader with a bad reputation, the reputation that had followed her to the shitty community college she tried to attend every other semester. I was the wrong brother in the car. She was coming clean about the disappointments of her life, and it should have been Kieran who was here to receive her confession.

She turned her head to look at me again. Her cheek against the leather seat. Her eyes seemed glassy, either from tears, or her previous drinks. "My life isn't what it was supposed to be."

"It never is." My body tensed as she reached across the console and rested her hand on my thigh.

"Truth or Dare?" she asked with a flirty smile, and the heat of her palm on my leg soaked through my jeans and stirred awake the man inside the lost places of my mind.

"Truth," I answered.

"I do things, Declan, things I shouldn't, to feel better about myself. I'm tired of being alone."

So was I.

The rise and fall of her chest drew my eyes to the low dip of her dress. My fingers ached to touch her. Something coiled inside my gut and all I wanted to do was tell her something real. Confess to her as she had to me. The air felt thin as I said, "I'm tired of waiting. Waiting to feel something. Waiting to burn. Waiting to fucking fall apart." I swallowed as her eyes locked on mine. They were bright as the first light of morning as she eased her body across the center console of the car.

My eyes on her mouth, my head full of the white noise of hope as I readied myself to kiss her. *Kate*. I'd only kissed maybe five girls in my lifetime and, as her lips met mine, the white noise parted and allowed the expectant quiet to bathe the space between us. She moaned a delicate breath as her hands wrapped into my hair. My hands found her hips as she moved onto my lap. Her skirt hitched up as she situated herself above me, straddling me. I placed my hand on the warmth of her thighs as she licked my bottom lip. She tasted like beer, and the plastic flavor of her gloss coated my tongue as I deepened the kiss with a groan. She rocked her hips against me and I hardened beneath her.

She's not her, and she's not for you.

She's dirty, can't you see her shadows.

Don't stop.

Stop.

Don't stop.

The pain of my arousal made my stomach contract as she moved her body along mine. Tortured. Wound up. Heated breaths and lost words drove the need I'd buried for so long. The whispers in my head grew louder. Urging me to feel, urging me to stop, the conflict flared inside me with an angry flame, and I gripped her hip harder than I should have with one hand as the other moved down past her skirt. It had bunched along her waist and her black underwear was visible. My thumb trailed just under the seam and Kate whimpered against my lips. She leaned back and dropped her hooded eyes as she pulled at my belt and quickly undid the button of my jeans.

What am I doing?

You're Feeling. You're burning.

Kate's clammy hands wrapped around me and my jaw clenched.

She's dirty.

She moved her thumb over the head of my dick and I groaned. I closed my eyes and tried to push away the guilt as she worked her hands up and down. The bile crept up my throat and I gripped her wrist. My eyes opened and instead of the light blue I had prayed for every night, the deep color of soil gazed back at me. The mud of a grave. There was no hope in her... she was full of shadows and the gray light of dawn was just an illusion sick with the perversion of her truth.

Stop.

Stop.

"Stop." I was breathless as I ceased the motion of her coercive hands with my own.

She leaned forward and brought her lips to my ear. "Are you not having fun?" Her teeth scraped at the lobe and it set my jaw on edge. The whispers turned to laughter.

"I need to go."

"Okay." She drew out the word, annoyed as she lifted her body and maneuvered back to the driver side of the car.

I fumbled with my pants and belt as I pulled myself back together with trembling fingers. The muscles in my arms flexed as I fisted my hands at my side once I'd finished, once I'd realized what I had allowed to happen. The whiskey had turned sour and my head was hammering out every vile thought.

You would have fucked her in a car. You want to. You need to.

I shook my head and mashed my molars together to stop from arguing with myself out loud.

"I thought you were into me?" She was hurt, angry. Kate pulled at the hem of her dress trying to make it longer, trying to cover up her shame.

"I'm sorry... I-I told you before I wasn't—"

"Available, yeah, I know, but—"

I opened the door. "Trust me, Kate..." I stepped out of the SUV and rested my hands on the frame of the car as I leaned down and looked her in the eyes one last time. "I'm... I'm sparing you."

She rolled her eyes. "From what?"

"From me." I leaned back and dropped my hands from the car. I didn't look at her when I shut the door. I didn't turn to watch her laugh at me, at my lack of courage, or my sad, fucked-up excuses. I didn't look to see if what I'd said had affected her at all, and I didn't care, because there was nothing I could do about it anyway. I belonged to Paige, and as I neared the familiar beat of Bellows, the phantom feeling of Kate's fingers evaporated. I was able to concede that seeing Paige again, even though it had pulled me back into the underworld of my own mind, had me feeling something other than despair. When I saw myself reflected in her eyes again, I was more than just a mirrored image of placid calm and cooled aggression. I was fire and want and rage.

I was feeling.

I'd felt.

The air in Bellows had thinned now that the expectation had disappeared into a messy mistake in Kate's front seat. Liam was sitting with a few guys from the shop, and Kieran's cool blue eyes met mine from across the room. He exhaled what looked like a breath of relief as he hurried toward me

"Where's Kate?"

"I think she went home. I walked her to her car," I lied and his lips formed a thin line.

"You were gone awhile." He gave me a once over and his shoulders eased for some reason. "Look, that chick. She's not a good girl, Declan."

"No?" I played along.

He shook his head. "She's got some issues, and I don't like to talk shit, but I'm pretty sure she's promiscuous."

I wanted to laugh at the word. He was only twenty-six. He should be drinking, sleeping around, and living life, living a life I sure as hell would never have. "Always the saint." I slapped him on the shoulder and gave him a sideways smile.

"Just stay away from her, Declan. She's an alcoholic. She was hitting on those assholes I went to high school with the other night, then came right over to you and flashed her smile. She was drunk. I should've said something then, but you seemed interested, and it's been so long since... don't buy into her, Declan, you've waited too long to just—"

"Don't worry." I hated that he did. "Kate's not for me. She's not my type."

She's not Paige.

I gave him my practiced chuckle and he smiled.

"Good." He nodded toward the back of the room. "Let's play a game of pool."

It was easy for Liam and Kieran to make believe I was normal inside the confines of the bar and the tattoo shop, but I was tired of pretending. This day wouldn't end in laughter and fake smiles. It would end with smears of paint as I sullied the eyes that haunted me from the canvas.

"Nah, I'm going to head to the studio. I've got some energy to work off. See you at work tomorrow."

"You sure?" The creases around his eyes deepened with concern.

I nodded.

"Chandler finally gave you the key to the place?"

"Yeah, I guess when you pay for two weeks of studio time he figures you're good for it. Tell Liam I left?"

"Sure thing, Declan." He shook my hand and pulled me into a side hug. "See you in the morning."

I tried to ignore that the tone of his voice hinted at a question as I turned to leave. It was a fact, my brothers, my mother, they watched me like I was a bomb and my clock was winding down and, at some point, I'd reach my detonation and rip our family to shreds.

PAIGE

His room was small with aged paint and brown shag carpet. His twin bed was pushed into the corner, the handmade quilt was oversized and threadbare. The whole space was covered in drawings and paintings. Declan's talent showcased on every wall and spilled from his desktop. It smelled like paper, citrus, and the slight scent of soap lingered in the mix. His space was warm, inviting, and I liked how the lamp on the table cast everything in a creamy light.

"You're pretty far from the bench." He took my hand, led me to his bed, and I sat down.

The bench of the mountain was where the rich kids lived. The doctors' sons and daughters. The accountants and finance gurus. Me.

"I always wondered why rich people build in such dangerous places. You know?"

I shook my head and pressed my lips together trying to fight my smile. I liked listening to the way Declan thought. He was so smart and most teenagers didn't care about the little things, not like he did.

83

"Beachfront property, mountain sides, it's crazy, think about it. Hurricanes, earthquakes, floods..." He noticed my small smile and smirked. "What?"

My lips curled of their own accord. "I like that you think of this stuff, Declan."

His smile fell and he sat next to me on the bed. I lifted and entwined his fingers with mine. "I'm fucking weird." His stare landed on our hands.

His fingernails were covered in paint; yellow and red and blue crusted under his nails and in the creases of his hand. His skin was rough and worn, like a real artist, and mine, it was soft and underused. Together they clashed, but I loved the feel of him. I thought it was a perfect fit. "I don't think you're weird, and my house, it's cold, Declan. We have all these big windows to look out over the valley, but the curtains are always shut. Sunsets hidden, starlight concealed... your house... it's a home, mine...you've seen it... it's staged. Always on display, but never part of life."

He raised our joined hands to his mouth and brushed his lips over my knuckles. I shuddered and closed my eyes as his hot breath tickled my skin. "I'm sorry I waited so long to bring you here, I was... embarrassed."

My eyes opened. We'd been together for almost eight months, and this was the first time I'd been invited to his house. I wanted to ask him why, even though I knew the answer. He was poor. His dad drank too much, from what he told me, and his brothers were rowdy, but he always spoke well of his mother. "Don't be. I'm excited to finally meet everyone." I turned and faced him fully, unlinking our hands so I could hold his face between my palms. His pale cheeks filled with color as I leaned in. "Thank you for letting me in. It feels... more official, for some reason."

He licked his lips, his blue eyes never leaving mine. "Just ignore my dad, okay? Anything he says... just forget about it."

84

My stomach dropped and I was sad for him. I could see the fear and rage behind his irises. "It doesn't matter what he says." I kissed him once and then again and he exhaled in relief. "I'm not going anywhere."

He kissed me, this time at his own fevered pace. Declan's mouth claimed mine as he leaned me backward onto his bed. The soft scent of him encircled me and each kiss he took pulled me deeper in—in love with him. I was in love with him. It was absurd, and juvenile, but I wanted to spend every minute in this tiny, ramshackle room with this boy who thought like a man, who painted like a god, and who made me feel like I was special... like I'd always be his.

It was dark in my room. The overcast sky gave little light and it didn't help I refused to open the blinds. After seeing Declan again, after seeing the hate in his eyes, I hadn't been able to go back to The Gallery. The next day I called in sick, and I didn't have another shift scheduled until this afternoon. It had rained the next day and hadn't stopped, fall pushed its way into the bowl of the valley. Cleansing the creosotes and sage, feeding the rivers, and bringing the cold of autumn with its crisp touch. Lana had tried to drag me out of bed with promises of food and tea. She'd tried to make me shower, tried to stuff me with Oreos and soup, but I wouldn't, couldn't budge. Her classes had kept her busy this week, and I was grateful for the privacy to grieve. I grieved for the loss of my child, for the loss of myself, for the loss of my life, my own person. I'd given into my parents and Clark and the damn church. I'd given up on myself. I lost my palette, my color, my individuality. I'd lost my love, my Declan, and I'd allowed him to fade. I'd fed him to the pack of wolves, to the demons in his head.

Seeing him in the studio, watching him war with himself, he was gone to them, to the voices. They plagued him and I let him go... nine years ago, after we'd split up, after he'd chosen to leave. He'd been so angry. But he'd come back for me, a week after the break up, and I refused to see him. I'd thought I was doing him a favor, doing myself a favor. We'd been cursed, damned, but after seeing myself on his canvas the other night, seeing my eyes, it was clear he never let me go. So I'd chosen to torture myself with memories. I'd succumbed to each one and fell into dreams of him and us. The summer he'd finally let me meet his family. His house was perfect, just like him, but his father had come home so drunk he'd puked on the porch and Declan had to ask his brother, Liam, to drive us to my house. We'd had dinner there instead, and it had taken him almost another month to finally let me back in.

I rolled to my side, the stench of body odor flared my nostrils. My eyes felt puffy and my hair was greasy and smelled like salt. This last dream hit me hard. It hit me like a train because it was the first time he'd given me his full trust and it was then that I realized I'd fallen in love with him. Teenagers don't really fall in love, my mother had said. My parents had played along with our relationship because they never thought it would flourish. But it had. And where we thought we were a blooming flower, my parents had thought we were a caustic weed. My parents joined the church my senior year and things only got worse from there.

You were young, you did what you could.

I exhaled a noisy breath. A sour film coated my teeth and my lips felt like sandpaper. My phone vibrated and the screen lit up casting a green glow to the room. I picked it up and stared at the face on the screen. I let it go to voicemail. Missed call. It didn't take long for her to call back. The screen lit up again and I swallowed past the empty feeling in my belly.

"Hello." My voice was stretched thin. I hadn't spoken in a day… maybe longer.

"Clark said he can't get a hold of you. Are you alright?" My mother's voice was full of fake concern.

"I'm fine. And, I told you I don't want to speak to him. He wants a divorce and so do I. He wants to be with *her*, Mom." I closed my eyes and leaned back into my pillow.

"I'm not sure about that, Paige. We've spoken to his parents, we all think—"

"I'm an adult, stop treating me like a child."

"Then stop acting like one!" She raised her voice and clicked her tongue. Her words held malice as she continued. "We did everything to assure your happiness, it's the least you could do, for your father, for me, he has to work with these people, Paige. We have a reputation to uphold. If you go through with this divorce... you'll be excommunicated. This is your deliverance. After what you did... well."

I could picture her in our white kitchen picking her manicured nails. Pastel pink, always pastel pink. Her blonde hair straight and her crème colored dress pressed. I grit my teeth.

"I know what I did, you don't need to remind me, and if getting excommunicated means I don't have to go to that church anymore.... if it means..." I sat up, my chest heavy and my voice building steam. "If it means I'm free of the false doctrine, the control of a man who would rather screw the nursery leader than be a good husband, then that is exactly what I want." I was out of breath, screaming, sobbing. I didn't speak like this. I didn't ever deny my parents' rule. But I was finished allowing people to dictate who I was supposed to be. "I'm done, Mom. I'm done paying for a sin I'll never be forgiven for."

Silence.

"Mom?" I choked out the word.

"If this is your choice," she spoke slowly with condemnation. "Then you have chosen the way of Hell, and may the fires burn away all your selfish needs. God forgive me, but there is no place in this home for you anymore, girl. You disrespected this house, your husband, and your father the day you left Clark, the church. And trust me... your father feels the same as I do."

He was probably sitting next to her, listening, throwing away his only child like the piece of garbage that she was.

I hung up the phone and stood from the bed. I had nothing left to say. My legs were lead stumps and as I stretched, the pain pulled like rubber bands along each limb of my body. I'd been avoiding that phone call for too long. I'd been excommunicated from a church that called me a murderer, from a husband who never loved me, and from a family that would see me burn before they ever allowed me to be happy again, to feel something other than mourning for the choice they'd never absolve me of.

I was truly alone. Utterly lost. And, even though I should fall back into the soiled sheets, never leave the filth of this room, something pulled me to the shower.

"I just draw what I see."

Sad eyes. My eyes.

"You see the world, Declan."

He was the only one who saw me... the only one...

I caught my breath and turned the water to scalding. The filth would wash away and I would be clean again.

The rain had subsided by the time I got to The Gallery. My stomach was empty, but after talking to my mother, after severing all ties to my family, I didn't have much of an appetite. I'd been at work for just about an hour and every time the bell on the door would ring my heart would fly into my throat. I didn't dare check the studio to see if his painting was still there. I seriously doubted he stuck around after seeing me. My whole body shivered. It was most likely the lack of sugar in my system or just straight-up anxiety. All I wanted was to see Declan again, but at the same time, I dreaded it. I had nothing left of me anymore. Nothing to lose. The layers had been shed and husked away into the trash.

"You look like shit. You've lost some weight?" Chandler's brown eyes assessed me with alarm. He'd been too busy stocking the shelves when I arrived to get a really good look at me.

The teal sweater I had on felt too big. It was supposed to hang off my shoulder, but it fell farther than it had before. My collarbones jutted out and my face felt hollow. I was starving, but not for food. I was hungry for something, someone, a love I didn't deserve... not anymore.

"I had a stomach bug. Sorry if I left you hanging the other day." I toyed with the thread on my sleeve and I kept my eyes on the counter.

"It happens. I was fine. But, listen, I think you should maybe go home? This little four-hour shift, it's nothing, I got it. Go rest."

If I had to go back to Lana's house and rot in the grime I'd created over the past few days I'd never survive. As hard as it was pretending to be a real human for a few hours, I didn't want to be alone.

"I'm feeling better." I gave him a weak smile.

His brows knotted. "Why don't I believe you?"

I puffed out a laugh. "Because you're too observant, I guess."

"Do me a favor. I'd rather not get..." he pointed his finger at my stomach, "Whatever the hell it is you have, so go home." His smile was lopsided, but he was being serious.

"Really?" I scrunched my nose when he nodded.

"Before you leave though, could you grab a few things from the studio for me while I finish up this last bit of inventory?

The customer who rented the place called earlier and he said he'd be by to pick up a few supplies he'd left last night."

My heart stopped.

Last night? Could it be Declan?

I nodded and he gave me a small cardboard box and a list of things to grab for the client.

He walked to the small pile of paints he had to shelve and left me to it. The studio door was at the end of my tunneled vision and, as I moved toward it, the room spun. Once I entered, and the smell of paint assaulted my senses, I practically stumbled over my own two feet as the canvas came into view. It was the same painting, his painting, but now mostly completed. I swallowed down my panic and let the vibrant colors pull me toward the larger-than-life blue eyes. It almost looked like a photograph. The detail was immaculate. The sadness nearly palpable.

The paints and brushes Declan had requested were sitting on the stool. They were his own. I didn't recognize the brush brand. My fingers trembled as I picked up the wooden handle of one of the smaller brushes. I might've been imagining things, but when I closed my eyes, I felt the heat of his skin, and the rough patches of his calloused flesh on mine. It was like he'd left his imprint, and the minute I connected with something of his I felt him, deeply, in my bones, my heart... in my soul.

"You're crazy," I mumbled.

"Paige?"

A small scream burst from my lips and I whirled around.

"Holy shit, I almost didn't recognize you." He was still a teenager the last time I saw him. He still looked the same, but older. His dark brown hair was cut short, his shoulders were huge and his chin was covered in a goatee.

"Kieran?"

He didn't answer, but his mouth twitched at the corners.

"I have the supplies, I mean, I was getting them—"

My hands shook so hard I almost dropped everything to the floor as I tried to gather them and place them in the box.

"It's alright. I can grab this stuff." Kieran reached out and placed his hand over mine. A calm energy hummed in the room, and my throat closed off as tears pricked my eyes. "Has he seen you?" He watched me with careful eyes.

I nodded and a small sob bubbled up my throat.

He swore under his breath. "That makes sense."

"What makes sense?"

"Declan used to go to St. Ann's Cathedral every month after you guys broke up to light a candle. He stopped going a while ago. But today, he left the shop early and asked me to come here to pick up some of his stuff so he could go pray. He was insistent. This week has been rough for him and he'd been doing so…" He shook his head as if he'd said too much. "It makes sense, because here you are."

"He lit a candle… every month?" I brought my fingers to my lips as the tears I'd been fighting finally fell. "What day?"

He narrowed his eyes. "The thirteenth, why?"

August thirteenth was the day we'd gone to the clinic.

"He's at St. Ann's?" I asked, my breath caught in my chest and pressed against my sternum, the rising need to leave, to find him, to connect, barreled through me.

He nodded. "Paige, listen he's—"

"Thank you." I dropped the brushes and box to the ground as I turned quickly to leave. It was the first sure thing I'd felt since I left Clark.

"Paige!" Kieran shouted and swore again, but I ignored him as I ran for the studio door.

11

PAIGE

The ornate wooden door, carved with angelic murals, was heavy and creaked as it opened. The sound was eerily loud and seemed to echo in the small chamber between the outside door to the church and the actual door to the cathedral chapel. The soles of my shoes squeaked against the ancient slate flooring as I took the few steps needed to enter the building. The rain had quit but the sidewalk was still wet. It was an off hour for the church, so I was able to park in front, but my shoes still suffered the wrath of the large puddles along the walkway up to the massive building. I felt underdressed in my sweater and jeans and, as my hand wrapped around the large iron handle of the inner door, my heart caught in my throat. I couldn't seem to catch my breath.

This door was just as heavy but made little noise, unaffected by the weather, it opened smoothly. The weight of it caused my arm to ache and, as the chapel was revealed to me, the honeyed scent of incense filled my nose. Each breath was difficult to take as my eyes searched the huge room. Pew after pew, my gaze lifted until it reached the altar. It was a massive sculpture of white marble, and just above it was a gruesome crucifix with a life-like version of Christ, blood spilling from his head, hands, feet, and side. I swallowed deeply at the mournful piece of art, and I was so transfixed by it I hadn't noticed the man kneeling at the left side of the altar until he spoke.

"Our Father, who art in heaven, hallowed be thy name; thy kingdom come, thy will be done, on earth as it is in heaven. Give us this day, our daily bread, and forgive us our trespasses, as we forgive those who trespass against us; and lead us not into temptation, but deliver us from evil. Amen."

Declan's voice was thick, as if he'd been crying, it seemed unsteady, and he kept his head down as he made the sign of the cross. He was kneeling in front of a table of candles, all lit and sparkling in the still air as if Declan's breath brought the flames to life. He hadn't heard me enter and he continued his penance as he began whispering again in prayer. This time, he prayed to the Virgin. He was wearing a black t-shirt and, as I inched closer, I could tell it stretched against his broad shoulders. I could see ink peeking up around the base of his neck just below his hairline. I wondered about what lay beneath the surface of the black cotton, what else he'd permanently inked into his flesh. I should have announced my presence, but as I grew closer, close enough I could smell his familiar scent of soap and citrus, my pulse thrummed so loudly I was sure it would be warning enough.

Instead, I quietly moved next to him and kneeled down onto the cushioned support. He didn't jump, but exhaled sharply as his head lifted just enough that he'd be able to see who was bold enough to kneel next to a man in an empty church while he prayed. Maybe he'd caught my scent too and had been prepared, either way we didn't speak. Both of our heads were bowed in respect. Respect for our loss, our love, and our God, the one thing that could possibly save us.

I licked my overly dry lips, my mouth was desiccated with nerves as I, too, began to pray. At first, I kept the comforting silence, but old habits die hard, and my words slipped easily from my lips in a beseeching whisper.

"Heavenly Father, I am wounded, and saddened. I am weak and miserable. Without thee, I am lost. I have sinned, dear Lord, and I do not deserve thy grace, but I seek it..." Tears spilled from my eyes and dripped past my moving lips. "I seek it." I was desperate. "Heavenly Father, I seek thy forgiveness, I seek the forgiveness of thee, and of the one I love, the one I have wronged," I mumbled the words over and over, and I didn't even realize it, but I'd begun to gently sway back and forth.

I kept my eyes clamped shut. I let the smoky scent of the candles, the incense... Declan... fill my lungs with each insecure breath. I prayed and prayed, this time in my head, the words repeated until I felt numb, until the sensation in my legs vanished and it was only when I dropped my hands to my sides, my head still down, that I felt him. His hand was at his side too, and my fingers brushed his as I'd lowered mine. Heat billowed up my arm when he didn't pull away. I felt his thumb trace along mine, and my heart pumped furiously and disjointedly as I wagered in my head if I should take his hand in mine. I didn't need to make the choice and, as Declan laced his fingers through my own, I exhaled a shuddered sob.

This was what home felt like, and a blanket of peace, weighted with his touch, covered me. There were no more prayers, just a mute calm. He squeezed my hand gently and I raised my head, our eyes searching each other's. His crystal blue irises were rimmed in red, and his cheeks were stained with earlier shed tears. His full lips parted as if he were about to speak, but instead, he raised his free hand and cupped my wet cheek. I didn't dare close my eyes and miss a second of this.

I kept them wide open as I leaned into the heat of his palm. I wanted to tell him I was sorry. He needed to know that I'd left it all behind, left the life I thought I needed to live to be saved. To save him.

I wanted to tell him I wished we would've kept the baby, gotten married, and lived in his tiny room with its shabby walls and brown carpet. At least it would've been love, at least I would've had the one person who always loved me for me. But, there was no reason to wish for a time that could never be, and the way he watched me now, with a tinge of terror, I had no idea where we could even begin.

He leaned in and my heart fell into my stomach. The room around me ceased to exist as the warmth of his breath played at my lips. He watched me as he slowly inched forward and, when I didn't move, his eyes closed. He kissed me so lightly, like I was made up of the fine marble of the altar. I was eighteen again and he was slipping through my fingertips. Our lips moved together in a last dance, a last chance at remembering before his mouth dusted a whisper of promise and he pulled away. I was dazed, and the vertigo of his kiss lingered over me keeping me captive. The blue in his eyes flickered as he dropped my hand and stood.

His other hand still held my cheek as he said, "You're poison, Paige. But, I'm tired of hating you. My father was a drunk, and I love you. It's my affliction, and I'll never be cured of it, never be rid of how I feel about you." His voice was hoarse as if he was holding back his emotion.

I swallowed deeply, the pain of his words seeped from my eyes. He dropped his palm from my face and his chest heaved with each breath as he stepped away. Was there any worse punishment then seeing the damage you'd created and there wasn't a thing you could do to change it, or make it better?

"Declan." I breathed his name, said the word as if it had to be spoken, as if I had to utter it to prove to myself this moment had really happened.

When I stood, he shook his head and turned. I watched his strong posture fall as he continued to the front doors of the church. He'd kissed me, he'd told me he loved me, but I was his sickness, and it would be selfish of me to feed his addiction.

Selfish.

The word throbbed behind my temples, and the panic rose and squeezed my chest with each foot of distance that fell between us. *Selfish.* I'd given up everything for Clark. Everything for my parents. I'd given up on Declan, I'd lost faith in the love we had. *Selfish.* I'd sacrificed our child, so we could be together. He would never forgive me.

After everything was said and done so many years ago, I'd thought we'd be able to make it. But he'd hated me for the choice I'd made. And, in some ways, he'd been right. I'd chosen to run. I'd run to the shelter of a church that offered absolution, to my parents who offered me up like a lamb to the man who was supposed to give me back my soul. I hadn't known Declan would come back to me a week later, a week too late. He'd despised me and I'd thought I'd given him his escape.

But, as the church door opened and Declan dissolved between the past and present, I was forced to make another choice.

And I was going to be selfish this time.

"He kissed you? In a church?" Lana's smile was ridiculous.

"He also said I was poison, remember?" I carelessly shoved the lettuce around my plate.

"He said he loved you." She quirked her eyebrow and popped a piece of grilled chicken in her mouth.

I nodded and the lump in my throat grew. Once I had gotten home from the church, all I'd wanted to do was to hide in my room, make a plan, figure out how I was going to try and repair the relationship I had destroyed. I wasn't so self-assured that I didn't realize it might be a battle I'd never win, but I had to try. Because if I didn't, if I didn't at least try to explain everything to him, explain why I wouldn't see him the day he came to my house after we'd split, then he'd always think himself worthless, and I couldn't let him believe that anymore. I'd hoped to fall into my dirty sheets and the despair of an impossible task. But Lana had made dinner, stripped my linens, and opened my blinds.

Lana poured us both a glass of red wine, and I eyed her as she sipped deeply from the glass. "Take a fucking sip, it'll relax you."

Lana had poured me a glass every night that we'd eaten together and I would leave it untouched. I lifted the glass to my nose and the aroma of wood, apples, and berries puckered my lips, and my mouth watered. I exhaled in defeat and took a small sip. The room temperature wine was bitter, and the urge to spit it out almost overwhelmed me.

"This is gross." I winced as I gulped my water and Lana laughed.

"Maybe you'll like white wine better. I'll get some for tomorrow." She gave me a coy grin and I shook my head.

"I work tomorrow."

"That's right... and you're hoping Declan will be there?"

I nodded once and bit my lip. "I need to talk to him."

"You could go to his brother's tattoo shop that he works at. Confront him on his own turf. Force him to listen. He might not show up at The Gallery, and could you blame him if he didn't?"

She was probably right. The way I'd let everything go to pieces... I was surprised he could even look at me.

"I would've married you, I want to marry you."

"I couldn't have married you, Declan. We'd end up just like your mom and dad. You would've had to get a job working minimum wage. There would be bills, and mouths to feed. You would've thrown away everything that is beautiful about who you are until you drowned your regrets in a bottle and ended up hating me for trapping you into a marriage that was doomed from the start."

His eyes turned cold and he gripped my arm.

"You're hurting me, Declan."

His lips moved but no words came out as he increased his grip. I whimpered and he released me abruptly, and I tripped backward nearly losing my balance.

"Declan?" I was breathless as he raised his hands to his temples trying to quiet the chatter in his head. He mumbled incoherently and when he finally met my gaze, Declan's blue eyes were blank.

"I hate you for this. I hate that you would rather kill our child than be poor, than marry me. Than live a life with me." He was yelling and he never yelled.

"No, no, Declan that's—"

"You're right. I'm sick and our baby could've been sick, and why would you waste your fucking life on me." He raised his voice and he gripped my arm again and led me to his bedroom door. He had to know I did it for him, for us. He was sick, but I loved him. His beautiful mind. Having a child, this young, it would ruin him. "I'll never for-forgive you for this." He croaked and stuttered as his emotions overcame him. My whole body felt empty as I looked up into his eyes. They were filled with tears and he clenched his jaw as he released me from his hold... from his life.

It was the first time he'd ever turned his back on me, but in reality it was me who had turned on him. I'd lost my faith in who he was, and I couldn't see past my own fear to make the right choice. I naively thought we'd be able to move on, move forward. That we'd eventually marry without the burden of a child, when we weren't just children ourselves, but when I saw the pure hate in his eyes that day I knew there was nothing I could do to change what I'd done or how he'd felt about me. So I'd left. And when he came back for me... I ignored his calls, he'd even came to my parents' home. He'd yelled and fought with my father, who threatened to call the police. I'd hid in my room, thinking the worst of myself, hating who I was and how I had destroyed his innocence with my selfish sin. So I sacrificed my own feelings to God, to the church, in hopes I could at least redeem him. Redeem Declan.

"I should've let him in, Lana. I should've taken his calls, I should've—"

"You did what you thought you had to do. You were a still a child yourself and your parents, you think they would've let you be together after you'd told them the truth. They would have hung you both by the rafters in that damn chapel if you had tried to stay together."

She was right.

"Do what you have to now, Paige. You're free to choose again, make it right. He loves you, he said it himself. He'll forgive you... and if he doesn't, at least you tried and you can move on." She sipped her wine and nodded.

"I'll give it a week. If he doesn't show up at The Gallery, I'll go to him." As soon as I declared it, the black feeling in my heart lifted.

"Good, now eat, because you're too damn skinny and no man wants a bag of bones." She giggled and I smiled.

I closed my eyes as the imprint of his kiss, his mercy burned across my lips. He'd charged me as his poison, but had pardoned me with the sweet taste of a promise.

DECLAN

The bus dropped me off about two miles from Paige's house and the walk was all uphill. It had snowed last night, but even so, by the time I got to her place I was sweating and probably fucking smelled like shit. I almost turned around when I pulled the piece of paper from my pocket to make sure I was at the right house. It was a palace, hidden within the mountainside. The house was three stories high with gray stucco and pine trim that blended the building into the frost-covered spruces and the wintered, barren Aspens that surrounded it. It was modern lines, but natural at the same time. Paige's home reminded me of something out of the Frank Lloyd Wright architecture book I'd borrowed from the library once. The driveway's steep incline was cleared of snow, at least. My calves were already burning, and the hike up to her front door didn't help.

The door looked heavy and had iron bars that covered a small, square window within its center. It seemed too medieval compared to the rest of the house. My eyes scanned the massive entryway as if I didn't already feel out of place enough.

The voices in my head laughed.

You don't belong here.

You're trash, can't you smell your stench.

The nervous vice in my chest tightened, and I swallowed hard as I rang the doorbell. The dense scent of pine pulled into my lungs as I tried to take a deep breath. There was no sound on the other side of the door, and the longer I waited, the more I began to believe the echoes in my head. Trash. She was too clean. This house with its manufactured purity, this girl with her perfect smile, slight curves, and small stature... she was too good for me, too much to hold. The insecurity bubbled up my throat and choked me.

"Declan?" Paige's voice was kind, soothing, and it was bright like the color yellow.

I lifted my gaze. She was wearing soft looking, black leggings and a large, Army green sweater that consumed her form. The sweat was thick on my brow as I rubbed the back of my neck. "Sorry it took me so long, the bus dropped me down on Elk Avenue."

Her eyes widened. "That's almost three miles. I should have had my dad come get you."

The thought of her father picking me up from the brown piece of shit, pile of bricks I lived in almost made me puke. "That's okay, I don't mind walking, it's how I get around." I gave her a sideways smile, and she stepped back, gesturing for me to enter her castle.

"You actually just missed my parents. My dad has some pharmaceutical dinner thing..." She winced as she took in my appearance. "They should be back in a few hours. I'll have one of them take you home if you don't mind hanging out that long. I feel bad that you walked so far... it's freezing outside."

I'd take as much time as she'd allow, but as I stepped inside and the faint smell of fresh powder hit me, I hoped my scent wouldn't permeate these spotless walls. White. Everything was white. White marble floors. White walls, white furniture, and white throw rugs. I stopped and looked down at my dirty boots. Crusted mud along the soles flaked onto the shiny surface of the floor and I cringed. There was no way in hell Paige, or her parents, would ever see where I lived.

"I should take my shoes off." It wasn't a question and the panic in my voice was evident.

Filthy. You're filthy.

Paige's quiet giggle broke through the venom spewing in my brain. "This place is ridiculous, right? The only thing with color are the paintings on the walls, which are pretty great, but I mean, I don't know, it's like living in a—"

"Funeral home?"

She laughed again, her pink lips curled at the corners and her eyes crinkled around the edges in such an easy way my stomach flipped. "I was going to say museum." She reached for my hand and laced her fingers with mine. "But funeral home works, too."

I kicked off my boots and attempted to bend down and place them neatly along the wall but Paige stopped me. "Leave them. It's fine."

The dirt from my shoes screamed at me.

Filthy. Filthy.

"Come on, I talked my mom into getting me some art supplies, I've set them up in the den." She squeezed my hand. "Thanks for coming today." She flicked her eyes down, her long lashes shadowed on her pink cheeks. "I was nervous."

Paige was all I'd wanted and we'd started hanging out all the time at school, and on our half-days we'd go to the diner down the street from campus. Sometimes with her friends, sometimes just us. I liked it better when it was just us.

I'd been stuck between her and reality. I wanted to ask her out, I wanted her to be mine, but we came from such different realms and seeing her home, seeing her in this crisp wealth of light, it only made my fears more tangible.

You shouldn't have come here.

You don't belong.

"Why are you nervous?" I was the one who should be nervous.

"I guess, I... I mean... I don't really know what this..." She stumbled her words as she met my gaze. "I mean are we friends?"

Friends.

I nodded. "I don't generally walk three miles up a mountain to see people who aren't my friends." My smile was wide as she rolled her eyes.

"That's not what I meant."

Friends.

I wanted more. I wanted to kiss her, to touch her face, to feel her mouth on mine. I hadn't ever kissed a girl before, and I wanted her to be my first. I wanted to do things I probably shouldn't, but the longer she looked at me like that, with big, expectant blue eyes, the feelings I had stirred into something vicious, and the male in me craved to feel any part of her.

"What did you mean?" I stepped in, closer than I normally allowed, and linked our other hands.

I was so much taller than her and I liked that she had to look up at me. Her back would arch just enough that it would close the space between our bodies and the heat made everything I hated about myself disappear. It was just her. Just me.

Her cheeks were crimson as she licked her lips. "Am I more than a friend?"

She was more than she would ever know.

I nodded. "Do you want to be?"

She sucked on her bottom lip before she spoke and I almost groaned.

"Yes."

I placed a strand of her hair behind her ear, leaned down, and brought my lips to her cheek. The connection made her shudder and I grinned as I said, "Good." The confident tone of my voice surprised me, and as I pulled away and saw the smile on her face, the lush red color of her cheeks, for the first time in my forsaken, shit of a life, I felt normal.

The music in the studio couldn't drown out the memory as I pulled my brush along the canvas. The spindly, bare branches of Aspens fit nicely in the background of the painting. Paige's eyes were surrounded by the color of summer sunsets and the night of winter. I'd told her today that she was poison and I'd meant it. I'd meant to stab her with the word. I'd meant to make her feel how I'd felt for the past nine years. Unsure, unhappy, lost. Tasting the tears on her lips, feeling her breath mix with mine again... I would suffer her noxious death, her unspoiled oblivion, her tainted kisses because I was sick for them. I was no better in my addiction than my father and his whiskey, than Liam and his useless conquests, and Kieran is his indulgent love of Christ.

The day I walked into Paige's childhood home I knew I shouldn't want her. We were too different, and when I'd felt that burst of confidence, that need of normalcy for the first time, I was hooked. I lived for the fix, for the silence and beauty Paige granted me with each touch. I hated her and loved her and just like the addict, with a monkey on his back, when I'd left the church today I knew I'd never be able to quit her.

The brush fell from my paint-covered hand to the floor. I hadn't realized how out of breath I'd become. The anger rushed through me with each rapid pulse of my heart. I closed my eyes and let the music surround me. I needed a break from those eyes, but even in the darkness she could find me. I felt her hand in mine, and the smell of the old cathedral filled my nostrils as I inhaled. Her prayer haunted me.

"I am wounded, and saddened. I am weak and miserable. Without thee, I am lost. I have sinned, dear Lord, and I do not deserve thy grace, but I seek it... I seek it. I seek thy forgiveness, I seek the forgiveness of thee, and of the one I love, the one I have wronged."

Her frame was so fragile. The devils in my head begged to see her bones, see what horror lay beneath, but the human in me couldn't hate the shell of the woman who'd kneeled beside me... not anymore. I opened my eyes and Paige's gaze watched me from the canvas. Everything I hated about her had vanished and all that was left was a woman I didn't recognize. Her youth and beauty had paled and she was a skeleton of her former self, a wraith, just like I'd always envisaged her to be. She hadn't looked so frail when I'd seen her here in the studio the other day. It seemed I'd ruined her as much as she'd ruined me.

I bent down, grabbed the brush, and took a rag from my pocket, wiping up the splatter from the floor the best I could. The studio floor was covered in paint anyway. The clock on the wall told me I'd been here way too damn long. I covered my paint and gathered up my brushes. I dropped them in the jar of thinner sitting on the back wall and disconnected my phone from the stereo.

"Shit."

My hands were still wet and left fingerprints on my phone case. I wiped the excess paint off my hands onto my jeans. As I wiped the back of my phone as well, I saw the blue notification light was blinking. I opened the lock screen and saw I'd missed a few calls from Liam and had a text from Kieran.

Kieran: *Dinner tomorrow at Mom's.*

It was too late to text and say I didn't feel like doing the Sunday dinner thing, but I'd missed the last few and I was pretty sure my mom, if capable, would've driven to the shop and dragged me there. I stared at Kieran's previous text. The one that warned me he'd accidentally told Paige where I was. I'd have to let him off the hook tomorrow. Kieran hadn't meant any harm, he never did, but sometimes I wished he could lie just like the rest of us. The whole *not being a liar* thing was inconvenient for him.

I flipped through my contacts until I saw her name, and I wondered if her number was the same. My thumb hovered over the call button. We'd been on neutral ground today. A truce had been called before God as we both felt our sin and heard the other's prayer. It was always that way with us. Her joy was my joy. My love was her love. Her pain was my pain. Paige and I were one, and we'd felt it today. I wasn't sure if she was still married. I knew nothing of her these past nine years but the memories I'd dwelled in. Today, I'd wanted to set her free from her pain. She'd sought me out for forgiveness, and I wasn't sure I'd be able to resist her lure.

I let the screen go black and placed my phone back into my pocket. I walked through The Gallery and locked the front door behind me. The bite of early fall sent a shiver down my limbs as I walked to the apartment. The city streets were abandoned for beds and lovers, and I was alone with my thoughts and the demons that twisted my rights into wrongs.

"Let me see her!" I shouted.

Paige's father curled his upper lip exposing his white teeth. "You're to never see my daughter again." His words moved like ice, slow and hateful. "You think I'd let her see you again after what you two have done. You've murdered an innocent life, and I will see to it that Paige pays for her sin, that she gets her atonement, but you..." He shoved me square in the chest, but I held steady and rolled my shoulders back. Mr. Simon stepped off the threshold closing the distance between us, so close I could smell his self-righteous breath. "You're worthless, Declan, always have been, always will be, and I will pay my own price to the Savior for ever allowing you to get close to my daughter."

Worthless. Worthless. Trash.

No.

I shook my head and shoved him back.

"Paige!" I called her name in a roar. She had to hear me, she had to know I'd come back.

"She told us what happened, Declan. She broke down to her mother three days ago. Did you think you both could just throw away a life without guilt... without consequence? She doesn't want to see you, and if you don't get off my front porch I'll call the cops!"

She's given up on you.

She hates you.

"Paige! Please!" I was frantic and I tried to pass him, but he blocked the door.

"Call the police!" he shouted over his shoulder, and Paige's mother glared at me as she pulled her phone from her pocket and flipped it open.

"Just..." I was out of breath, out of chances. "Tell Paige I forgive her."

I didn't wait for a confirmation, he'd never tell her and if I stayed I'd end up in jail, or worse, the psych unit. I should've never told her to leave last week. I should've never shut her out... I'd let her believe that I hated her and now I'd lost her.

The city loomed above me as I neared my apartment, and the laughter in my head was sardonic. The hate inside me had won the day I broke up with Paige. I could twist and turn the story over in my head a thousand times. She'd given up on me, didn't think I was good enough to marry, and when I'd told her I'd never forgive her, I'd been still freshly wounded. But over the next few days, it had started to become gangrenous with regret, and I'd been able to see what I hadn't seen before. She'd said she didn't want to destroy my future, *not* hers. She'd said she wanted to protect *me*. And maybe it had been a lie, and maybe it hadn't. We'd both been too fucking young, too caught up in our own pain to be capable of dealing with any of that shit, and over the years I'd lost touch with the truth, and I'd let the wound rot. Her father had been right.

I was worthless.

"I seek the forgiveness of thee, and of the one I love, the one I have wronged."

She didn't know.

I'd been a coward to walk away from that porch without telling Paige the truth. Without trying harder to tell her in person that I'd forgiven her. Instead of trying to get her back, I'd bowed out. I'd let her go. For years, every month on the thirteenth, I'd go to church and I'd light a candle for our child, for Paige, in hopes she could feel its healing flame. I'd stopped going a few years ago in an attempt to move on, in an attempt to heal the festered wound, but it only made it worse. Not until today, when I felt her hand in mine, her lips against me, had I ever thought I'd be pardoned of our sin. I'd left the church with anger, fear, and uncertainty, but I'd also left with a peace I couldn't explain, like that part of my life, the hole caused by the choice—the loss of our child, had finally been sewn shut.

Kneeling together, as one.

It was as it should've been.

It was as if God had finally heard the call, and our prayers had finally been answered.

The tree branches were intricate, and the odor of fresh paint might've been undetectable to others, but as I stood just a breath away from the perfection of the painting, I could smell it. The sharp scent tickled my nose and the pain, it was everywhere. It was in each brush stroke, each dark color. I stepped backward and the sullen tree branches blossomed in front of me in a wide panoramic. The eyes that watched me from the canvas were now surrounded by wintered bark. The branches and twigs jutted out in every direction. It had been winter the first time Declan had come to my home, and I wished he was here now so I could ask him if this was, in fact, the tree line of my parents' house, if he still cherished the old days like me. I wished so much to go back to that day. A simpler time.

I brought my hands to my lips and sucked in a deep breath. I felt him. The tingle of his lips, and his beard, it was new to me, but I could feel it like I'd always known this man, like he was a part of me, like I had no other choice but to find him, be near him.

"Paige, it's time to go." Luca stared at me with annoyance. I only worked with her every once in a while. She was part-time like me so I rarely saw her.

"I'll be right there," I said with as much civility as I could muster. I wanted to stay.

Three days had gone by since our small armistice inside the church, and I still hadn't seen him here. But Declan's painting continued to get more detailed, and I wondered if he came afterhours to avoid me. When I'd checked the rental log earlier, I'd noticed that Chandler had booked Declan another week. According to the log, Declan had paid cash, up front. The idea of sneaking back to the shop later was risky, and my throat was tight just thinking about it as I tried to swallow.

I wanted to see him again, talk to him, but I wasn't ready to stroll into Avenues Ink to do so. Lana had said she'd go with me, she'd just book another tattoo and I could go with her. It would all be very innocent and *oh shucks, fancy seeing you here*. It would be fake, and the last thing Declan and I needed was a façade to hide behind. I was glad to see he still came here each night and poured his heart, his thoughts onto canvas. I was intruding on something very private every time I'd take a sneak peek to see if he'd been here the night prior. This seemed to be his sanctuary, and I worried I'd been wrong to step foot in his place of peace. But seeing each new brush stroke, each new color, the painting was drawing us closer. I nodded my head as I came to terms with my decision to come back tonight in hopes that he would be here.

"I was about to lock you in." Luca's face was dead serious. "But I remembered you have the stupid keys."

Luca didn't talk much and, if anything, it was her only good quality. She was stunning though. Tall with long, silky blonde hair, artsy black-rimmed glasses, and a personality as cold and dull as the color of steel. She was waiting for me by the front door as I walked out of the studio. I grabbed my bag and gave her an apologetic smile as she glared at me while pushing open the shop door.

The night air was dry and cool, and I wished I lived closer so I could walk home. There was a certain fragrance to the shift in seasons. When summer still clung tight to the soil, but winter begged to differ. It was a mixture that created such vivid colors on the mountainside, as the leaves turned over their last breath to the changing weather. When I used to paint, it was always in warm, earth tones, and Declan was always dark. We had always been total opposites, but it worked.

"Goodnight. See you next week," I tried, but she just waved over her shoulder as she walked in the opposite direction.

I waited till she was gone and contemplated just going back in, but it was early still, just past eight. I walked slowly to my car, the pull of the studio was much stronger than the need to eat, but I caught my reflection in the glass of the neighboring store's front windows and brought my hand to my stomach. I really was skin and bones.

"That blouse is too small, change it." Clark narrowed his gaze as he eyed me through the mirror and adjusted his tie. "You're gaining weight, Paige."

I pulled at the hem of my blouse trying to get it to cover my belly. I dropped my eyes to the bedroom carpet. "The doctor said if I put on some weight, it might help with regulating my ovulation. I won't get above one-fifteen."

He turned and his lips twitched on one side as he moved toward me. My heart sank in my chest as he brought his hands to my waist. He'd always wanted a taller wife, a thinner wife... children. I was such a disappointment.

"Look at me," he demanded, so I obeyed. He searched my expression, and I hoped he wouldn't be able to discern the fear

in my eyes, the sound of my heart was like a bull-horn in the silent room. "One hundred and fifteen pounds is acceptable."

I exhaled a small breath and he brought his mouth to mine. His lips were thirsty and his breath was warm with a stale mint. He lifted his hands to my face and tilted my head backward, as his tongue pushed into my mouth without grace or permission. He always just took. There was no romance, no lust... no love... I was his and that is all that mattered. He pulled away and took a step backward as he appraised me and narrowed his brows. "Take your place, Paige."

"But, we'll be late for church." My mouth went dry.

He clenched his jaw. "You've already caused us to be late. I asked you to change for a reason, did I not? You can't wear that, it's too small, and now... you've gone and riled me up... take your place." His command was dripping with disdain, and his lips were in a firm line as he loosened his belt, untucking his dress shirt. I brought my eyes back to the floor as the familiar feeling of dread spread across my skin in a damp, cold sweat.

The cool air turned to ice in my veins as I hurried to my car. I *had* lost too much weight. The divorce, Declan, it was all taking a toll on me and, if I wasn't careful, I'd let my memories turn me to dust and ashes. *My place.* My place had been on my back, always still, no sound, no enjoyment. Three nights a week or more if he deemed it necessary. We were to have sex for procreation not pleasure, so Clark had always said, but he'd slept with Cheryl. I was sure that was specifically for pleasure. My hands balled into fists. When I was with Clark, I'd let myself forget what it was like before... I'd let myself think that was my worth, that I was no better than a prized horse. I'd exchanged love for ownership. I'd forgotten what it was like to enjoy physical touch. Clark had destroyed any notions of romantic attachments. Our marriage had always been about him, his needs, his wants, and how I'd never measured up.

I grit my teeth as I sat in my car and slammed the driver side door. I'd let him control my life, my mind, and my body. *He used me.* Tears pricked at the corners of my eyes as I remembered how soft Declan's lips had always been, how his touch pulled feelings from me, from my body that Clark had never been able to attain. Declan loved me... he *loved* me, and when our lips met again in the church, it had briefly washed away all the ugly Clark had covered me in.

There was no question anymore. My past was linked to my present, and if I didn't try to talk to Declan, try to fix the wrongs I'd committed, then that girl who stared at me from the store front window... she would win, and even death wouldn't be enough to end my suffering.

"Um... are we eating for two? Is there something you need to tell me?" Lana's eyes were wide as I shoveled stir-fry into my mouth.

"It's really good," I spoke around a mouthful of rice.

"I can tell you like it... are you in a hurry, because if you eat any faster I don't think it'll digest, and you'll be shitting full pea pods."

I choked down a laugh and struggled to swallow my bite.

"You haven't eaten in days and now... are you binging?" She gave me a knowing look and I narrowed my eyes.

"No," I said with an exasperated exhale. "I'm thinking..." I fiddled with my napkin as I diverted my gaze to the table. "I'm thinking I might go back to The Gallery tonight, he booked another week."

"Declan?" Her fork scraped against the plate.

"Yes."

It was quiet for a few moments before either of us said anything. She watched me push my food around my plate before she said, "I think this is good. I mean after what happened at St. Ann's... you guys need to reconnect, get all this shit... out... in the open... done."

My eyes locked on hers. "I'm scared."

"But you have to try, right?" She speared a carrot and brought it to her lips. "It can't get any worse than it already is?"

It could, but at least now, I had a twinkling of hope. "We'll see."

"Well, I'm glad you got your appetite back, even if you're eating your emotions, you need your kick ass curves back. I need a hot wingman." She smirked as she nibbled on the carrot.

"I'm not ready for wingman status." I stood from the couch and brought my plate to the sink.

"No? But look how far you've come. You've left the tyranny of a controlling, cheating bastard to live with the sinner of your past..." She paused and drew a halo over her head with her finger. "And now you're about to take the bull by the horns and win back the love of your life. It's like a Shakespeare play."

"He liked to write tragedies."

"Ahh. But he wrote a good sonnet I hear." She grinned.

"Lana, you're making me nervous." It was the truth and all the food I'd just shoveled down my throat flipped and threatened to come back up as I walked over to the couch.

Her smile faded and she took my hand. "If you need me, text me. I'll wait up for you. I've got nothing going tomorrow, so if Declan turns out to be a dick, I'll be here for the rescue mission."

I gave her a confidant smile, even though inside I was screaming in terror. "I'll... I'll be fine." I squeezed her hand in reassurance, but I wasn't sure if it was for her or for me.

My stomach was still a battleground as I pulled to the back of The Gallery and parked. The full feeling weighted me like a boulder to the front seat of my car as I turned off the engine. There were no other cars in the parking lot, but I'd seen a pale light shining from the back of the shop through the windows when I'd driven past the store front. My legs were like jelly as I made an attempt to stand from the vehicle. All my doubts bubbled with the bile in my throat. What was I doing here? What would I say? My hands trembled as I wiped them on my jeans. The thin, light blue sweater I wore hung off my left shoulder, and the cool air tickled my skin, but did nothing to calm the heat brewing in my blood.

My face felt hot all the way to my ears as I used my key to enter The Gallery. Music played and I recognized the song, *"Evergreen"* by Broods, it was one of Lana's favorites. She'd played the album almost every day since I'd moved in. The notes were slow and menacing, drawn out and sensual, and I wondered if the melody matched his mood. The studio door was propped open with the stool that normally sat behind the cash register and, as I moved closer, my heart fluttered like a trapped bird in a cage. The light from the open door cracked through the dark and my eyes were drawn to it. My gaze followed the warm yellow silhouette, and before I had a chance to take a breath, my eyes lifted and saw him standing in front of the canvas.

My cheeks flamed and my muscles tightened and went weak all at once. He was shirtless; his paint-splattered jeans hung low, his hands rested on the top of his head as he stared at his painting. His body was not what I remembered. He was carved stone now. The only word that came to my mind was powerful. Powerful, beautiful strength etched out each muscle.

I tried to swallow as I watched his hands fall to his sides, but my mouth was ash. He turned just enough that I could see the ink that covered his chest and the perfect V that disappeared below the top of his jeans. I tried to breathe, but the boy I'd known had transformed into a magnificent statue, and I was just a shadow, a voyeur... and I couldn't look away. I shouldn't be here; my courage evaporated as I made a move to step back. My footing was off, I was dazed, and I gasped as I stumbled. Declan's eyes darted to the door and trapped me.

He looked at me, his blue eyes wide as if he wasn't sure, as always, debating his own mind.

"Paige?" he asked. His voice was rough and sent a warm shiver up my spine.

I had nowhere to go, he'd caught me, so I walked through the studio door with my heart in my stomach. "I-I wasn't sure if I should, but I needed to see you."

He grabbed a rag from his work stool and rubbed off the excess paint from his fingers. The muscles in his arms pulled, and the power I'd seen a moment ago seemed to ripple off of him in waves.

"Why?" He threw the rag onto the work stool and winced, as if his own abrupt tone shocked him.

Because I wanted to tell you I'm sorry. Because I lost myself and I think you're the only one who could put me back together. Because, I still love you, always have.

The air grew tense between us, his citrus scent muted my thoughts, and I had to close my eyes. I had to speak, I had to say something. "Because, I miss you."

I heard him exhale and my eyes opened, but fell to the thick, black cross he had tattooed in the middle of his sternum. The rise and fall of his chest was noticeable as he sucked in each ragged breath. He took a step toward me and I lifted my gaze to his.

"I'm not sure where to go from here, but I miss you, Declan, and—"

He lifted his hand and for minute I braced myself for his touch. I longed to feel the heat of his palm on my cheek, let the forgiveness feed my pulse, but he'd raised his arm just to run his fingers through his hair roughly as he stared at me with bright blue eyes.

"Grab a canvas." He flicked his gaze to the door.

"You need another canvas?" My heart skipped, was he dismissing me or letting me in?

"No, but you do."

PAIGE

The slight hiss of the storm was competing with the delicate sound of guitars. The music was lazy, and the slow strum fed my heart, and fed my mind as I painted. It was days like this that I lived for. Days when the snow was three feet deep and still coming, and I'd become a captive of a beautiful artist. My smile spread warmly across my face as I sat down on the white marble next to Declan.

"I really love this band." He turned his head and smiled at me.

"Me too. It really helps me concentrate on the work." I leaned to the side and turned up the music.

We'd been sitting cross-legged, side by side for about an hour and a half sketching. We'd spend most of our time like this, sitting in my den working on something. Today, I had originally planned to draw something Dali would've been proud of, but instead, I penciled the curve of Declan's jaw, the slope of his nose, and before I knew it I had almost a complete portrait.

"You're getting better." He gave me a sideways smirk.

"I have a good teacher," I said as he leaned in and my heart sputtered.

We'd had our first kiss a few weeks ago and since then we'd been stealing kisses whenever we could. It was silly, but I loved when Declan would take a few minutes between classes at school and kiss me thoroughly in an alcove or an abandoned hallway. The warning bell would ring and being tardy would be the last thing on our minds.

Our art projects were forgotten as his mouth moved eagerly against mine. I didn't care that my parents were in the kitchen and could possibly catch us. He tasted like toothpaste and something sweet, just him, and as he wrapped his hand around the back of my neck and pulled my lip with his teeth, I exhaled an unsteady breath. I'd lost myself in the feel of his lips, and the way his fingers tangled in my hair. I whined when he pulled away and his chuckle heated my cheeks. He might've been laughing, but he was just as out of breath as I was, and something told me he was holding back on purpose. We were too young to want more.

Tell that to my heart.

"I like kissing you." I scrunched my nose in embarrassment as the truth slipped from my lips too easily.

His chuckle turned into a hearty laugh and my stomach filled with butterflies. I made an attempt to swat his shoulder but he grabbed my wrist gently and brought our hands together by wrapping his fingers with mine.

"I hate it when I have to leave." His smile fell and the color of his eyes deepened.

I looked down at our joined hands and how they fit together. My hand was so small compared to his, but it didn't feel awkward.

"I hate it, too."

I did. I missed him too much when he wasn't around, and I worried that his moods turned dark when I was gone. He struggled so much between his real thoughts and the voices that he heard. He'd told me about them before we were official, and I had to admit to myself that it scared me at first, but he was always so honest with me, and if I was being truthful, I kind of liked that he was special like that. I'd told him as much, and since then... our relationship... it changed, and he'd become more than just a friend, he'd become important to me. We'd become important to each other.

The music switched and the sound of Low turned over to Interpol and the mood lifted.

"If it keeps snowing like this I might hide in your closet and stay the night." His smile was mischievous.

I leaned over and pecked him on the cheek before I said, "Promise?"

"Over the Ocean" by Low played and reverberated off the walls of the studio. The song washed over me. The wave of it crashed and consumed me as my eyes stung with unshed tears. I inhaled a deep calming breath as I pushed away the memory. Declan had invited me to stay tonight, he'd let me in, and as my eyes found his and the familiar music played, I wanted to go back to the den on that snowy day. Start over and never let him leave.

"I can't believe you still listen to this." I placed my canvas on an easel he'd set up for me with shaky hands.

He nodded before he pulled on his white t-shirt. He ran his hand through his messy hair and his eyebrows knotted. "Sometimes... sometimes it's the only thing that will help me paint."

I brought my eyes to his, grateful for the cotton that covered his chiseled chest. I wasn't sure I'd be able to speak like an actual adult if he'd stayed shirtless the whole time.

"I... I haven't painted in years." My throat felt tight, and my tongue was like sandpaper as he dropped my gaze and turned to his own canvas.

"Start with the basics, Paige." He sucked in a breath. My name affected him and I wasn't sure if that was a good or bad thing. "Paint what you know." He wouldn't look at me as he scanned his depiction of my eyes.

He scooted the work stool that stood between us closer to me. His palette was filled with blue, purple, gray, orange, and red. I wanted to lift my brush and dip it into the paint, I wanted to see if I still existed. See if Paige Simon had truly died, or had I just been hibernating. I was scared stiff. Declan started to work and I couldn't help but watch him. His hands moved across the painting like a skilled musician played the piano. My pulse was a mess and my stomach had torqued itself into knots. My canvas stared back at me, just as blank as I'd become.

"Declan, I—"

He stopped mid stroke, his head tilted down, and he asked, "Are you nervous?"

"What if I've changed too much?" My voice was a shell.

"I think it's all still there." He kept his eyes fixed on the floor, but his voice had grown strength, and I felt the hope ignite inside my veins. It blossomed in my chest like a brilliant red rose. "Talent doesn't fade away."

Talent.

I'd let myself believe we were talking about us, not my ability to create art.

He didn't speak again, and the lump in my throat turned to shards of glass as I turned back to my canvas. I wasn't ready. I stepped back from the easel and watched Declan from the corner of my eye. He resumed his work as if I wasn't there, and if I hadn't been so selfish I would have left. But, I couldn't, so I went and sat in the back of the studio against the wall. I sat and watched him. I admired him from afar like I'd once done as a teen and, as the music of our youth poured from the speakers, everything had seemed to come full circle. I only hoped that this time we'd both get some sort of resolution.

I checked my phone and it was fifteen past one in the morning. My tailbone ached from sitting on the cold, concrete floor for so long. But I'd refused to budge until now. Declan covered his paints and wiped his hands on his towel while he looked at my unused canvas. He stared at it, his lips parted and his fists clenched. If this had been us back in high school I would have asked him what the voices had just said. He would've looked at me with sad eyes before he told me something awful. The voices had always been cruel and, if there was only one thing I would change about Declan, it wouldn't be to get rid of the hallucinations, it would be to make them helpful, make them tell him just how amazing he was.

I stood from my private vigil and stretched my limbs. Declan's eyes moved over my body, and I shifted self-consciously under the weight of his gaze. I pulled nervously at the hem of my sweater and then rubbed my hands on my jeans as he stalked toward me. It was difficult to wrap my head around how much he'd transformed over the years. Here was this gorgeous man, walking toward me, and I was nothing but bones and hollow eyes. Declan grabbed his phone that sat by the stereo and pocketed it. The music died and the room became claustrophobic. I'd come here to talk, and all I'd done was hide in the corner all night. This was a huge step, a white flag, but I was still sick with nerves.

He paused and took a deep breath, steeling himself before he looked at me again. I bit my lip unsure of what to do or say as I stood there like a mute. He glanced over my features again, and his brows dipped with what seemed like worry.

"Are you hungry?" he asked.

My stomach threatened to empty right here in front of his feet at the mere mention of food. I shook my head. "No."

"There's a place, just up the street. It's open twenty-four hours."

I shook my head again. As much as I wanted to talk with him, a restaurant wasn't the place, and besides, the way he watched me, his eyes filled with a mixture of fear and uncertainty, I didn't want to force this... us.

It fell quiet and all I could hear was his breathing... it soothed me and gave me a bit of courage. "Thank you for letting me stay."

He rubbed the back of his neck and a sliver of his skin was exposed as the hem of his t-shirt lifted. I dropped my eyes to the floor as I spoke, "I won't bother you—"

"Don't."

His tone was harsh and I raised my head and met his cool eyes. "What?"

"Don't play the victim. We've both lost enough to hold that title." His jaw constricted when I puffed out a shuddered gasp. His anger was radiating off his shoulders.

I took a step backward toward the door and stuttered, "I-I—"

"Wait." He swore under his breath. "I didn't mean... I mean... fuck, Paige, you're here." His eyes held me in a bewildered stare.

My bottom lip started to tremble without my permission, and I had to take several short breaths. In and out. In and out to maintain my emotions. I'd learned with Clark crying got you nowhere. "I shouldn't be, but I had to say—"

"Say what?" he asked. His voice raised.

"I had to say..." My throat contracted and, when I tried to speak, the pain of the words caught in my throat.

"Say what?" His eyes softened and he moved toward me.

The dam broke and spilled over and I realized I was gasping, swallowing air down in giant sobs. The heat of his palm on my cheek eased each breath until I was able to see past the blur of tears.

"I'm sorry." His tone was full of comfort and sadness, longing, and the guilt I held ripped at my heart until I was just pieces.

He framed my face with both of his hands.

"Forgive me," I managed to say and when he looked at me again I was sure I was the one having hallucinations. He was the boy again. Innocent and wide eyed. "I'm so sorry."

He pulled me into a hug and, when my damp cheek dried against the cotton of his shirt, I felt safe again.

"I know."

We stayed like that for a while. His arms around me, holding me tightly against his chest. No promises or big discussions. Just two people who needed each other in the moment more than they needed the blood that pumped rapidly through their veins.

It was cathartic.

A possible renewal.

There weren't any smiles or kisses. No more words needed to be exchanged tonight. There was just a peaceful balm of acceptance. We were at mile one and I would make sure he knew everything, but right now, I needed his scent filling my lungs and his heart beating in my ear. And as he let me go, I knew, at some point, he would figure out that the Paige from the past was gone, and I had to be prepared that he may not care about me beyond this apology.

It wasn't a weird silence as we locked up the store, and when he offered to walk me to my car, I accepted. It was late, after all.

"Will you be here tomorrow night, too?" I asked as I opened the driver side door of my car.

"Will you?" He held the door for me as I sat down. I wanted to look up at him one last time, but my heart thundered, and the butterflies swirled and fluttered. "I've booked the week, I think that's enough time for you to find your inspiration again."

I couldn't be sure, but I almost heard humor in his words and, as I lifted my chin and let my gaze search his, there was a hint of a smile in the creases around his eyes. I leaned back and decided what I would paint tomorrow. I'd paint his eyes, just as he'd painted mine. But instead of the winter, I'd surround him in the spring, in the bright light of the sun and vibrant greens of summer grass. I'd paint him as a starburst, as something to worship, because I'd only known one deity and he'd left me to fend for myself.

"I think I'll be ready tomorrow." My statement held so many meanings and truths, but as I offered him a small smile and his Adam's apple bobbed nervously, it was clear we had a long journey ahead of us.

He nodded, edgy again, as he started to close the car door. "I'll be here around eleven."

He shut the door before I could answer, and I turned the key in the ignition as I watched him walk away. I closed my eyes and offered up a thank you in hopes someone was listening. I prayed that this was just a beginning. That the path we would forge from here on out could heal us both. And I prayed to be lucky, because I didn't deserve anything better than just a chance, but I prayed that maybe Declan could love me again. It was selfish to wish for such light to be wasted on a lost soul, but I kept my eyes shut tight and prayed for it anyway.

DECLAN

My eyes were tired, my mind—fuzzy as the machines hummed in unison, and the white noise of it lifted above the clamor inside the shop. I hadn't slept well last night, and it was almost closing time. Today had been a long one, and if it wasn't for the fact that Paige might be waiting for me at The Gallery later, I'd go home and crash.

You can watch her bleed.

You liked it.

The muscle in my jaw stretched and pulsed as last night's nightmare flickered in my twisted brain again. I'd been forced to watch Paige die over and over in my head all damn day. In the dream she'd been naked, laid out on my bed, silent and still. Her light blonde hair, feather soft, spilled in fluid torrents on my pillow—the strands shadowed her face. It felt so real, seeing her like that again. It'd been too long and I'd wanted her, I'd been able to feel the heat in my stomach, the flash of need in my veins as I'd approached her. I'd moved toward her, my mind filled with the thoughts I'd suppressed for years,

126

thoughts about her body and how it had felt to be inside her. She was just for me, just like always.

As I got closer, I could see her more clearly. She looked too frail, too thin and before I'd been able to reach her, feed her with feeling, fatten her flesh with my touch, breathe life into her frozen lips with my breath, her ribs had begun to break and puncture through her transparent skin. The gore of it, bright red, had been too surreal to look away, and I'd been shocked still into watching her bleed out onto my sheets. Liam had shaken me awake. Saved me from the horror. I'd been screaming, he'd said. I had woken up covered in sweat, and my fingers burned as if I'd been clenching my hands into fists as I'd slept. I'd told him everything about seeing her last night, about the dream, about her apology, and he'd listened with weary eyes.

"Declan, come look at this shit." Kemper's loud voice did little to ease my thoughts.

I flicked my gaze to his station, his client, who I wagered was probably younger than her ID had said, was lying on her back holding her bare breasts. As I stood I made an attempt to push the nightmare aside. Seeing Paige last night in the studio, having her cheek against my chest, that was real, and I didn't want to admit how much I had wanted it. She'd looked as if she was falling apart and, despite my fears, my need to hear her say she was sorry, I'd wanted to help her, feed her, and get her talking. It hurt too much to see her cower before me, like she wasn't worthy of my presence. Shit, I wasn't worthy of hers. I shook my head. We'd both had enough pain, we'd both done wrong, and I wanted to talk to her, see what had changed, why she'd chosen to come there... why now?

The girl smiled at me as I walked over to Kemper's station. "What am I looking at?" She had a complex looking web of stenciled flowers that bordered the bottom curve of each breast. It was beautiful.

127

"What do you think?" Kemper eyed me before lowering his gaze to his work and I smirked. He was new to Avenues and he always doubted himself.

"It's amazing," I said, and the girl's smile split into dimples. Definitely too young.

Liam approached us and his smile died as he looked at the girl, his lips in a firm line. "How old are you?"

The girl's voice was saccharine. "Eighteen."

"Yeah?" Liam looked at Kemper and scowled.

"Hey, man, I checked her ID." Kemper's face paled.

"I bet you did." Liam let his eyes linger along the girl's body. "Always thinking with your dick. After today, find another place to get your ink, little girl." Liam lifted his chin at me and I followed him, giving Kemper a smirk. He mumbled something under his breath, and the girl's smile was nowhere to be seen.

"Way too young," Liam grumbled as we walked to my station. "We're all headed to that the new pub on Broadway after closing. Kemper said it's badass but Kieran doesn't want to go."

"Mom been alone all day?" I asked.

He nodded, and his chest rose and fell heavily with the burden of being the oldest son. His words were tight as he exhaled. "Yeah, Mrs. Detwiler's daughter hasn't been stopping by as much anymore now that she's got classes."

Our mother wasn't sick with an illness, she was sick with age, sick with life, sick from being married to an alcoholic. She only knew that house, with its stained walls, us boys, her need to make sure we were okay and raised right, despite the circumstances. She was lucky to have her faith, and the new priest, Father Becker, was good to her. He'd found Kieran some help, someone to keep Mom company when we couldn't.

She was so used to waiting on others and now, her legs were too weak, her mind was going, and it was our turn to help her.

"I can check on her so Kieran can go out, too," I offered, and he shook his head.

"He's not into it tonight, you should come, let him take care of Mom. We've been doing it for years." His smile was for my benefit, halfcocked and hiding his true feelings.

Liam has had to take care of me just as much as her.

"Nah, you guys have fun, I'm almost finished with the piece I've been working on… and I kind of already made plans." My tone was even as I rubbed the back of my neck, but Liam narrowed his eyes as he sat on my work table.

"With *her*." The venom in his voice coated his lips.

He's right, she'll just hurt you again.
Don't be stupid.

I ignored the voices. My mind was a cage and I was tired of being trapped inside its deceiving walls.

"Yes, I told her I'd be there tonight. Besides, I've booked the studio for the week."

His jaw ticked. "So you're just going to let her destroy you again. I'm telling you right now, Dex, I can't go back there with you. You were nearly hospitalized the last time and—"

"I know," I said in a loud whisper. The people here, they didn't need the details of my shit. "Hell, I don't know what's going to happen, but she looked so broken, and we've been through too much. She apologized, she—"

"So that's it, she walks in, apologizes, and the past nine years don't matter. What about everything you've fucking been through!" He roughly raked his hand through his hair, and his eyes pierced straight through me. "You owe yourself more than that, you were a train wreck and she left you for dead. She fucking married another man, Dex."

The pressure in my chest consumed the space and my lungs fought to breathe. "I love her."

"That's not enough to fix the damage she's caused."

"We caused... me *and* her. I'm just as guilty. I'll work through this shit on my own, you're not my damn caretaker, Liam!" Anger colored my words in black and the buzz of the shop had silenced. I turned to look over my shoulder and everyone was staring at us. Kieran, who was sitting at the front desk, shook his head as he looked at us with a disappointed glare.

Liam's eyes creased around the corners as he winced. "I've done everything I can for you, for this family... plan your own goddamn funeral, I'm done." He stood abruptly and the table scratched against the tile floor. He didn't look at me again as he walked away.

Kieran stood and moved toward me with sorrow-filled eyes. "We just worry about you, Declan. He'll be fine, don't stress it. I'll talk to him, okay?" He patted me on the shoulder and nodded before he took off after Liam.

Liam had been burned just as badly as I had by love, and I didn't blame him for hating Paige, for hating Kelly, for hating his life, but I had a chance to heal, and I was fucking taking it.

She'll cut you open.
She'll bleed you dry.
Maybe...

But, at least the poison would at last be free from my system and maybe then the death she'd give me would be sweet, because I'd have tasted what it felt like to live again one last time.

Paige's corn silk strands were balled and twisted and placed on the top of her head in a messy knot. She wore a long black dress, the color at odds with her alabaster skin, but the fabric appeared soft, casual, and it flowed smoothly along the line of her figure. She'd always been petite, her stature delicate, and in the past her curves would've filled out the dress just enough, but now the fabric drowned her as she stood in front of her canvas. Paint covered her hands, and had dripped onto the floor and her dress. A smudge of green traced her jawline, and my lips broke into a smile. My chest filled with warmth and my head emptied. All my usual shadows dissolved by the beacon of light before me. Its white hot heat scorched through me as I watched her paint my profile, my eyes, everything in vivid color. She wasn't the same, but the woman in front of me was just as tragically beautiful as the girl I'd once loved, I still loved.

The music she'd chosen to play wasn't anything I'd heard before, but it was quiet, light and sweet, and the female vocals lifted as Paige's lips twitched with a smile. She'd finally noticed my presence. The front of the dress dipped low enough I could see the rise and fall of her breasts as she struggled to breathe. She pulled her bottom lip through her teeth and gave me a nervous wave. My nightmare last night a forgotten horror story.

"Hey," she said, and her voice, it sounded just as anxious as I felt.

I lifted my chin in greeting as I took a few more steps into the studio. The closer I got the more her scent and the mixture of paint almost dragged me to the past, but I focused on her eyes and how they'd aged with pain, and I remembered, in that moment, that we were two people... broken and battered, meeting for the first time. Everything before this moment couldn't matter anymore. If I wanted to move on, if I wanted her, I'd have to love this version of Paige, and as her lips trembled, I knew that I could... that I would.

"You found your inspiration?" I asked and she lowered her eyes for a flash before raising them back up to mine.

The honesty shimmered within the azure color of her irises and she spoke, "You've always been my muse." She turned and looked thoughtfully at her canvas. Paige lifted her brush as if to continue to work but stopped and dropped her arm. "It's unbelievable," she whispered.

The air was cool inside the studio, and a slight draft stirred the stray pieces of her hair. I rolled my hands into fists in an effort to not reach out and touch her.

"What's unbelievable?" I asked and took another step closer. My eyes closed briefly, as my nose filled with the scent of rain, the scent of her.

"When I was with Clark, at first, he allowed me to paint." Her eyes fell to the floor and my shoulders tensed at the word 'allowed'. "But I had nothing to paint, and I think he enjoyed that I'd lost that part of myself because it was connected to you." She flicked her eyes to mine and her smile banked the rage that was building in my chest. "I'd thought I'd never paint again, but after all this time, all it took was you, and my mind opened with color and ideas, and after I'd left here last night I was able to see exactly what I wanted to paint."

She stepped toward me and I brushed my fingers against hers. The paint that coated her skin, red, yellow, and green, was still wet and transferred small splotches onto my knuckles. The promise she offered in her words scared me, but she had to know.

"You never lost it, Paige." I brought my thumb and forefinger to her chin and tilted her head back so she wouldn't drop her gaze again. "It's right in here." I released her chin and traced my fingertips along her forehead. Her body relaxed under my touch and I wondered what the past nine years had been like for her. "Did he hurt you?"

She nodded. "Not physically, but he broke me, nevertheless."

She took a step back, and the heat of her body evaporated from between us and her face blanched. Did she still have feelings for him?

"Did he leave you?" I asked.

She stood taller and shook her head. "No, I left him..." She placed her brush on the work stool and stared at my painting. "I was given to him, Declan. I was a gift from my father. A perfectly packaged sinner ready to be saved. I was something to control, and when I couldn't give him what he wanted he looked for it elsewhere."

"You were gifted?" My brows furrowed, and all I wanted was for her to look at me, but she wouldn't. She continued to stare, seemingly lost in her own thoughts.

"I had to tell my parents everything, and you know, Declan, you saw how the church had taken over their lives. I was cattle to be bartered for status. I was to marry the pastor's son. I was to atone for my murdering ways."

My heart was like a jackhammer as I watched her shiver. She rubbed at her arms until the blood pooled below the surface of her flesh. Her words strangled me, and the light drained from my periphery. The darkness came back with a vengeance I'd never felt before, and my fists begged for answers.

"Clark was a façade at first. The doting husband to the pitiful wife who still longed for her past. After a while, I assimilated. I did exactly as he wished, as my parents wished. I was the perfect Stepford wife, except for one flaw... I wasn't able to bare Clark a child. He hated me for my sin and how it ruined his chances at the family he thought he deserved, so he sought comfort in another woman."

"So you left him?" My fury was barely contained and she could tell.

She finally brought her eyes to mine and they were wide open. "Yes." She turned to face me fully and took my hand in hers. "I'd thought for so long that I deserved every rotten minute I spent with Clark because of what I'd chosen to do and then, when I wasn't able to conceive, I knew God thought so, too. I didn't deserve happiness, and I'd told myself I never deserved you." I wanted to tell her she was wrong, but she said, "I wish..." she choked. "I wish I would've kept our baby and married you. Created an existence that didn't involve pain and heartbreak, only art and joy and family. I wish I would've had faith in us, in you, and I should've never let you leave my house that day thinking I didn't love you... want you—"

"Paige." I dropped her hand and cradled her face between my palms. "There's no going back." She'd been wishing for things we'd never get back, living in shit, just like me. Mine was self-imposed, but hers, my head throbbed, what else had she had to live through?

"I understand." She sounded defeated. She pulled away and my arms fell to my sides.

The voices in my head smiled, and my heart cracked and spilled through my veins in wet, sloppy beats as my palms cooled, the heat from her cheeks an afterthought. "I don't think you do. I have no clue what you've been through, or who you are now, but I want to. Our past is gone... we've changed, Paige... I've changed."

You're the same, Declan.

See how she watches you, she knows it... you're still worthless.

I brought my thumbs to my temples and pressed as I closed my eyes willing the thoughts away. *Not now.*

"What are they saying?" Her fingertips were light on my shoulder and, as I lowered my arms, I opened my eyes. She was so close. The voices whirred and hissed as her fingers trailed down, dusting along the line of my arm, until the warmth of her hand tangled in mine.

I was a kid again, and she was the only thing able to heal me. "They say I'm worthless." I swallowed as her lips parted with a soundless gasp.

She squeezed my hand. Her smile was compassion, it was faith, and it spread a deep burgundy glow in my chest. "All you have to do is take a look behind you..." She flicked her gaze to my painting. "And you'll know that's not true."

DECLAN

"Don't worry, honey," my mother spoke with her usual kindness, but I didn't miss the anxiety that highlighted her tone. "I'll get you some water."

Paige was pale and lying on my bed, my mother sat at her side with a warm smile as I hovered in the doorway. I lingered as my mom stood. My head was pounding; the voices I'd forgotten about polluted my peripheral vision again.

"She looks really tired, sick... maybe she should head home? Her mother could tend to her." My mom took my hand and squeezed it. "She doesn't have a fever."

We'd come back to my place after we'd left the clinic. Paige was too afraid to go home, she wasn't ready to tell her parents, and I sure as hell would never tell mine.

"She's just tired, Mom, it's been a long day. I think maybe a stomach bug. I'll take her home in a little bit."

She nodded and whispered so only I could hear, "Your father is passed out, use his car, she shouldn't have to ride the bus like that."

"Thanks." I leaned down and kissed my mother's forehead, I towered over her now. Almost a man, but still a boy. A boy who'd just lied to his mother, who'd just made the most adult decision of his life, and who watched his girlfriend quietly leak tears onto his pillowcase.

You hate her.

No.

You hate what she's done.

No.

I was lying more today than I ever had before, to myself, to my mom, to Paige. My mother closed the door behind her as she left my bedroom. It could have been two minutes or twenty, but I stood there and stared at the girl I loved, and as time ticked by, as each one of my heartbeats slowed to a grind, a painful ache grew... for her... for what we'd done, I wasn't sure I would ever move again.

She sniffled and opened her eyes. They were void of color. The soulful blue had been snuffed out.

"Are you in pain?" My voice scratched in the open air, dry and flat.

"I deserve it." She closed her eyes and I was grateful for the reprieve.

I didn't contradict her as my fingers clenched at my side.

"I'm damned, Declan, I've condemned us both." Her voice splintered into bruised purples and my feet moved at her silent cry for help.

I kneeled at the bedside and ran my fingers through her hair.

She betrayed you.

I exhaled, sifting through my venomous thoughts and kissed her cheek as I whispered, "Maybe we were damned from the start."

The heat from her touch radiated up my arm, fighting off the voices that still screamed *worthless, worthless, worthless,* as the memory flickered behind my eyes.

"Do you still feel damned?" I asked. Her words, my words still fresh in my head from that day.

Her eyes glimmered in crystalline waves of blue as she said, "On most days... yes, but I've come to terms with my fate."

"Your fate?"

"I can't have children. I tried, for years, to conceive again, and I think God gave me a gift and then I discarded it. I—"

"We did, Paige, we both did. I let you suffer alone, and there are days I fucking drown in that choice. I want the illness, the blackness in my brain to swallow me up so I can't remember how I'd treated you that day." Each breath burned as I spoke past the lump in my throat. I'd let her believe she was damned. I let my own anger punish her with silence. "If anyone has a one way ticket to Hell it's me. I let it fall apart... I was the one who went quiet, when all you needed was noise."

She exhaled an unsteady breath and I released her hand.

"I'm sorry I left you alone, captive to your thoughts. I didn't save you like you'd always done for me, and I'm sorry for not fighting harder to get you back."

I held her face and drew her watery gaze to mine.

"Did you mean it, Declan? Did you mean it, what you said that day... that we were damned from the start?"

I shook my head. "I was angry and confused, and if I could go back—"

She wrapped her arms around my waist, and I dropped my hands as she brought her cheek to my chest. Out of instinct, of self-preservation, my body stiffened, but then melted as her palms lay flush on my back. The familiar embrace calmed the unnerving feeling of being touched by her again.

"There's no going back, remember?" She breathed and I felt her smile against my chest as I draped my arms around her small frame. She leaned back but kept her hold on my waist. Having her hands on my body again, it set the pilot light ablaze in my heart. "You and I, we made so many mistakes, and I could let myself fall into each one until I could no longer find a way out, but I'm too tired to get lost, I'd rather just move forward."

As I cupped her cheek, she closed her eyes and leaned into the touch. The rational thoughts, the dark thoughts, they became a piece of parchment held above a flame. They flaked and burned and blew away into the thick, studio air, and all I could think about was kissing her. Her top lip was fuller than her bottom, and I wondered if she'd kiss my upper lip first like she used to. I could almost feel it, her hesitant breath would brush the skin of my lips. Would I get to smell the sweet mint of her mouth, feel the damp heat of her flesh against mine?

She was once my ruin, and she could easily rip me apart again, and I think I'd let her.

I waited for the hateful hallucinations, the malicious thoughts to grip me, but there was no sound... nothing to cool the warmer thoughts that had begun to brew inside me.

She stared at me, her eyes brilliant under the studio lights, waiting for me to make the choice, to choose the path forward.

I nodded, and her features softened as my lips curved into a smile. I caught a piece of her hair and softly placed it behind her ear.

"Let's paint."

"Do you like working at Avenues?" she asked as we packed up for the night.

We'd spent the majority of the past two nights in silence. It was the way it had always been with us. Paints, pencils, charcoal, oil pastels, it didn't matter the medium, we'd mix it with music and fall onto our own planets, each orbiting the other. She was the Earth, and I was always her night. Working next to her again was no different. I think we purposely didn't ask questions, knowing it could disturb the weak foundation of the treaty we'd both agreed to. We had discussed nothing but art until now. Paige's body, still thin, seemed fuller somehow, and she even had color in her cheeks as she stood with her bag already over her shoulder, staring at me, awaiting a response. She was opening the next door, and there was a part of me that didn't want to cross the threshold, because what if what I had become still wasn't good enough to keep her.

"I do. It was weird at first, permanently placing a piece of myself onto another person, a stranger, but I love it. I like it best when they don't give me a reason behind what they pick. I tend to make my own assumptions." I smiled as I covered my palette.

"So you and your brothers all work there?"

I nodded. "Kieran runs the books and Liam owns it. He bought it six years ago, just after my dad died. The place was going bankrupt, so he—"

"Your dad died?" The blush in her cheeks faded as she took a step toward me. She reached out her hand in comfort, but I turned away and headed to the stereo to grab my phone. He was one of the reasons I'd lost her to begin with.

"He was nothing more than a drunk." The sentence was a rapid fire machine gun to the white flags we had raised.

She thinks you're just like him.

"But he was your father."

I clenched my jaw. "Liam was more of a father to me than he ever was."

She lowered her head and whispered an apology.

"I'm sorry," I said as I shook my head. "I didn't mean to raise my voice." I moved to where she was standing and lifted her chin. "It was more of a relief when he died, Paige. He wasn't something any of us were proud of, and Liam, he had to give up everything to help with his medical bills." *And mine.* "Kieran gave up his quest for the priesthood to stay with Mom, and—"

She took my hand. "I wish I could have been there for you."

A spark of anger snapped behind my eyes, and I shrugged out from under her touch. She hadn't been there.

"After we split, it got pretty bad, Paige, I was in and out of treatment, different docs. I was a fucking head case. They said I had a mild psychotic break about a year after we'd broken up. The voices, they'd eaten me alive, I'd lose time a lot, still do when I get really depressed, but I'd been able to pull out of it without hospitalization. It cost Liam. He took care of me when I couldn't do it for myself. I would have rotted away in that house with my mother, but after Pop died, it was like Liam finally got the freedom to fly, and thank Christ he took me with him."

The guilt painted dark circles under her eyes and they began to deepen into black and blue hollows.

"I-I worried about what it had been like for you." Paige's voice was fragile. "There were many times I wanted to reach out, talk to you, but it was forbidden, my past was erased the day I married Clark. I was his to have and he did what he pleased. I wasn't allowed to paint, have friends outside of the church. I wasn't allowed to hold a job. If I ever mentioned you, or anything... even Lana, I was told to pray away my demons. Clark made sure I always remembered what my place was." She exhaled and I let her take my hand. "I wasn't there for you, and I wasn't there for myself."

Everything she was saying cut me open, churned in my gut, and made me see red. Clark had owned her as much as my sickness had claimed me. "I didn't mean to make you feel guilty."

She smiled without malice. "You did. But it's okay. We've both hurt each other and the damage, it's done, but we're not beyond repair. At least I hope not. I'm just glad you don't hate me anymore."

She cast her gaze down and a small gasp slipped from her lips. She turned my arm over in her hand and traced the ink with the tip of her finger as she mumbled the words "*You see the world.*" The hair on my arm stood and a shiver ran up my spine as she circled the "O" in the word you.

I watched her cheeks fill with pink again as she continued to move her finger slowly, delicately, over my skin. "I-I." She struggled to speak past her trembling lips.

"You told me I saw the world, and it was the first time anyone ever looked at my sickness with anything other than sadness. You saw me as something unique and special, not twisted and fucked up. It was one of the first tattoos I got. Even though I was pissed, and part of me thought I'd never forgive you, I needed to remember you. Your eyes, they were always honest, and those words... they were the only piece of reality I had to hold on to for a long-ass time." I weaved our fingers together, and the silk of her skin stole away any lasting trace of irritation. She looked up at me, her guilt still heavy. "I might have hated you, Paige, but that hate, it was the lie. This..." I lifted our linked hands. "This is the truth."

I brushed my lips across the back of her hand, and the blush of her cheeks heated into a deeper shade of red.

Her eyes sparkled as she spoke, "You've always known how to make my heart beat, Declan." She bumped her hip into mine, lightening the mood between us, and that sassy, teenage girl I fell in love with emerged with a full-blown smile, making me chuckle.

There you are, Paige Simon.

She had finally shown herself. My pulse quickened at her easy laughter, and I squeezed her hand.

"You make it easier to breathe." The sentence tumbled from my mouth before I could stop it.

She raised up on her tiptoes and kissed my cheek, and the fear of losing her again, of pushing us too fast, and derailing the progress we'd made niggled at the back of my throat as I swallowed down the urge to ask her what she was doing once she left here tonight. It was late, and she needed to sleep. Fuck, I needed to sleep, but the idea of having her next to me again, of taking her home and kissing her until her lips were bruised and her chin was raw from my beard, marking her with my touch, my lips... *shit*... as good as it sounded, as much as I needed that, I wasn't ready.

"Will I see you tomorrow?" I asked as she pulled away, my hand in hers still.

Our week at the studio was almost over, and I didn't have enough money to extend the lease. I'd been cutting back my hours at the shop, pissing off my brothers so I could get here earlier, have more time with her, but after everything we'd hashed out over these past few days, I'd suffer the wrath of Liam, and I could always just paint in my room.

She tugged on my arm. "Of course." She said it as if it was a fact, as if I was nuts to even fucking ask, as if she hadn't had anywhere else more important to be, and my lips broke into a wide smile.

The cold air snaked around my body as I walked her to her car. The sky was a cloudless, stark midnight blue with bursts of yellow stars. Everything seemed more vibrant. I could even smell the bakery a few blocks up. They must've started baking their sweet breads for the early morning rush. The heat of her skin pressed against me and I took a chance and pulled her under my arm. She burrowed into me as we walked the last few steps to where she'd parked behind The Gallery.

Paige lingered in my embrace once we got to her car. I turned her at the waist so she was facing me. We were just a hair's breadth away from each other, and the need to kiss her fueled my rapid pulse once again. The monster in my head was asleep, and each breath she took curled in white steam from her lips, pulling me closer. She raised her hand and placed it at the nape of my neck and brought her lips to my ear.

"Good night, Declan."

I held back my shudder as she pulled away and her fingertips dusted at my hairline. Blood pumped and filled the deep, dark recesses of my heart. My body responded to her body as I watched her blush fall past her chest, disappearing beyond her sweater.

As I let go of her hips, I steadied myself. My voice was even, and there was no trace of the fire, of the red, lashing flame she'd created as I said, "See you tomorrow."

PAIGE

The door clicked shut behind me as I walked into the studio. Declan was already there, dressed in torn jeans that hugged his thighs and a tight, white t-shirt. His skin always looked so touchable next to the soft white of cotton. He was pulling out my supplies, but his work stool was empty.

"Hi." The syllable was meek as I approached him.

We'd started something again, I wasn't sure where it would go, but the relief I felt in his presence was more than I had ever received while on my knees in prayer.

He took my hand in his and the calm I'd been craving all day trickled down my spine. "Hey."

I reveled in the feel of his hand, and I took a moment to admire his work. I'd not had a chance lately to really see it up close, because I'd been too enveloped in my own work. His painting, it was raw and real and stunning. The texture was thick with surreal strokes and lines that blurred but blended into each other in a perfect dance. The center piece, my eyes, encased by trees, surrounded by giant swirls of dark grays and purples. Each whorl was its own cosmos encased by tiny specks of yellow... stars.

I felt breathless as I let the intricate details soak my vision. "Declan, this is so much more than beautiful."

His eyes filled with an ocean of blue. It was unnerving and familiar at the same time, watching him melt in front of me, watching the life of the boy I used to know color his cheeks.

He was quiet and let me admire the pieces of his soul that had been splashed onto the canvas.

"This should be in a museum, lit for everyone to see. Are there more?"

He nodded.

"I'd... I'd like to see them sometime... if that's okay?"

"Most of my work is dark, you might not like what you see." His jaw pulsed slightly, but I smiled through the nerves.

"I've always liked your dark, Declan."

He squeezed my hand and said, "If we finish up a little early we could swing by my place, all my paintings and drawings are there. I try to frame the most important ones."

"I'd love to." I let my eyes linger on his painting for a few seconds before I met his gaze. The air between us seemed to fill with static, and the scent of him, the strength of his fingers wrapped with mine, made my heart feel hollow and full at the same time and it beat with uncertainty as his lips spread slowly into a grin. A grin I knew, a grin that transferred heat from his body to mine.

He looked down at our tangled fingers. "Should we paint?"

His voice was firm and strong and sure and I hoped that we would eventually, fully mend our broken hearts. I wanted him to look at me like this again and again. The idea of *us* was a treacherous river to forge, and our past, a rushing rapid, eager to tear us apart, ready to shred away our skin and bare our bones. It was too soon to think myself worthy of a future, it was foolish, but Declan had forgiven me. He'd held my hand the other night and told me that, together, we were the truth. Not the rules I'd been given by the church I had chosen to blindly follow in order to find some speck of hope. I'd wanted to excel and become something holy, worthy, but with Declan I only ever needed to be me. Mercy... it was thick and somber and resided inside the storm of his eyes as he watched me now. It was fresh and new and beautiful and I'd missed him.

I wanted him.

"Yeah, let's paint." I smiled and he slowly released my hand.

I could paint my life in golds and greens and begin to heal for myself, for him. With Declan, I was able to just be—be me, even if it was only for tonight, or this past week. I couldn't allow myself to think beyond this moment.

He was quiet as he rustled through the brown leather satchel that was always sitting at the foot of his easel. He pulled a sketch pad and a box of charcoal from the bag.

"Are you not going to paint?" I asked when he sat on the cold, concrete floor in front of his work stool.

"I think it's finished," he said as he flipped the sketch book to a blank page.

I awaited more explanation, but none ever came. He sat on the ground for the majority of the night, moving the charcoal quickly over the page, stopping every now and then to smooth his thumb over the paper, shadowing, contouring... what, I couldn't say. Conversation was minimal, and it was difficult to concentrate on my own project. At times, I'd feel him watching me. It would start out as a tingle of goose bumps that would spread along the line of my arm. His eyes lifted the hairs on the back of my neck, but when I would finally allow myself to look at him, his head would be down, his arm muscles taut and determined as he drew whatever masterpiece he'd thought up along the page. The urge to ask him what he was working on almost consumed me. I realized I'd barely worked on my own painting. I exhaled a sharp breath and he chuckled. The sound of his deep laugh, mixed with the light bass of the music stirred the dormant butterflies in my belly.

"What?" I asked, unable to contain my smirk as his eyes raised to mine. A hint of mischief colored his sea glass irises with a speck of caramel.

"It's killing you, isn't it?" His smile erased all the dark shadows from under his eyes.

My eyebrows formed a dubious curve. "I don't know what you mean?" I shook my head and turned my attention back to my own work. I ignored the smug smile he had. It felt too easy... this whole night did.

"It's you." His voice was smoke and flame and my stomach flipped.

I closed my eyes and took a deep breath.

"Would you like to see?" he asked.

I did, but I didn't. Declan had a way of recreating reality. He'd show you who you were, he'd give you a glimpse into his mind, he'd paint you with veracity and passion and there would be no way to deny the truth. I was terrified to see how he saw me now.

He didn't give me a chance to say no as he turned the sketch pad toward me. I was there but I wasn't. It was shadows and mist and my body had been stirred by the air. My profile the only strong line. My head was tipped down, my arms slightly raised as if in prayer, my silhouette lost into the gloom behind me. It was sad, and striking... it was perfect. I kneeled down in front of him and took the sketch book from his grip with trembling fingers. I stared at the girl in the picture. It was sure and clear and abstract. It was steadfast and fleeting... it was exactly how I felt. I was Clark's wife, but I was also Declan's heart, and I was stuck between worlds, just as he'd depicted me.

My eyes found his and I was anchored. He lifted his charcoal-stained fingers to my face. I closed my eyes and let my body incline to his. His citrus scent was mixed with earth and rain. And, as he held my cheek, I licked my lips, ready to feel his mouth on mine, ready to feel awakened, ready for him, but his hand fell, and my eyes opened as he eased the drawing from my hand.

"Are there parts of you that are still his?" Declan's voice was a deep whisper and it hit me hard in the chest, cracking me open.

I shook my head, but I knew it was a lie. There was so much I still needed to work through. A marriage to a man like Clark didn't just fade away.

"I want to wash him away, make it as if he never existed." I stood, my knees aching from the chill of the concrete.

Declan sat completely paralyzed.

"Nothing of Clark remains here." I pointed to my chest.

But there were some things I thought would never go away.

My eyes closed as his body hovered over me. The weight of him was suffocating. The damp feel of his breath on my neck curdled my stomach. I wanted to lose myself in something else, thoughts of Declan, thoughts of his mouth on mine, his hands on my hips, but Clark had robbed me of that. His brutal grunting distracted me from the fantasy, keeping me chained to the present. The painful pinch of his body moving inside of me had to be a sign this wasn't right, this wasn't love. Clark's eyes avoided mine as he growled through his release. I should pray that this time his seed would take, but God doesn't listen to liars.

"Nothing of mine was ever his." The memory turned my heart to ice.

Declan stood, closed his sketchbook, and then held my face with his free hand. His thumb moved with a gentle touch across my cheekbone. "I'm sorry that you ever thought you had to give yourself over to him."

"I lost sight of myself, Declan, but I'm getting better. I'm still in here..." A nervous laugh erupted from my lips. "At least I think I am."

"You are, I see it sometimes. When your guard is down, the Paige I've always known... she's still there." His smile was comforting as he lowered his hand from my face.

"'I took a deep breath and listened to the old brag of my heart; I am, I am, I am.'"

"The Bell Jar," he said with a sideways smile.

"You remembered?" I shook my head in disbelief.

"It's your favorite book, Paige. How could I forget? You know, you could get that quote as a tattoo."

"No way." I laughed again, but this time with feeling.

"No?" He quirked his eyebrow. "I could do it for you, if you wanted." He ran his hand through his hair and dropped his gaze as he grabbed his satchel and placed his pad inside.

My heart flapped out several shuddered beats before it found its proper rhythm again. "Maybe?"

"Tonight?" He grinned and I laughed once.

"I'd rather see your paintings, if that's all right with you." My smile was brightly woven within the words.

"Then let's go."

He'd said he lived walking distance from The Gallery, but I'd driven us to his apartment anyway. I'd had a small panic attack when I'd first seen the tattoo shop because I was certain Liam would most likely hate me. We'd pulled around back, down a narrow alley and parked. The shop was closed and when I'd ask Declan if Liam would be home, he'd said he'd texted his brother earlier and he'd gone out with some girl. From our conversations at the studio, I knew Kieran lived at home still, so when Declan lead me up the rickety and rusted stairs behind Avenues Ink, I had a small wave of relief that we would be alone. Declan's hand was wrapped tightly in mine as he opened the apartment door. Once inside, he flipped on the lights, and the shade of the night evaporated, illuminating the entire space in a white glow.

The ceiling was high and, from what I could see, the apartment was very modern. Everything felt cold except for the beige area rug. I only glanced around the place briefly before my eyes landed on Declan's paintings. They were in various sizes, hung in steel frames against the exposed brick of the industrial-themed apartment.

"Declan, this place... it's like your own personal exhibit." I couldn't hide the wonder in my voice as I pulled him to one of the paintings.

My eyes devoured the linear form of the triangles and circles clashed together in black paint. The shapes seemed to bleed in white lines down the canvas.

His laugh was soft and he squeezed my hand. "Liam lets me hang most of the stuff I do out here. The weird shit is reserved for my room."

"The weird shit?" The swear word sounded foreign on my tongue and he laughed a little louder.

"Yeah, it's more personal, and I don't know, I'd rather it not be on display for just anyone." He tugged me away from the abstract painting. "Come on, I'll show you."

He led me past the kitchen and down a short hall. There were only three doors. One of which was open. The bathroom was small, and it, too, was decorated in mostly gray and black. Declan opened the last door and it felt ridiculous to be nervous, but I was. Fear and excitement, though fear was winning, covered my skin with expectant goose bumps, and I wished he hadn't released my hand as we walked through the door. Declan pulled his phone from his pocket and placed it in a docking station. He turned on his stereo, flooding the room with a smooth rhythm. I should've kept my eyes on him, I should've known what was coming, but I was barely able to conceal my gasp as I took in my surroundings.

Every wall was covered with us. *Me. Him. Memories.* Most were twisted into painful images. There was only one painting that stood out from the anger, the hate, and the sadness. It exuded light and the entwined forms were in love, and kissing, surrounded by a buttered warmth of yellow. If I allowed myself to close my eyes, I'd hear *"Have Yourself a Merry Little Christmas"* playing in the background. I'd smell poultry spice and my mother's yams. I lifted my fingers to my lips and I felt his mouth on mine as if I was in that hallway again on Christmas day.

"That's a new piece." Declan's voice sifted through the memory pulling me back to him, to the present. "I painted this a little while ago. I'd had a nightmare, and then I fucking blacked out, and when I woke up the next morning..." He pointed to the painting. "I was covered in paint."

"It's our first kiss," I whispered.

Declan didn't confirm my statement, he just sat on his bed and watched me as I stared at each painting. My eyes always present in each. Sometimes I could sort out the memory and some I couldn't. I wanted to ask him about each one, but it felt wrong to do so. Each piece was a private moment, a secret thought carved out by his hand, and the torment... I felt it to my very core.

"I can see your suffering." I turned to look at him. "It haunts this room."

His eyes focused solely on me. "It was the only way I could exorcise the demons after you left. I had to paint them, Paige, I had to set them free anyway that I could, or I would have lost myself to my psychosis. Liam encouraged it, cheap therapy." He laughed without humor.

I sat next to him on the bed. "I'm glad you had Liam."

He moved just enough that he was facing me. "You didn't have anyone, did you?"

I shook my head fighting back the tears. He shouldn't have to pity me, he had enough misery of his own. I lay back, my arms at my sides, closed my eyes, and let the smell of Declan's black comforter pull me under. His room was saturated in the scent of him, of paint and his detergent. "When I married Clark, I deluded myself into thinking it could work. I ignored how he treated me, how his touch made me physically ill. I forgot what it was like to feel real love. Declan, I just let it go. It hurt too much to remember. I was lucky not to have anyone, because I'd been able to pretend it had always been that way."

The bed shifted, and I felt the weight, the heat of his body settle next to me. His fingers dusted along mine, and each breath I took became a fight for survival. My heart hummed out uneven beats as our fingers danced and teased and then finally wound together. I felt the bed shift again and I opened my eyes. Declan was lifted on one elbow looking down at me.

"You deserved to be loved, no matter what you thought of yourself then, you deserve to be loved." His voice was low and rich, and I held my breath as he leaned forward.

He hesitated, just above my mouth, and his eyes watched me cave to his will as our breath mingled for two agonizing heartbeats before he stilled my shaky lips with his own.

He kissed me with a gentle edge. My lips rediscovered his, starting with the top and then tasting the bottom. He groaned as my tongue licked at the seam of his mouth, and his hand moved from my cheek only to cradle the back of my head. He deepened the kiss, his tongue sliding easily into my mouth, just like always, as if we'd never parted. He still tasted of spearmint, and the bristles of his beard against my skin had me begging for the burn. I twisted a hand into his hair and I pulled him closer, kissed him harder, as I placed my other hand on his chest curling the fabric of his shirt with my fingers. The beat of his heart drummed just below my fist and its tempo matched mine. Fast. Wanting. Free. Two people finding their way home.

I didn't want to wake up from this new dream. I'd been stuck in a nightmare for almost ten years, but the landscape of it had changed with this kiss and its splashes of red mixed with the pink sweetness of remembering.

He pulled away, but not before nipping at my upper lip. His eyes were alive, his pupils fully dilated, almost completely eclipsing his flawless shade of blue. He kissed me again, but this time the urgency was gone. He painted my lips with soft strokes of heat as I brought my hands to his face. The coarse feel of his scruff was different under my fingertips and, as I kissed his upper lip one more time, I smiled against his mouth. He leaned back and gave me a smile of his own before he buried his face in the space between my neck and shoulder. His lips trailed a short path before he exhaled. The combination of his breath and his beard tickled my neck and I giggled.

I giggled. I hadn't giggled in forever.

"Fuck, I missed that sound." His voice vibrated against my neck and down every limb, and echoed in every pore.

"Me too."

18

DECLAN

Breathe.

The tip of my nose trailed along the deep hollow between her shoulder and collarbone.

Breathe.

She'd left me fucking breathless.

Paige's nails scratched at my hairline and I let my eyes fall shut. I'd surrendered to the moment. She'd tasted different. The sweetness of youth had become something more feminine, more real. I couldn't describe it, but if I could paint it, it would be in a vibrant purple. *Lush.* It'd been the only word that spun through my head as my mouth consumed hers.

She giggled again, and I lifted my head once more to look at her face. Her chin was red from my beard and her lips were swollen. Even her nose was pink. The blue in her eyes turned to shadow and smoke as she waited for more, waited to see what I would do next. Every muscle in my body wanted her, needed to feel the release only she was ever capable of giving me. My hand rested on the flat plane of her stomach, my thumb just under the hem of her sweater. Her skin was too soft, inviting me to taste it, to do more than I knew either of us was ready for. I tried to ward off my thoughts, calm my raging pulse, and cool the need that was building quickly.

Breathe.

She's so close.

I lowered my mouth to hers again and let the ache snap at the flesh of her lips. Her moan increased the drive as I inhaled her and pulled her closer... *too close*... until I lifted my body over hers and braced myself with my hands on either side of her head. She whispered my name, and without thinking, I pressed against her seeking relief. Wound up and hard, the friction nearly set me off. She gasped and I pulled away rolling onto my side to face her. I'd gone too far. Paige's cheeks were crimson as she panted through each breath.

"Why'd you pull away?" she asked and raised her fingertips to my mouth tracing a line across my bottom lip. "Tell me what's going on in your head, Declan, you look... sad."

I lay down on the pillow, removing myself from the temptation. She moved with me, resting her cheek against the right side of my chest and placed her hand on the left. I covered her hand with mine and draped my right arm over her hip keeping her tight against me as I spoke, "I don't want to push you."

"You're not." Her voice rumbled in my ribcage.

Paige's jeans were a size too big and, as I ran my fingers along her hip, her sweater began to rise up. Her skin prickled under my touch and I followed a path to her bottom rib.

You can feel her bones.

You'll break her.

The image from my nightmare, my fear, the blood and gore, flashed behind my eyes. My breathing increased and she noticed.

"You're not pushing me, Declan, I chose to come over here." She made a move to lift her body from mine, but I held her tighter. I didn't want to see her face when I told her what I was about to say.

"I have this nightmare, where you're naked and all I can feel is the pull to be inside you, but each time I take a step toward you..." I swallowed past the thick silence between us, "Your ribs pierce through your skin and you bleed out right in front of my eyes."

I felt her lips quiver against my chest. "I bleed out?" she asked quietly, tentatively.

"My head's a fucking horror show."

"Don't be afraid of me," she said as she wiggled out of my hold and leaned up on her elbow.

"I'm not."

Her brows furrowed as she scanned my face, as if she could feel the lie, and after a moment, she shook her head. "You are, that's what the dream is about. I hurt you, Declan... and maybe it's your head's way of telling you to be careful."

She was the one who needed to be careful, it'd always been that way. My sickness could turn on me. I'd be a monster without meds.

"I just don't want to rush this. I haven't been with anyone since you... and maybe—"

"You haven't?" The set of her mouth was skeptical.

I ran my hand down her arm. "No, not really. I've kissed a few girls, but nothing ever panned out."

Nothing ever compared.

She dropped her gaze and the color left her cheeks. "You really have been so alone."

It drove me fucking crazy thinking about her with another man, thinking about her trying to give *him* a child, thinking about what he'd done to make her so timid. From the little she'd shared with me, he'd been a prick, and as much as being isolated from others, from touch, almost brought me to the edge of my sanity, I somehow think I'd had the better life.

"It was better that way for me, no one would ever understand me." I tugged at her hand and she lifted her chin. "No looking back, right?" I gave her a sideways smile, and she exhaled an unsteady breath.

Paige's eyes gleamed as she met my stare. "I let him have my body because it was all I had to offer him. I was the sinner, and he just took what he wanted, justifying it by saying it was my place as his wife." My jaw clenched and fury clouded my vision. She placed her left palm on my chest as I sat up. "Listen." Her voice was a calm, pale green. "I want you to know, you need to know, I never really wanted to have his child. And even though I struggle between my own salvation and whether or not I think God, or whoever is up there, has forgiven me, I thank him every day that I never got pregnant."

It was selfish, but I was thankful, too.

She shed one tear and I watched as it dripped down her cheek.

"I'm not looking back, Declan, all I want is to move forward, and I needed you to know I never stopped loving you, and being here with you again, it's the absolution I've been begging for since the day my father sent you away."

My heart punched out loud, rushed beats and trapped itself inside my throat. I needed to hear her say it, to hear her say she still loved me. I'd been without feeling for years. I'd caged it inside of my head, let the voices coil any emotion I'd had into knotted branches of self-loathing.

"When I said you were poison, at the time I meant it. I meant it because I never stopped loving you, but I'd let myself, let my sickness turn what we had into something twisted. Since you've been back, the voices, they've diminished. My meds, they've been working, but it's you, Paige... you're the remedy and you always have been."

Her lips parted with a faint breath, and I leaned in to kiss her on the cheek. She closed her eyes, and I kissed her wet lashes first, her forehead, and then her mouth. My fingers held her at the nape of her neck and my thumbs found their place along her jaw. She opened up to me. This kiss wasn't about physical need. This kiss was an affirmation.

She was the first to break away. A few inches separated our lips.

"Should I stay?" she asked.

I nodded. "Yeah."

"What about Liam?"

Liam could fuck right the hell off. "Let me worry about him."

I lay back onto the pillow and she followed, placing herself in the exact same position as earlier.

"Okay." She yawned.

"Do I need to set an alarm?" I didn't have to be awake until eleven so I wasn't worried about me, but I wasn't sure if she worked tomorrow.

"Mmm?" She nuzzled closer aligning her body along the side of mine, and the hand she had on my chest curled around the fabric of my shirt securing her hold on me.

I chuckled. "Do you work in the morning?"

"No."

I reached to the left and hit the light switch on the wall next to my bed, hardly moving her at all.

"Goodnight, Paige." I kissed the top of her head.

"Love you." It was just a murmur, but the heat of her breath saturated through my t-shirt and hit me square in the heart.

"She's a good girl, Declan." My father's speech was slurred as I walked past the couch.

He was wearing his uniform still, his boots were covered with filth and sat on the coffee table without care. His legs were crossed, and he seemed at ease, even though the color of his skin around his left eye was turning an angry shade of blue. I'd just came in from saying goodbye to Paige. Liam offered to give her a ride home this time, so we wouldn't have to take the bus. She'd said her parents could come get her, she said it every time, but I wasn't ready for them to see this shithole, or even worse, ask to meet my parents. Besides, Liam needed some time away to cool off.

"I mean it..." He attempted to sit up, but he burped, dry heaved, and then sat back and closed his eyes.

"I know she is, Pop."

He didn't respond. Passed out, just like always.

I wanted to shout at him, "I wish you could really see her. I wish you weren't always drunk, breathing whiskey down her throat every time she was here."

She'll never come back.

The voices had been so quiet lately. But tonight the malice in my head was right. She'd never come back, not after tonight. Liam and my father had really gone at it. She looked terrified. I was pissed at Liam for not controlling his temper.

"I'm sorry she had to see that." Mom, placed her hand on my shoulder.

"Did Liam really drop out of school?" I turned and looked at my mother. Even though she'd had us boys late in life, being married to Pop, it must have aged her twice as fast. Her hair with strands of gray already, her eyes surrounded with deep wrinkles... she looked spent.

"I'm afraid he did, that boss down at the tattoo parlor offered to teach him how it all works, I suppose. He said he'd make more money, and I told him we didn't need it, but he insisted we did. I guess he saw one of your doctor bills. It got sent to collections."

Guilt drowned my lungs.

Your brother has to suffer because of you.
Look at the trouble you cause.

"I'm feeling better, I don't need—"

"You know as much as I do that once that boy gets an idea in his head he can't be stopped, and honestly, I haven't told anyone yet, but your dad, he got demoted. We really could use the money, and Liam has always been good at everything he does. I have no doubt he'll shine and be the best artist there." She smiled but it didn't reach her eyes. "All my boys are so creative." She gave me a light pat on the shoulder. "Stop worrying. I can see those gears grinding."

"Mom, can you help me with this math homework?" Kieran's hair was messy, as if he'd been pulling at it. He had been lucky enough to miss the fight, stuck in his room doing homework.

"Sure, honey." My mom gave me a smile before she left to help my brother.

I looked at my dad again and something inside me snapped. When Liam told him he'd quit school, he didn't even care. It wasn't until Liam called him a fucking waste that he threw the first punch. He hit my brother in the jaw. Paige had cried out, and Liam attacked Pop in a fit of fists and screams. It took both me and my mom to separate the two of them. It was when everything had calmed down I'd remembered Paige. She was huddled in the corner of the kitchen, terror in her eyes.

I'd finally found the one thing worth living for and, in one heated flash of an impulse, she could be gone.

The sun hadn't risen yet and I'd only slept for about three hours. My night, after I dozed off, was plagued by dreams of my childhood. I hadn't thought about that day in such a long time. I harbored a shitload of guilt when it came to Liam, and I knew he was going to flip when he woke up to find Paige was here. I'm guessing I was even worried in my sleep. His temper could get out of hand, and if he did anything, said anything to hurt Paige, it was going to be one hell of a morning.

Paige was still out cold as I rearranged the covers around her. She rambled a few incoherent words and pulled the comforter up to her chin. I shut the door as easy as I could and the click hardly echoed in the hall. The light was on in the kitchen, and the smell of coffee got stronger as I made my way down the hallway in the same clothes I'd had on yesterday.

Liam was leaning against the counter with just a pair of sweats on staring at the coffee maker.

"You're up early." I kept my voice down in hopes I wouldn't wake Paige.

"I haven't been to bed yet." Liam looked at me with bloodshot eyes.

I laughed. "Good night?"

He scrubbed his face with is palm. "Fuck, no."

"What happened?"

He stared at me.

"Liam?" My brows knotted. "What happened?"

"Kelly called me." His jaw pulsed.

Kelly was Liam's ex-girlfriend. They'd been together since he was nineteen, but after Pop died, and he bought the shop, things changed. She'd left him about three years ago. Moved to California. Liam was going to ask her to marry him, but he'd said she wanted to be a model and that marrying him would have stifled her dreams to finally leave this town. I sometimes think, if he wasn't strapped to our family financially, he might've gone with her.

"She did? What did she say?"

"I don't know, I was with Tana, she's sleeping, by the way. Keep your voice down."

"You didn't answer?"

"We were fucking, Declan, hell no I didn't answer." He ran his hand through his hair in frustration.

"Well, shit."

"Yeah." He shrugged his shoulders. "Why are you wearing the same clothes as yesterday?"

"Paige came over to look at some of my finished work, it got late so she... she stayed over." I kept my eyes on his.

"She's in my apartment? Right now?" The challenge in his voice was a bull stuck in its pen.

I didn't back down. "Our apartment."

His jaw set in a stubborn line and he shook his head. "You're just asking for it, aren't you? That chick is married, do I need to remind you again that *she* left you, she –"

"Lower your damn voice." I exhaled an aggravated breath. "She's getting a divorce, and the asshole she was married to... she's had it bad, Liam, worse than I originally thought. We're trying to work it out."

"Until she decides to run again." He laughed without humor, turned, and grabbed the pot of coffee, pouring the brown liquid into his mug. He sighed as he put the pot back on the burner and dropped his head.

"She's not running. He controlled her, her parents basically sold her to him for a shiny spot in the front goddamn pew of their church. They took her shame for what we'd done and used it against her. They told her she was a sinner, that she was damned, that she wouldn't be able to have the forgiveness of God unless she married him and saved herself through the

163

church." I spoke in a rough, hurried whisper. "You can't judge her, you don't know shit."

He raised his head, but braced himself on the edge of the counter, his back still facing me. The muscles in his shoulders stretched with tension, but he was calm when he said, "You're my life, Declan, this family, Kieran, Mom, you're all I have, and I'm not just going to sit by and watch her fucking break you again."

"I love him, Liam." Paige's voice wavered and she startled me when she put her hand in mine.

Liam turned and focused on our linked fingers. He knew what Paige and I had been through, he was aware of it all, but still his cold, brown eyes assessed her as he said, "You fucking better." She stiffened at my side as he took a step toward her. "I almost lost him because of you... if you're not in this for the long haul, then I suggest you hit the damn road, because if I—"

"That's enough!" Paige was shaking at my side and I was about two seconds from clocking my brother in the jaw. "Can't you see you're scaring her?" I pulled her under my arm and Liam frowned.

"I think that's the point," she whispered.

Liam flicked his gaze back to her. He watched us both for a moment and his shoulders sagged.

"It's too early for this shit." He ran his hand through his hair again. The dark strands were at odds with each other as he turned and grabbed his mug.

Paige released my hand and moved out from under my arm.

"Paige, don't."

She rested her hand on his arm. The tiny fragile bones of her fingers begged him to give her a chance. "I-I know you're worried, but I can promise—"

"I don't want your promises, save those for God, just don't hurt him again." He snapped his eyes shut and pinched the bridge of his nose.

"I won't."

He stepped away from her touch and moved toward me. The severe line of his jaw, the creases around his eyes, they relaxed. "I'll see you at work."

Paige watched him as he disappeared down the hall. "What did he mean he almost lost you?"

"I told you, it got really bad after you left."

A flash of panic flickered across her features. "Did you try to—"

I shook my head. "I thought about it, but nothing ever concrete."

"Liam hates me and it's for good reason."

"Come here." I held out my hand and she took it. "He doesn't hate you, he dropped it, that's a good sign. If he hated you, he would have tried to throw you out, and then I would've ended up in jail for assaulting my brother. I think it ended well." I pulled her to my chest.

She huffed.

"Just give him some time, he'll come around."

At least I hoped he would.

PAIGE

Declan's computer screensaver danced with bubbles casting the room in a blue glow, and as the sunlight peeked out of the bottom of the closed window shades, my surroundings became clearer. I sat up, pushing the heavy black comforter to the side. It had tangled around my jean-clad legs. My hair was a little damp with perspiration, my mouth was sticky with thirst, and I was alone.

Declan's side of the bed was disheveled. I placed my hand on his pillow and the cold fabric sent a chill up my arm. I wondered how long he'd been awake or if he'd been able to go back to sleep at all after our early morning encounter with Liam. Liam had been so abrupt, and he had every right to be, but I hoped he'd give me a chance. He'd been almost like a brother to me once. Being an only child, even if Declan hated it, I loved going to his house most of the time. His father was a drunk, but his mother was the sweetest person I'd ever known. Her paper-thin, frail hands had a history. A history of laundry, housework, and raising three strong boys. Her sapphire eyes were Declan's and they held secrets, pain, and longing. Their

166

house lived and breathed and creaked and groaned and, over the years, it became mine, as well.

"I guess you think you're better than us?" Liam was still breathing heavy, his hand gripped the steering wheel so tight his knuckles were white despite the cuts and bruising.

My heart was banging and clanging, and the blood whooshed behind my eardrums. "W-what?"

The car rolled to a stop as Liam pulled to the side of the road a few blocks from the O'Connell's. He shifted in his seat and looked at me. His features were the hardest of the boys, the darkest. His deep brown eyes pinned me to the cushion of the passenger seat. He was attractive, just like his brothers, but in a scary, too manly sort of way. His hair was almost black and too long, dipping past his left eye. He was built bigger than any sixteen-year-old boy should be.

"Is he your charity project?" He raised his hands in question. His knuckles were raw and the image of him taking his father's punch, his face shocked and pained, blinked vividly in my mind.

I was confused, and as my brows furrowed, his jaw relaxed and he lowered his hands. "We're a fucking freak show compared to your palace on the bench."

It was my turn to be angry. "Excuse me?" I sat up straighter and my own hands balled into fists as they sat on my thighs.

"Dex is special. He always has been and if you—"

"Declan is more than special, he's brilliant, and beautiful, and..." I paused as Liam's mouth twitched with a budding smile. "I suppose you think I'm just some dumb kid? I care about your brother. He's the only one who gets me." I dropped my eyes to my lap. My fists were now a tangle of nerves as I threaded my fingers in and out.

"I'm sorry." Liam's brusque voice had taken on a soft edge. It was deep and the timbre of it soothed my steel spine, and I exhaled a shaky breath.

"I'm sorry you had to see that tonight, it's... it's fucked. This whole life... it's not right."

He drifted away. His eyes now out the window, thinking about things I'd never ever be able to imagine. The hardships he'd endured at such a young age... it wasn't right.

"Are you hurt?" I asked.

He shook his head, cleared his throat, and said, "Declan told me you're a real Picasso."

My lips pressed together and my smile hid at the corners, shy and new. "He did?"

Liam's smile was warm and surprisingly... soulful. "Yeah. You make him happy. Keep it that way." His smile danced as he put the car in gear.

"I will. I promise." It was too quiet for him to hear as he concentrated on pulling back onto the roadway. But he exhaled, and the set of his shoulders relaxed, and I thought, for just a moment, that maybe he had heard me after all.

I grabbed my phone from the night stand, shaking off the memory. I'd failed Declan... and I'd lied to Liam. I hadn't kept my promise, and the lump in my throat turned to ash, making me nauseous. I looked at the door to the bedroom. I was too scared to just walk out of his room. Liam and I had a huge bridge to build, and I wasn't ready, or equipped to do it on my own. At least not today, not after this morning. My thumb had just opened the lock screen so I could text Declan, when he walked in.

He was wearing only a pair of faded, touchable blue jeans that hung low on his hips. That very perceptible V dipped below the denim waist line and, as I continued my free perusal of his bare chest, I noticed a glint of metal. My eyes widened, I hadn't

168

noticed it in the studio the other night. Both of his nipples were pierced, and I had to drag my eyes upward before I blushed. He was watching me as the door closed behind him. Declan's dark blond hair was still wet, and his cheeks were pink from the shower. The smell of soap and deodorant filled the room, and the hummingbird in my chest took flight. I'd seen his tattoos, briefly before, but seeing him now, muscles and ink on display, I nearly swallowed my tongue. I'd been kept in a glass box for the past nine years. Need and desire had been prayed out of me, leaving duty and servitude in its place.

"Good morning." His voice was coarse and worn and honey at the same time. It was the hammer, the breaking point, and my glass cage shattered to pieces all around me.

"Hi." My breath hitched as he moved toward the dresser.

I watched him through the mirror as he opened his top drawer and dug through it. His back was free of ink, but the wide expanse of it, the strength, it heated my cheeks. He caught me staring through the mirror and as our gazes collided his blue eyes lit with a hungry flame. Declan's arms and chest were teasing me within the reflection. I stood from the bed, running my nervous hands through my hair. My feet moved forward without my bidding, driven by pure curiosity and the need to touch and trace every line on his body. He'd made his flesh a canvas, and just like his art, I was sure each piece had a meaning.

I raised my fingertips and, as I dusted his shoulder, he went rigid. A flash of fear darkened his irises.

"May I..." I placed the palm of my hand flush to the skin of his bicep and he melted.

The humidity of his shower still lingered around him like an aura, and his citrus scent was intense as he turned to face me. His posture was calm, and his arms hung with ease on each side, granting me silent permission. I was eye level with the thick black cross that was tattooed in the center of his sternum just right of his heart. My hand began to shake as I lowered it to his chest and traced the symbol. He shivered under my touch, as the tips of my fingers followed along the inside of the tattoo, making the sign of the cross.

"It's for protection," he said, so low it was almost a reverent whisper.

"Protection?"

He took a deep breath. "From the evil in the world... and... in my head."

"Nothing about what goes on in your head is evil, Declan." I brought my eyes to his and watched in awe as the color cleared back to light blue. Maybe it was the shadows of the room, but as he stared at me, I felt his mood shift.

He leaned down, pressed his lips to my forehead, and I laid my hand flat against the ink, pausing momentarily to feel his heart rate increase below my palm. He pulled back and allowed me to continue my perusal. I gently trailed along his skin to the next tattoo. Everything on his left arm was geometric and, if you looked closely, you could glean shapes within the tangled knots of black. Faces, clocks, everything was intricately sewn together along the flesh. I brought my fingers to his right arm, the one with my eye, with my words, and traced along the inner hollow of his elbow. He exhaled a shuddered breath as I drew lines up and up until I was back at his shoulder again. I wanted to ask him why he'd chosen the things he had. What did the quote on his rib cage mean to him? He was a walking tome of secrets and I wanted to decipher each one. My fingers feasted upon each swirl as my hand moved down his left pectoral muscle. But, when my thumb accidentally brushed his piercing he groaned and grabbed my hand. He held it against his chest for a few seconds until the flame flickered and ebbed away.

"I should get dressed." He gave me a small smile that was at odds with the strain apparent in his tone.

He released the hold he had on my hand and I let my palm fall away. He turned and grabbed a black t-shirt from his dresser. His muscles pulled tight as he lifted it over his head. It was overwhelming to watch him like this. It felt blatant and rude, but this was the boy I'd shared everything with, and the man he'd become was too tempting, and it shook the very foundation of what *I'd* become. We'd always been two different spheres, always drawn to the other, but this time, he was more than I could handle, and it wasn't a question of if. It was when... when would we crash, when would this man unleash, and when would I succumb to the power of his release... to the power of the fall?

"May I use your bathroom before I go?" I ran my hand through my hair again. My reflection confirmed my suspicion. My cheeks were splotched with red, my hair was untamed. I was wrinkled, and ruffled, and most likely smelled as such.

He nodded. "I'll be in the kitchen when you're ready."

"Is Liam—"

He frowned. "He left already. I told him I'd be down in a little bit. Paige... he's just overprotective."

"I know. Doesn't make what I did any less horrible."

"What we did." He scrubbed his hand down his face. "I'll talk to him, it won't be—"

"It's okay, Declan, let him come around on his own terms, it's how he is." The corner of my lip lifted. "He's just as gruff as I remembered. If not more."

Declan laughed. "He's an asshole on most days. Don't let him get to you."

"I won't." I'd almost convinced myself.

"See you in a few minutes." Declan grinned just before he turned and opened his bedroom door.

The bathroom was just across the hall, and once I was under the bright lights I cringed. I was worse than I thought. I reached into my jeans pocket and pulled out a hair tie. I quickly assembled a top knot and secured it into place. After splashing some cool water on my face and patting it dry with a towel from under the sink, I stole some toothpaste and brushed my teeth with my finger. The sour taste of my mouth rinsed away with cold water and, as I took another cursory glance in the mirror, I decided this was as good as it was going to get.

Declan was sitting on a bar stool doodling on a piece of paper in the kitchen when I emerged with my bag over my shoulder. He glanced up at me and gave me a gorgeous smile that reached his eyes. His full lips spread even bigger as he assessed me.

"You look nice." He stood and pocketed the drawing.

"Thanks." I laughed.

"Would you like to see the shop?" He placed his left hand in his pocket and motioned with his right toward the door.

"Sure."

I tamped down the fear of seeing Liam again so that I could let myself enjoy the invitation into Declan's new world.

The air was crisp and dense with the electricity of autumn as we descended the stairs. I shivered and Declan wrapped his arm around me as we walked the short distance from the bottom of the stairs to the back door of the tattoo parlor. The heat of his body was an instant relief, as well as the gesture.

He squeezed me once before dropping his arm to open the door. Once inside, my eyes devoured everything. The art on the walls, some of it I could tell was Declan's, but the rest were mish mashes of style. From the typical tattoos to the more intricate. Some pieces drawn with an obvious delicate hand and others angrier. The floors were stark white and each station had red leather tables. We'd passed a few empty spots, but as we neared the center of the shop I felt the eyes of everyone in the room. The hair on the back of my neck stood at attention as I heard Liam's deep voice.

"It's just a fucking chick, Kemper, calm the hell down." Liam laughed and smacked who I assumed was Kemper on the shoulder.

Declan linked my hand with his as we approached them and my heart began to sprint. "Hey, Kemp, this is Paige, an old friend of mine."

Declan's tone was jovial, warm, unburdened. He was in his element. I gave Kemper a wave and marveled at all the jewelry in his face. Both nostrils were pierced along with his eyebrows. He even had a piercing in his lip. He was reed thin, tall, and his black Mohawk was flat and slicked back.

"It's a girl," he said with wonder and Liam smacked him in the back of the head this time.

"Of course it's a girl, you fucking idiot." Liam laughed and nodded his head at me. I noticed a slight narrowing of his eyes before he turned away. He didn't trust me, but he wasn't kicking me out either.

Declan chuckled and the sound of it vined around my heart and gave it a squeeze.

"It's nice to meet you." My voice was too timid. Avenues Ink, with its clean lines, blood-red furniture, and black counter tops, it was bold and I was just a spectator.

"She speaks." Kemper winked and gave me a goofy, lopsided smile. "I don't think I've ever seen you with a—"

"First time for everything," Kieran's familiar voice sounded right next to me and I jumped. "Hey, Declan..." He smiled at me. "Welcome to the shop, Paige." He continued past us as if it was just like any other day.

"Good to meet you." Kemper leaned in with a conspiratorial grin plastered to his face. "I was starting to think Declan didn't like girls." He laughed at his own joke.

"Get the fuck to work, man." Declan shoved Kemper's shoulder in jest and he grimaced.

"Easy, meat head." Kemper gave me another once over before he walked away rubbing his arm.

Declan tugged on my hand. "This is me." He nodded his head to the station to the right and then led me to the work table. "Have a seat." He let go of my hand with a mischievous smile.

I took a seat on the table, and the stiff leather gave way to my weight. It was comfortable and inviting and I suddenly could see myself lying here, eyes closed, letting Declan cover me with his art.

"I was thinking." He reached into his pocket and handed me the drawing from earlier, but it was more than a drawing. The quote *"I am, I am, I am"* was written in his handwriting and just below it was a heart rhythm. Something you'd see on a monitor in a hospital. The line was jagged with actual marked beats... three, to be exact. "I could do this... if you wanted."

I flicked my gaze from the paper to his eyes. His hand rubbed at the back of his neck as if he was nervous, but the smile that played at his lips suggested otherwise. I'd never really wanted a tattoo, but this... I looked at the paper again and then back at Declan. This was perfect.

"Where would you place it?" I asked and his smile widened.

He drew a line with his finger along the left side of his chest just along his heart line. "This is where I can hear your heartbeat the loudest."

The butterflies in my stomach tipped and twirled until they escaped and fluttered in my chest. "When?"

His eyes were crystalline and his smile... it was endless. "Now, whenever you want." The excitement in his voice mirrored my own.

"Maybe next week? I can request off a few days to heal?"

"It heals pretty quick, but—"

"Can I wear a bra after?"

He chuckled. "Probably not for twenty-four hours."

"Then next week it is, I'll see if Luca will trade with me." I hopped off the table and wiped my hands down my jeans.

"You're serious?" he asked and I nodded. He lifted his hand to my cheek and let the pad of his thumb trail along my jaw. "I can't wait."

I wanted him to mark my flesh with ink, make the false purity I'd clung to for so long vanish. I wanted to be bonded to him, his handwriting permanently on my skin, a constant reminder that I *was* alive... that this heart still beats, and it belonged to Declan.

Declan introduced me to a few more staff members. Each a carbon copy of the other. Male, muscles, tattoos. There was one female, Ronnie. She was tall, and thin with china white skin and red lips. She was like a Gothic supermodel with black hair and perfect curves, and when she'd shaken my hand with disinterest, I'd felt mousy, at best. The wind had been removed from my sails as Declan walked me out to my car.

"She's a lesbian." Declan's voice was filled with mirth.

I exhaled and turned to face him leaning against the driver side door. "She is?"

"Yes."

I bit my bottom lip and his eyes fell to my mouth.

"I'm glad." The two words slipped out as Declan closed the space between us.

He framed my face with his palms, his eyes still on my mouth and mine on his as his thumb pulled across my bottom lip.

"You don't ever have to worry about that shit with me, Paige, you never did, and you never will." He leaned in and I could smell the mint on his breath.

I licked my lips. "I don't?"

He exhaled and the warmth of it intoxicated me. "No."

He covered my mouth with his. His lips eager. I leaned my head back and parted my lips for him. His tongue was sweet and soft, and the feel of him, his body pressing me into the metal of my car, I was putty. Free for him to shape and form at his own will. My hands wrapped around his neck, drawing him closer, and the tips of my fingers slid into his hairline. This kiss could have lasted for minutes, hours... days. The sun could have set and risen, the world could have stopped, and we would've never noticed. The wet heat of his mouth on mine, my hands in his hair, his powerful form aligned along my body, each feeling took everything we'd been through and wound it around our limbs in sighs and shadow. The loneliness, the regret, the pain, it weaved through each breath, each taste, and made us one again. One in past, in present, and in love.

Declan softly bit my bottom lip before he broke away. I licked my lips, still desperate for his taste as he leaned back to look at me. His hands still held my face as he said a little breathless, "When can I see you again?"

Now, tonight, tomorrow, every day, every night, I didn't want to miss another minute of him. "I have to have dinner tonight with Lana, I promised her, but I live with her, I could—"

"It's okay." He kissed my forehead just at the bridge of my nose, just like he used to. "I'm booked late with appointments all week. Do you work tomorrow?"

I nodded.

"I'll see you then, I'm coming by to pick up my painting. I'm going to frame it this weekend. If you want I could frame yours, too?"

I was still rusty and I wasn't sure my painting deserved a frame. "I'd like to take it home, work on it some more."

He took a step back and nodded as I reached into my bag for my keys. I hit the unlock button and the car alarm chirped. He opened the door for me and assured me he'd text me later. As I pulled away with the sting of his kiss still on my lips, and his eyes on mine through my rearview window, a shiver of loss skittered along my spine.

I'd been a trophy, placed on the shelf for display, no one cared that my shine had been dulled by years of dust. No one, not until Declan.

The boy I'd ruined had become the man to save me from my oblivion.

DECLAN

Fire spread across my chest and arms as I lifted the bar above my head. Liam's smug smile hovered above my face egging me on as he spotted me. He added twenty more pounds to the barbell, bringing me up to two hundred and forty-five pounds. The most I'd done for reps and I was struggling through my last set.

"Don't be a pussy, Dex, push through it." Liam's smirk twitched as I growled through the last rep.

The bar clanged loudly as I set it back into the rack. "Fuck you." I choked out a laugh as I sat up completely out of breath. "Shit, I'm done."

"No way, Kieran isn't even here yet." He slapped my bare shoulder and I flinched.

The gym was almost a daily thing for all of us, but we tried at least once a week to meet up at the same time. It was our sanctuary, and it was where everything about each of our lives didn't matter. This was where we'd strip ourselves down to the beasts we'd learned to hide every day. All the shit we'd gone through, in here... it fed us, made us stronger instead of tearing us apart second by second.

"Why'd you push me?" I wiped my face with the bottom of my shirt.

"Here." I grabbed the towel he handed me and wiped my face. "It seems like you're getting soft." Liam's smile fell just enough I caught his meaning.

I exhaled a sharp breath. "Don't be a jealous dick. She came back, I can't help that Kel—"

"Don't!" The word clipped through the air and silenced the other people around us. He lowered his voice to a menacing whisper, "There is no damn difference between her and Paige. They both saw us for what we were and tossed our sorry asses to the side."

"I'm tired of your bullshit, Liam. Paige is nothing like Kelly. Paige and I... we both made some shitty choices, and now we have a chance to make it right. Stop pushing your baggage onto everyone else. It's getting old." I stood and threw the towel at his chest and he caught it, his face like a stone.

"I leave you two alone for twenty minutes and you're at each other's throats. Come on, guys, leave this shit in the locker room. We're here to shred, right?" Kieran glared at us, but the longer the silence between us grew, his glare turned to pleading.

"You're late." Liam moved his eyes to Kieran and rolled his shoulders as he sat down on the bench. He clenched his jaw once before turning his eyes back on me. "For you, Dex, I'll give her a chance, for *you*, because it's you I fucking care about, and I know she does, too, but sometimes... that shit isn't enough."

"I think this time it is."

The scars she'd left behind still hurt. They pinched and begged to tear open every time I looked at her. But, yesterday morning, she'd looked at me like I was worth the worship of her touch. We'd kissed in a way that connected us again. In a way that had torn my heart and hers into ribbons, and once we'd pulled away there was no going back. All the pieces had blended as a whole and she'd taken a few of mine, and I'd taken some of hers. Our scars had merged, and it felt... right.

"Maybe. For your sake, you better hope you're right." Liam exhaled and dropped the towel I'd thrown at him to the floor as he lay back on the bench.

"I know I don't know everything that happened, but I know Paige. And she's always been a good person. What happened is between you two. And no matter what this asshole says, we'll both be here if it all goes to hell." Kieran shoved my shoulder with little force and turned his stare onto Liam. "You going to lift that shit, or just stare at it?"

"I'll spot you," I said with a smirk as I moved behind the bench. "You need me to remove some weight?"

Kieran laughed and Liam narrowed his eyes. "Just shut the fuck up and spot me."

The rest of the morning was business as usual at the gym. Pushing, shoving, breaking each other's limits and setting tempers on edge. It was how we did it, and after we'd finished and showered, ready to leave, it was just us O'Connell boys again.

"You want a ride back to the shop?" Kieran asked me and I shook my head.

"I want to walk."

"Don't be late." Liam snapped on his helmet and straddled his Harley. The signature sound of the bike roared to life and echoed inside the back alley parking lot behind the gym. He gave Kieran and me a wave before he drove off.

"You sure?" he asked again as he pulled a set of keys from his gym bag.

"It's only five blocks, and it helps clear my head." I pulled my bag over my shoulder.

"You seem happy, don't let Liam ruin it." Kieran's blue eyes creased at the corners as he smiled. "You going to stop by The Gallery on your way back?"

"No, I need to stop by later and pick up my painting. I could use your help this time, it's bigger than my normal pieces"

"Sure, we can take my truck. The framing supplies are still in Mom's garage. What time you want to head over?"

"A few of my later appointments called yesterday and canceled, so probably around six. I should be finished by then. You think Liam will be okay with us both leaving though?" My brows dipped with doubt.

"Do you really care?" he asked with a laugh.

My lips broke into a full smile. "Nah, not really."

I'd opened my phone about five hundred goddamn times today. I wanted to text her, but every single time Liam, or Kemper, or a client would interrupt me. I could still feel her hands on my body. Every inch of my skin lit with the color of orange under her touch. She was silk, and at first I feared her softness. She could bring me to the brink and I'd forget myself, lose my control. Lose myself in the wake of her kiss; her body. Paige had been curious about my ink, but as she'd innocently traced the lines, she'd ignited the violent need that threaded through my veins. That deep, forgotten blood had boiled and churned with each beat of my pulse, and the apprehension, it'd turned to something else... something primal, and if I hadn't pulled away, I would've fallen victim to her new taste, the scent of her, the feel of her, the memory of what it was like to let go inside of her.

"I'm going to grab the truck, pull it around front. You about ready?" Kieran asked.

My last client had run a little late. It was the third time I'd seen him this week. He was getting an entire mural on his back. "Yeah, just finishing cleaning up. Dorian was late."

"That back piece is going to look sick though. The decayed trees you did, they're amazing."

I laughed as I shut the black tool box full of my equipment. "Says the guy who only has a tattoo of a rosary around his neck."

He shook his head with a smile. "Hey, it goes all the way down to my chest."

"You need more ink." I teased him all the time about this. He was our desk guy and the kid had no visible tattoos. It was bad for business.

"Tell me something I don't already know, come on, let's go before Liam realizes we both left."

"I'll meet you out front."

After he left, I pulled my phone from my pocket. The weight in my chest lifted as I opened the lock screen. Paige's number had changed, and after the first few studio sessions, I'd finally gotten enough nerve to ask her for it. I hadn't once called her or texted her yet, I hadn't needed to. She had just been there, every night, ready to paint.

My thumbs moved quickly over the keyboard.

Me: *Hey, it's Declan. Are you still at work?*

I did another quick look around my station, everything was in its place, and I headed for the front door.

"You're off tomorrow?" Kemper asked as I walked past his station.

"Yeah. I'm taking a couple of days, working on a project."

"Sweet, see you in a few."

I waved and just as I past Liam's station I said, "I'm out, I'm headed to pick up the painting."

Liam shut off his machine and raised his head. His purple gloves were covered in ink. "You framing at our place or Mom's?"

"Mom's."

"Kieran taking you?" he asked.

"Yeah, he's waiting for me out front. Ronnie said she's got the desk. I'll see you later?"

He nodded. "I'll be around. I might go out to Bellows tonight though, that weird as fuck band I like is playing. Maybe if you finish early you and Kieran can come out."

"Maybe." My phone vibrated in my hand, and when I looked down Paige's name flashed across the lock screen. "See you later."

He lifted his chin before bringing his attention back to the half-naked customer lying across his table. As I moved to the front door I opened the message.

Paige: *When you tell someone you are going to text them later it usually means later that same day... just an FYI.*

I laughed.

Me: *I'm sorry, did I make you worry?*

It wasn't right, but I liked that she might've worried. If she was worried then that meant she had something to lose, and if losing me scared her... I knew we'd be okay, because I wasn't going anywhere.

Paige: *Yes.*

Hurt her.

Hurt her like she hurt you.

My smile dimmed as I opened the door to the shop. I'd forgotten to take my meds this morning, and this was the first internal stimulus I'd had in twenty-four hours. When I was with Paige, I didn't need them as much. I didn't like how they dulled my senses. When I was with her, everything felt magnified and it felt too fucking good. So good I'd completely spaced taking my pills today.

Kieran was at the curb and as I got into the truck he asked, "Why do you look like someone just punched a kitten?"

"Nothing, just drive."

He didn't respond to my irritated demand, instead he turned off onto the road.

Me: *I'm sorry that you worried.*

She responded immediately.

Paige: *I'm being a girl, it's okay.*

I smiled at my screen as I typed.

Me: *Are you avoiding my question? Now I'm starting to worry.*

I pictured her in my head. Standing behind the counter at the gallery. Her phone in her hand, her head tipped down, and her mouth spread into a coy smile. I hoped her hair was up so I could see the fine strands that had fallen loose dust the slope of her neck. That was my favorite thing. Every time I was near her, all I wanted to do was lean in and inhale.

Paige: *What question?*

I laughed again and I noticed Kieran glance at me from the corner of my eye.

Me: *Are you at the Gallery? I'm on my way there.*

Paige: *I am.*

I hadn't realized how anxious I was until she confirmed that she was there. The knots in my shoulders untied. Kieran hit a pothole and I raised my gaze. He was pulling into the back lot of The Gallery.

Me: *Parking now.*

Paige: *I'm the blonde in the overalls.*

I grinned. Paige was emerging again in the fun, light planes of color that had always seemed to brighten my shadows, meds or no meds.

"You want me to wait out back or come in?" Kieran asked as he cut the engine.

I pointed to the emergency exit. "Wait there, I shouldn't be too long. I'll have Paige turn off the alarm. It will be easier than trying to maneuver it through the store."

"You don't want help packing it?" He lifted his right eyebrow.

I wanted as much time with Paige, just me and her, as possible. I didn't want my brother to make her uncomfortable. "Nah. I got it."

He shook his head. "Alright, just text me if you change your mind, I'll head in."

I nodded as I turned to head around the front. The sun was already setting and, as I walked toward the front door of The Gallery, the street lamps lit, illuminating my path to her. The chill in the air didn't faze me as I stopped in front of the window to the shop. She was laughing with Chandler behind the counter. Her hair was up, like I had hoped, and she was wearing a short sleeve, white t-shirt under her worn overalls. She was warm with flushed cheeks and rose-colored lips. I caught my own reflection in the glass of the window. The dark circles under my eyes were gone and my irises swirled with specks of green and white. She was changing me.

She caught me staring and her smile turned timid as she bit the side of her lip. I ran my hand through my hair as I opened the front door. The bell jingled somewhere in the background of my mind as I made my way through. The overalls she had on were spotted with paint, and I wanted to know what she'd been working on. I wanted to know what she was thinking as she watched me approach her. Her chest rising and falling a little bit faster with every step. I wondered if she noticed how Chandler looked at her. He saw what I did. He saw the spectacular work of art standing behind the counter and he wanted her, but she was oblivious because all she wanted... was me.

"Hey, Declan, I didn't hear you come in." I kept my eyes on Paige as Chandler continued, his voice a little less confident than before. "I was just going to call you today, I need you to move your piece, I've got another renter."

"Hi." Paige's voice made my lips turn up into a smile.

I braced the counter with my hands and nodded at Chandler. "Paige and I are boxing it up today."

"Paige?"

"Yeah, you still have those preassembled shipping crates?" I asked not missing his confusion. He wanted to know why Paige was looking at me like he wished she would look at him.

"Yeah, they're in the back, I'll show—"

"I got it," Paige chimed in with a wicked smile, and her eyes teemed with excitement.

We both ignored Chandler's stare as she made her way around the counter. She took my hand in hers and all the blood in my head rushed and pounded as I leaned down and kissed her once on the lips. "I'll never make you worry again," I whispered only for her to hear.

She bumped me with her hip and grinned. "Come on, I'll show you where the packing supplies are."

She led me back to the studio and once we were inside, she gave me instructions on where the packing supplies were in the storeroom. I'd asked her to disable the back door alarm for Kieran, and she didn't seem to mind that he was here. Everything was set out and ready to go by the time she turned off the alarm.

She stood in front of me, her head down, and I took her hand in mine. "I was afraid I scared you off."

"Not going to happen. I should've texted you, but I guess I didn't want to crowd you." I lifted her chin with my free hand.

"Please, by all means, crowd me." She smiled. "It's hard because I know this is new, but it feels like it's not... time passed, things have changed, but it's still just me and you."

We couldn't pretend like nothing had ever happened. Things had changed. She was fragile, and I was terrified of breaking her, but as her eyes searched mine, I could see her point. Underneath all the bullshit... it was just us, me and her, and starting from scratch was impossible. I leaned down and let my nose graze the slope of her neck. I inhaled her scent of rain and powder. She was still Paige. Scent and smile, color and soul, and as I brought my lips to her cheek, then her nose, and finally her mouth, I kissed the girl I had always loved.

I leaned back so I could see into her eyes. "I don't want to start all over, I still love you. You from nine years ago, and you now."

She expelled a shuddered breath. "I like that you know the not-so-bright spots of my soul, and you still love me regardless of them."

"I love you even more because of them." I squeezed her hand and the excitement from earlier nearly brimmed over her lashes. "It's impossible to think when you look at me like that."

"Like what?" She tilted her head slightly and furrowed her brows.

"Your eyes, any lingering color of regret... reluctance. It all vanishes and all I can see is you. You looking at me like I'm the only thing that matters."

She pinned me with those sure, bright blue eyes. "To me, you're everything."

PAIGE

"So you guys are an item then?" Lana twirled her lo mein around her chopsticks with ease.

My head had continued to swim long after Declan had left The Gallery, even after I'd come home for the evening. Declan and I had packed up the painting, and with Kieran's help, the process had gone too fast. He'd been there one second and then gone the next. His lips had been too brief, and as much as I liked Kieran, I'd wished he would've stayed outside.

"Paige?" Lana giggled. "Did you hear me?"

Walking on air had always been a side effect of Declan's kisses, but now his mouth promised more... his touch promised sin and relief, delicate and rough. I wanted all of him. I brought my fingertips to my lips; they still felt raw.

I nodded. "Yes."

"Yes, you're an item, or yes, you heard me?" She scooped another huge bite of noodles into her mouth.

"Yes. We're together. Again." I smiled and shook my head. "Is it crazy?"

"No, not if it makes you happy. I'm just glad you guys are working through things. It's healthy, especially after all you've both been through. What changed from last night?"

Lana and I had dinner last night at this wei l restaurant that one of her many conquests had taken ler to once. Everything was picked fresh from the chef's garden, made to order. The place was small, homey, and it felt like we'd been eating dinner in some stranger's house. Only four tables, very exclusive. Lana seemed to know the chef personally. We'd talked a little bit about Declan, but then, everything hadn't been fully processed. And when he didn't text me, I'd thought for sure he'd chosen to pull back. I'd thought maybe he wasn't ready. But today, at The Gallery, it felt like old times. We'd laughed and smiled, and teased and flirted. His brother watched us with a huge grin on his face. We weren't kids anymore, and navigating this new us... it was going to be interesting.

"I can't really pinpoint it, Lana, but something clicked today. We... we love each other, and it's new but it's not. See, it's crazy, do we start over, or just keep going?" I poked my noodles with my chopsticks. My stomach too full of butterflies to eat much.

"I say fuck it, do both." Lana's lips broke into a huge smile and I laughed.

"Both?"

"You eat, I'll talk." She pushed my plate closer to me and stared. "Eat."

I picked up my chopsticks again, swirled the noodles into a ball and popped it into my mouth. She nodded in approval.

"So here's my diagnosis. You're married still, right? But, not really. You never were truly married to Clark. You've been..." She held up her hands and made air quotations with her fingers. "'Married' to Declan this whole time. You've both changed, and yet you're both a little emotionally stunted from the past." She looked at me with wide eyes, as if this all had suddenly dawned on her. "So." She held the syllable longer than necessary and I smiled around my noodles. "I think you can just keep going. Go with what feels right. You guys separated, nine years is a long ass time, so you'll have to start over on some things, but other things will be the same. You love him?"

I nodded.

"Then love him, Paige, and get that asshole ex of yours out of your life."

I swallowed the giant ball of noodles. "You're pretty smart."

"I'm a professional student."

"Not for long."

She groaned. "Don't remind me." She stood from the couch and grabbed her wine glass from the table. "One glass? In celebration of the long lost lovers' reunion?" Her nose crinkled as she smiled.

Why not. "One glass."

"Yes!"

I giggled as she pranced into the kitchen.

Declan and I *had* changed. I was learning to live and he was learning to trust. But, there was absolutely no reason we couldn't do it together.

"Clark... he still hasn't answered yet about the papers?" Lana handed me a glass of white wine and sat next to me on the couch.

Maybe there was still one reason I couldn't fully commit.

"No, and my parents are radio silent. It makes me nervous, like the calm before the storm. I keep thinking they'll just show up and demand that I stay married to him." I sipped the wine and the sweet flavor surprised me. It was tangy and tasted almost like apples. "This is good."

"See, I told you. Jesus didn't turn water into wine for nothing." Lana raised her eyebrows as she drank deeply from her glass.

"You're going to Hell," I joked.

"We can hold hands on the way down." Her smile was lopsided. "But, in all seriousness. You're twenty-eight years old, Paige, you never have to talk to your parents again if you feel like that's the best option. Adult perks... sometimes they're lovely."

Everything she was saying was true. I was an adult. But, at times, I didn't feel like one. I'd spent so much time trying to be something I wasn't. I worshipped at an altar that told me I wasn't good enough. I was married to a man who used me to make himself feel more important, and I had parents who treated me like I was still the teenage girl who had committed an unforgivable sin. I *was* emotionally stunted. I sipped at my wine and my limbs filled with gauze.

"I'm an adult," I whispered.

"That's what I just said." She narrowed her brows.

"I think... I think it's time I went home and talked to my parents. It's time I tell them they can't control me anymore."

"I think that's the best idea you've had since you moved in." Her grin pulled up at the corners and she appeared almost proud.

"I'll call them sometime this week, set up an appointment." I nodded as a confirmation to myself. I wouldn't let them scare me, guilt me any longer.

Lana's eye brow lifted. "An appointment?"

"It's the only way they ever really made time for me." My parents had always been a little cold, but as they fell deeper into the status of the church, it had only gotten worse.

"Don't get mad, but I never really loved your parents. They always seemed good at pretending." She set her glass down on the coffee table and picked up her plate.

"They were."

I was about to set my glass down and grab a few more bites of my Chinese food when my phone vibrated against the wood of the table. I picked it up with my free hand and saw I had a text from Declan. My breath caught and my stomach flipped. I stood abruptly and the wine in my glass sloshed.

"It's Declan."

She laughed. "I figured when you almost spilled the wine." She shooed me with her hand. "I'm heading out soon anyway. Bellows has this amazing band playing tonight. You could come?"

I raised my glass. "I think one glass of wine is a good start. Bar hopping maybe next week?" My sarcasm was welcomed and she raised her glass.

"Baby steps." She smiled and I turned to head to my room.

I waited until I was behind my closed door to breathe. Everything with Declan was moving fast. I was giddy one minute and felt at home the next. I drained the glass in one shot, and set it on my dresser before sitting down on the bed. He'd said he would text me tonight, and I knew he would, but seeing his name on my lock screen, it was ridiculous how happy it made me.

Declan: *Come out tonight.*

It wasn't a question. It was an offer.

Me: *Where?*

It was only a few seconds before he replied.

Declan: *Bellows. My brothers are dragging me out, but I want to see you.*

He wants to see me.

I chewed on my lip as I looked in the mirror. The wine had flushed my cheeks and my hair was up in a messy knot. I was in overalls, for crying out loud. Not to mention, I'd never even been in a bar.

Me: *I'd need to get ready, what time?"*
Declan: *Come as you are. I'll be there around eleven.*
I smiled at myself in the mirror.
Just keep going.
Me: *I'll be there around eleven.*

I dropped my phone onto the mattress as I stood, calling out to Lana as I opened my door. "He wants me to meet him at Bellows at eleven."

"Then get your ass in the shower."

Even though I couldn't see her, I heard it. She was smiling ear to ear and so was I.

Lana had tried to talk me into another glass of wine, but someone needed to drive. I wished, however, as I walked into Bellows, I'd had the glass after all. I was out of my element and the liquid courage would've been nice. The music was metal and bass, and the room was packed from wall to wall. The air was hazy and the clothes were skimpy. I pulled my oversized black sweater at the hem with anxious fingers.

"Stop it, you look hot." Lana's ruby-painted lips broke into a devious smile.

I had on my dark blue skinny jeans and a black sweater. Lana had pounced after I'd taken the fastest shower of my life. She'd dried and then curled my hair into loose waves. The kohl around my eyes, I felt it was too dark, but she'd said it made me look edgy. Right before we got out of the car, I'd pocketed my ID and debit card as she'd handed me a light pink, sparkling gloss. I'd taken a moment to catch my own reflection, and I couldn't believe it. I didn't seem plain for once. I looked... almost sexy. But seeing some of the girls here tonight, with their short skirts and cleavage, maybe I overestimated my sex appeal.

"I don't think hot is the right verbiage," I shouted loud enough for her to hear over the music and crowd.

"There's your man..." She pointed just after the crowd parted a bit, and there he was, sitting in the back corner, sketch book on the table, and eyes on me. "And the way he's looking at you, I think hot is an understatement." She smacked my ass. "Good luck, let him eat you alive," she growled in my ear, and I giggled nervously as I rolled my eyes. "I'll be at the bar."

I didn't drop his gaze as I stepped forward. The color of his eyes deepened as I advanced, and his smile pulled up on one side. I was almost to his table when another woman approached him. His eyes flicked to hers and his smile dropped dead as his jaw set in a tight line. She looked younger than us, her dark black hair was shiny and straight. Her dress fit her curves and as she leaned down to whisper in his ear, my heart stopped. My feet fumbled along the concrete surface of the bar floor as I came to an abrupt halt. The young woman leaned back and seemed to sway on her legs as she placed her hand on his shoulder for support. Did he know her or was she just some girl who'd had too much to drink, hitting on the hot guy in the corner? I smoothed my hands down the front of my sweater, took a deep breath, and swallowed down my unease. His smile... it had been for me.

Declan's posture was rigid once I got to his table.

"Hey, Declan." I kept my smile small, quiet, and private... for him.

The girl noticed me and dropped her hand from his shoulder. As soon as she relieved him of her touch, his eyes lit; the blue seemed to shimmer under the low light of the club as he looked at me. The moment should've been tense, filled with an awkward silence, but it wasn't. We both watched each other, ignoring the girl, deciphering, and feeling. His eyes followed along my face, my body, and back to my gaze before he said, "I'm glad you decided to come."

"I'm Kate." Her voice wobbled and my earlier assumption seemed accurate, she was, at the very least, buzzed.

I was reluctant to lift my eyes from his appraisal. "Hi." I held out my hand. "Paige."

She ignored my olive branch and I let my hand fall to my side without letting it bother me. I was used to cold receptions. I'd lived in a constant state of winter for over nine years.

Kate narrowed her eyes. "How do you know Declan?"

I knew Declan from soul to bone. "We go way back." I gave him a grin and he smiled.

"Have a seat." Declan motioned to me with his hand to the seat next to him.

I wanted to ask her how she knew Declan, but I wasn't sure she really did, and the way his body naturally leaned away from hers, as if she repulsed him, it made me think she didn't know him at all. I sat down and rested my hands in my lap. Declan surprised me. The warmth of his palm encapsulated mine under the table. He leaned over and whispered into my ear, his breath tickled down my ear and neck, "You look sexy."

It was bold and the pleasure of his timbre vibrated down my flesh and pooled inside my stomach, setting my cheeks on fire. I whispered a thank you as I turned my face to his, our noses almost touching, and Kate long forgotten. It wasn't like us, public displays. My heart thundered as he pulled me in, so close, our lips if we spoke, would touch, take flight, and I'd be lost to the height of it. He exhaled and it was strained as he leaned back, his eyes on my mouth. Kate cleared her throat, and for a split second, I marveled in the thought that maybe Declan was marking me, letting her know she had no chance.

"Good to see you, Declan," Her tone proved otherwise. She gave me a snide grin and turned, almost tripping over her own two feet.

She swayed through the crowd and I watched her until she was swallowed whole by the sea of people.

"Do you know her?" I asked, and immediately wished I hadn't as Declan almost winced. As much as the thought of him kissing this woman made the pleasant warmth in my stomach turn to ice, I had no right to care. "You know what, it doesn't matter."

"I haven't been with anyone since you, Paige. I was honest when I told you that. There were times…" Guilt flashed across his features. "I tried to move on, but like I said before, it never went far."

"I shouldn't have asked."

A waitress came to the table then. "Can I get you something?"

"Just a glass of water, please," I said.

"What about you, Declan?" she asked him with a knowing smile. "Water, as always?"

He nodded.

"Two waters," she confirmed before she turned and headed to the bar.

"Kate doesn't matter." Declan squeezed my hand under the table.

Again we were almost nose to nose, the charge between us crackled over the loud grind of guitars.

I shook my head. "She doesn't."

His lips brushed mine not once, but twice, and the flavor of mint flooded my senses as his mouth captured me. It was a quick stolen kiss, and when he pulled away, my face burned crimson. The room was loud and yet we were trapped in our own bubble. He glanced to the bar and his expression went flat. I followed his gaze and my eyes widened. Lana was practically draped across Liam and he didn't seem to mind.

"Lana's always been… aggressive." I frowned.

"Then they'll get along great."

"I think she's determined to try out every member of the male species. Too bad Liam has a girlfriend."

Declan laughed. "Liam? No, he's trying to fuck away Kelly's memory."

"What about the girl I heard you guys talking about the other morning?"

"She's just a regular." Declan's eyes darkened with a sad shade of blue.

I watched as Liam took a long draw from his beer bottle, his eyes locked on Lana's. The intensity of his stare would have crushed me, but Lana basked in it.

"What happened with Kelly?" I'd known her briefly. Her and Liam hadn't been together long before Declan and I had split.

The waitress dropped off two glasses of water, and Declan lifted his and took a drink with his free hand. "She took a modeling job in L.A. and he didn't go with her. If it wasn't for me and Mom though, he would've left with her."

That same spark of guilt flashed across his features. I bumped his shoulder with mine and nodded my chin at his sketch book trying to deflect the clouds I saw brewing in his eyes. There wasn't much on the paper, a few lines and some shading. I stared at it and realized it was the outline of the bar. I looked up from where we were sitting, and from his viewpoint, he could see everything perfectly.

"What are you working on?"

"This?" He released my hand and brought his fingertips to the rough lines of the paper. "This is shit, I was bored, just waiting for you."

"You come here with your brothers a lot?" I asked.

He nodded. "Yeah, I sit here and sketch usually. I like the bass, it helps with the voices. Liam and Kieran, they do their own thing."

I glanced around the room again, Liam and Lana were still flirting at the bar. His hand was on her hip, her mouth at his ear. I didn't see Kieran. "Where's Kieran?"

"He's around, probably closer to the stage. He really likes this band. So does Liam." His brows furrowed.

I laughed. "But you don't?" I raised my eyebrows and watched his lips turn up at the corners as I sipped my water.

"No, not really."

Setting my glass down, I said, "Then why are you here?"

"I wanted to see you." He pushed a piece of my hair behind my ear and I shivered. His touch was the fire I'd needed for so long, the heat my body had lost.

"This is my first time in a bar, you know." My laugh was soft and his smile widened. He reached for my hand again and I gave it to him. The feel of his calloused palm in mine was simple, and I sighed in relief as that fire stoked higher.

"How do you like it?"

"Honestly?" I quirked my eyebrow.

He nodded.

"It's loud and smells weird... and I'd rather be somewhere quiet, drawing with you."

"Then let's leave." He stood and I was forced to stand as well as his grip tightened in mine.

The black sweater I had on fell farther down my arm exposing more of my shoulder. Declan admired the exposed skin.

"Where are we going?" I asked, a little dizzy as we moved toward Liam and Lana.

"My place."

DECLAN

Liam and Lana hadn't seemed to care that we'd decided to leave, and I'd told him to tell Kieran I'd see him tomorrow at work. The front door of Bellows shut and the sound evaporated into the vacuum of pandemonium behind the glass door. The ice in the air coated my lungs as I sucked in an anxious breath. Paige gave me a shy smile and laced our fingers together. Her smell mixed with the fog of her breath as she leaned closer to me starving for heat. The bare skin of her shoulder and arm was covered in goose bumps as I wrapped my arm around her waist and pulled her close.

"Where did you park?" Her voice was muffled. She'd hidden her nose in the warmth of my thermal shirt.

"I walked, I don't have a car."

She stopped and looked up at me. "You don't?"

I shook my head. "No, I use TRAX. Public transportation is easier, everything I need is within walking distance most of the time anyway."

She shivered again. "I wished I hadn't driven Lana's car tonight, we could have used mine."

I chuckled. "My apartment is just a few blocks."

She frowned, but conceded, snuggling back into my side as we crossed the street. "Alright."

The sky was empty of clouds, the midnight blue soaked the atmosphere with pinpricks of light. Even in the well-lit city, you could see the stars. This was how it should've always been. Me and Paige, together. A wash of regret chilled me, and I pulled her, if possible, even closer.

It took about ten minutes to get to my apartment. Paige's teeth were chattering as I opened the back door. She practically fell over the threshold and sighed once the heat of the apartment surrounded her.

"You're lucky I love you. I wouldn't walk that far for just anyone, especially in the freezing cold." She hugged her body and I shut the door behind us with a quiet laugh.

"Do you want anything to drink?" I asked as we moved through the kitchen.

She shook her head and her stare took on the edge I'd admired when she first walked into Bellows earlier. It charged my pulse. She hesitated at the mouth of the hallway.

"Did you want to work on something? I'd love to see more of what you've been up to all this time." She fidgeted with the hem of her sweater and I wondered if she could feel that charge too.

"Sure, head on back."

I followed her to my room. The light of the hallway illuminated a path along the floor of my bedroom as we walked in. Paige stood inside the cast of yellow light as she dropped her arms to her side, her back to me. She paused and stared at one of my paintings on the wall. She'd already seen it, but she tilted her head as she considered it. Her sleeve fell again and that perfect slope of skin was visible. I thought about walking up behind her, pulling her body against me, and pressing my lips to the bare flesh. I liked her without make-up and artifice, but the dark power she wielded tonight, I was weak for it. My legs moved me forward until my hands found her hips. She exhaled and leaned back as I slid my arms around her waist.

"It's so gruesome, the way you used the red like you did. She looks like she's bleeding." The painting was a black and white silhouette of a woman's form with one bright red splatter of paint cutting across her body.

It wasn't a critical review, it was just her observations, her thoughts. I smiled before I kissed the top of her head and then lowered my lips to her ear. She trembled as I spoke, "It wasn't supposed to look like blood. It was supposed to be a burst of feeling." I raised my right hand and pulled the waves of her hair away from her neck.

She lay the back of her head against my chest and I could feel her struggle to breathe, feel each intake and exhale as I brought my mouth to the hollow just below her ear. The heat of her body absorbed into my lips and ignited the empty space with pressure and pulse.

My heart raced and my mouth watered.

"I'm nervous."

I lifted my lips from her neck and set my hands back on her hips. "Don't be. Nothing has to happen, Paige. I just get carried away when I kiss you."

Her breath hitched. "What if I... I mean, is it wrong if I want something to happen?"

I dropped my hold on her and stepped away enough so that she could turn and face me, but she didn't. Her head tilted down, and her fingers shook at her side.

"Will you look at me?" She finally turned, reluctantly, insecurity written in the crease of her brow. "Is it because you're still married? I can respect that."

I didn't have to like it, but she was still legally bound to him.

Her eyes searched mine. "No... and yes." Her bottom lip quivered as the color drained from her cheeks. She dropped her eyes to the floor. "When I was with him, it wasn't like me and you, Declan. My body... it was a vessel for birth, not for pleasure." Her stance became submissive as if she was trying to crawl inside herself.

"Paige—"

"It hurt, most of the time. I hated every second I was with him. I tried to think my way through it, nights with Clark... but even thoughts of you never made it better, so instead I'd chosen to fade. I'd become numb. I'd vanish inside myself until he had... finished. Until I couldn't remember who I'd been or what it was like to feel."

I felt sick. She was withering, right here in front of me, falling back into the hell she'd been imprisoned in with him. My anger flared, and my molars threatened to crack as I grit my teeth. But, Paige didn't need a warrior. She needed to be comforted, and my concern for her cooled my rage temporarily as I took a few steps toward her. I steeled my expression, breathed deeply before I lifted her chin. She didn't resist the gentle command. If I could I would erase her past, rip the self-righteous flesh from his bones, watch as his blood pooled at his feet. I'd find the color to match it and paint his death a thousand times in victory.

The demon inside my head was on the verge of awakening, but I closed my eyes and reigned myself in before I said, "A vessel..." The words strained through tight teeth. "He hurt you."

Her eyes were wide, her history unable to pollute the innocence of the crystal wave of blue and she shook her head. "He couldn't really hurt me, because I had you the entire time."

Her smile was timid as she placed her hands on my biceps. "Your whole body is shaking."

I hadn't realized it, but once I let myself fall into her gaze, every muscle in my body relaxed. She raised her hands and placed them on either side of my neck, the tips of her nails slightly grazing my skin.

"I want to kill him." The real threat had evaporated under her touch.

"He's not worth it... I don't want to think about him anymore... I want... I want—"

Her cheeks filled with blush.

"Tell me," I said in a low whisper.

"I want you to show me, Declan. Show me I can still feel. Show me I'm more than just flesh and bone. Show me I still have a soul." Her cheeks turned that final shade of need, crimson, and hot.

The sound of the oncoming train rumbled outside my window. I leaned in as her lips parted, taking her mouth slowly, letting the feeling overwhelm her until all the tension evaporated, and until her mouth moved against mine with eager strokes. She was alive against my body, her breasts pushing against my chest, her arms around my neck.

"Shut the door," she whispered against my mouth.

I kissed her one more time before I broke away to close the door. The train began to pass, and as I turned back to Paige, she was lifting her sweater over her head. Black, white, black, white, the light through the blinds blurred and flashed. It was as if someone was flipping the pages of a comic book. She was drawn out with graceful lines. She wasn't wearing a bra and the teardrop contour of her breasts made my mouth go dry. Her nipples were pink and stood out in a sea of colorless light. Her eyes were veiled with shadows, hooded, and the blood in my veins begged to be warmed by her, mixed and close, calling out to the other. My lungs burned as I held my breath. None of this seemed real. She was too still. Was this my nightmare all over again? I needed to wake up before the pink of her nipples turned the color of—

Paige shifted, moved toward me, and grabbed the hem of my white thermal shirt, lifting it with her fingers. I helped and removed it over my head, tossing it to the floor with her sweater. She placed her hot hands on my waist, pulling me in, bringing our naked flesh together. Her soft breasts gave way to the steel of my chest, and I pressed myself into her stomach. She gasped as she felt the hard length. My hands gripped her hips with a surge of need, holding her still, denying myself the overdue friction.

My tongue plunged into her mouth, stealing her breath, her taste, her moans. Our lungs together, expanding and contracting as we walked backward toward the bed. The train still vibrated the foundation of my room. The chaos of the light, the sounds, and her quiet plea—this wasn't my nightmare, it was Paige, and she was showing *me* what it was like to feel again.

I lay her back and pressed her into the mattress as she pulled at the buttons of my jeans and I quickly undid hers. I slipped her out of her shoes and the rest of her clothing, pushing off mine as well. I stood at the end of my bed fully naked as the train finally passed. The moon poured in from the half-opened blinds and bathed her nude form in an eerie, white light. I had to close my eyes.

This is fucking real.

"Declan?"

Without opening my eyes, I said, "Is this what you want?" My voice was gravelly and craving.

"Yes." It was just a breath and my eyes opened, no longer feeling vulnerable.

Her arms were at her sides, bent at the elbow, and her hands covered her stomach. The blonde waves of her hair fanned out around her head, absorbing the light and creating a halo. It spilled over her shoulders and breasts. Her lips were swollen from my kiss, her chin and nose rubbed red from my beard. She wasn't a phantom. She wasn't a perverted piece of my homemade fiction, she was here, warm and waiting. My eyes lowered, lingering between her legs. She was bare and she shuddered under my stare. I trailed my eyes along her thighs, the alabaster color was flawless, nothing marring the surface of her skin. I swallowed as I thought of how my fingerprints would look on her inner thigh.

Paige sat up, and moved to her knees, bringing us eye to eye. I wrapped my fingers around her waist with my left hand and brought my lips to hers. She whispered my name as I slipped my other hand between her slightly parted legs. She was slick against my fingers, and the familiar feel of her body made me groan. Her hands grasped my shoulders as if she was already bracing herself for the fall. I teased her sensitive skin and she shivered against me. Our mouths moved easily together. Instinct, teeth and taste, sound and sensation. I nearly came when she dropped one of her hands and wrapped it around my cock. My hand bruised the skin of her hip as I grasped her tighter, sliding two fingers deep inside her.

Her legs began to shake and she leaned into me for support. Her hand was working me into a frenzy, bringing me closer.

Breathe.

Closer.

Breathe.

She was riding it out, breathless, telling me not to stop and speaking my name in soft sighs. Her nails dug into my shoulder as she *became* feeling, as she gasped and whimpered and came on my fingers. Her eyes locked on mine and her hand stilled around my length, leaving me aching and raw for her. Paige's kiss was aggressive as I eased my hand from between her legs and settled it onto her hip. She nipped my lip as a small aftershock rocked her against me. I growled into her mouth as I brought us both down onto the bed with a gentle crash. She was pinned below me as I raised myself up onto my forearms so I could see her face.

Her eyes swirled with bits of green, her chest was red, her lips ruby, and her climax was still present along her goose pimpled skin. "I forgot how colorful you look after you come." My smile quirked up on one side as her blush deepened further.

She bit her lip as she lowered her hands slowly down my chest, her nails leisurely moving past the line of hair on my stomach. She brushed her thumb over the head of my dick before guiding me between her legs. "Do it again."

"Do what?" I asked.

"Remind me who I am." She moved her hips beneath me and I was gone to over nine years of waiting as I pushed inside her.

A growl rumbled in my throat as her body welcomed me. My stomach clenched as she took me in, and a thick relief washed down my spine as the color of her eyes turned that unique color of blue. That color was reserved for me, and only when we were connected like this. I didn't blink as the azure waters with honey around the rims brought me home.

PAIGE

His eyes turned a shade darker as he'd slipped inside me. He watched me, holding me with his stare. His jaw was tight, his control steady as I breathed him in with a kiss. He brought his hand to my cheek and whispered into my ear. His taste lingered on my tongue. My name on his lips, his teeth on my neck, his smell of citrus mixed with sex, he stroked each sense as his slow movements started to become powerful.

I slid my hands down his back, feeling the raw muscle stretch and burn beneath my fingertips. I rested my hands just below his waist pulling his backside harder against me, pushing him, and feeling him all the way to my core. His groan turned to a growl as he raised up onto his arms just enough to roll our bodies together as one. I sat astride him and, for the briefest of moments, a glimmer of insecurity flickered, and I raised my hands to cover my breasts. He lifted his hands to my wrists, gently lowering my arms as I leaned forward and my palms covered the large black cross on his sternum.

"You don't ever have to hide from me." His voice was rich and filled with a decadent command.

I wasn't used to the intense way Declan looked at me as I traced my thumb along the edge of the cross. Clark's eyes had always been shut, but *this* man, he gripped my hips, eyes wide open, lifting me, pulling me forward, and then bringing me back down, filling me with feeling, again and again, with each forceful thrust. I gasped as he opened me, moved me, and created something new inside me. I'd forgotten, I'd shoved it all away, but now I was giving myself over to the resurrection.

"Oh, God." The two words spilled loudly from my shaky lips as he cupped my breasts with strong hands. He rocked his hips, hitting me deep within, in just the spot I needed to feel every bit of him.

His hands skimmed the curves of my body, settling around my rib cage, feeling every one of my breaths, and with each drive of his hips, my breathing hitched and became uneven. My thighs began to tremble on either side of him as he dropped one of his hands between my legs, his fingers touching me, bringing me just to the edge of reason, and that delicious building ache spread into my stomach, and my muscles tensed as I came closer to falling. The room was full of plush purple light, suggestive sounds, deep breaths, whispered whimpers, and skin touching skin. My eyes were on his when my climax hit. His jaw clenched and his brows furrowed, but he never dropped my gaze. My eyes almost closed as that ache ebbed through me in ripples, and I cried out, unable to hold it all in. Unable to harness the incredible, and overpowering wave. He found his release inside me, shuddering below me with a gritty growl.

I moved my hips, pulling him in and then out one more time, and he groaned, stilling my hips under the dominant grasp of his fingers.

I leaned down to kiss him and he brought his hands to my face. His fingers pressed along my hairline, and he paused. For a few seconds, he just looked at me. His forehead was beaded with sweat, his lips were parted, and his eyes were molten as he pulled me in for another kiss. I was thoroughly out of breath as I broke away from his lips and our connection as I collapsed next to him on the bed. My cheek rested against the left side of his chest, and my right hand covered the cross as his fingertips drew long, slow, shiver-inducing lines along my arm and hip.

We rested in a peaceful silence at first. My fingers trailing down his stomach and back to the cross a few times before I said, "I've blamed myself for so long, never thinking I was worth more than what I had, waiting for God to grant me some sort of reprieve, and just when I thought that final piece of myself had faded away, he gave me back to you." I raised up on my left elbow and reverently kissed him on the chest right in the center of the cross.

He brought my right hand back to the tattoo and I felt each inhale and exhale—he lived just below the ink.

"You've always been there, you're right here, in each breath. You belong to color... to me. This... this is the only religion you need."

His lips found mine before I could speak, before I could say I loved that, loved him, everything about him was my favorite thing, but as he eased me onto my back, his body, his muscle, his heat covering me again, all I wanted to do was show him.

Our lips didn't separate as he aligned himself within me again. He made love to me until all I could see, smell, and hear was him—until I fell asleep enveloped in strong arms, covered in his scent, in his warmth, and bathed in the pastel of the early morning sun as it trickled through his blinds.

Every muscle in my body was alive the next morning. My arms ached and my thighs burned. I was sore everywhere. Declan's bathroom was chilly as I turned on the shower. I caught my reflection in the mirror and noticed that my skin was peppered with his touch. A few fingerprints here and there, but mostly on my hips and thighs. My chin was red, my cheeks were pink, and my hair was messy. I bit the corner of my lip trying to suppress my smile. I brought my hand to my collarbone and traced a line where he'd just kissed me not fifteen minutes ago. My eyes closed as I let myself remember the bristle of his beard on my overly sensitive skin, and the way we'd woken up together, snuggled beneath the comforter, my back still to his chest, drunk on each other and lack of sleep.

If I could I would've stayed with him in that bed all day, but at some point, reality won, and Liam banged on his door warning Declan that "his ass" better be to work in an hour.

The door to the bathroom opened and Declan walked in, shutting it behind him. He wasn't wearing a stitch of clothing and I admired him under the bright lights of the bathroom. The only trace of the boy I'd once known was evident in his lopsided smile as he, too, admired the view. I tried to comb my fingers through my hair, but it was pointless. His eyes trailed along my body, stopping at each mark he'd left behind. His smile wavered.

"They don't hurt," I reassured as I moved toward him.

"Are you sure?" he asked.

I nodded.

"Good," he said with an exhale and then kissed my cheek before pulling back the shower curtain.

The small space of the shower was filled with steam and Declan. I huddled in front of him as the hot water hit my back, unraveling each knot. Declan's hands covered my body with his soap, the brand the same as I'd remembered, as he washed me. His fingers worked against the muscles in my shoulders, his touch leaving me limp. I washed him as well, exploring his ink and his piercings. His body reacted as my fingers traced the V of his hips. Declan had always been quiet, but I liked that I could see how much my touch affected him. I could see it in the way his pupils dilated, the way his stomach twitched, and how his jaw pulsed, amongst other things. It was intoxicating knowing I made him feel as much as he did me.

He smiled as he leaned down and kissed me. Water trickled in past my lips as his tongue licked at the seam of my mouth. He groaned and rested his forehead against mine.

"I wish I didn't have to work," he said, and I laughed.

"You could come to The Gallery when you're finished. The renter fell through, and I picked up a few of Chandler's shifts if he promised to let me use the studio for a few days. I started something yesterday, on my down time at work. I haven't had a chance to do much with it, but I'd like to show you."

"I'm closing tonight, it wouldn't be until after eleven."

"That's okay," I said and gave him a broad smile. "I don't work at all today, so I'll probably go home and nap... I was up really late last night, I could use the rest." My nose wrinkled as his lips slid into a slow smile.

"I'll be there." He leaned in and brushed his lips across mine before reaching behind me to shut off the water. "If we stay in here any longer, I'll never make it to work."

We dried off and he let me borrow one of his sweaters to wear home. The soft gray material would have hugged the wide breadth of his shoulders and fit snug along the washboard of his stomach, but it swallowed me. I brought the sleeve of it to my nose and inhaled the smell of his detergent. I lifted my eyes and caught him staring at me. He was relaxed, his mouth slightly curved at the side, in jeans and a dark blue, fitted sweater. The morning sun poured in through his open blinds. His hair seemed blonder under the light. Gold flecks highlighted his full beard. He was symmetry and stone, masculine and handsome.

We stood about ten feet apart, him on one side of his room, me on the other. I reached inside my jeans pocket and pulled out my hair tie.

"Leave it down," he said softly.

"Why?" I narrowed my brows and placed the hair tie back in my pocket. The strands were starting to air dry in wild waves.

He moved toward me closing the distance. "Remember that time... it was spring, and we'd only been together since that winter. We'd gotten stuck in the sprinklers, out in the middle of the lawn at school. You were soaked, head to toe."

I smiled as I remembered. He had laughed, and I had pouted, but he'd kissed me anyway, ignoring the frigid wet clothes.

"Your hair, by the end of the day, it had taken on its own life. It was waves of corn silk, and I remember the exact shade of yellow I'd painted you in that night." His smile touched his eyes. "I was infatuated with you... and fuck..." He exhaled a long breath, and my heart skipped and hammered for him. "Looking at you..." He raised one of his hands and fingered a piece of my hair. "It's like I've gone back in time."

He pulled me into a hug, and his arms engulfed me. My cheek pressed against his chest. The rapid beat of his heart matched mine. "I remember." I laughed and he let me lean back so I could look into his eyes. "It was a good day if you disregarded the soggy clothes we had to deal with for two whole periods. Wasn't that the same day we made-out in the art supply closet and Mrs. Birch caught us."

His head tilted back as he laughed, the full body sound of it filled my heart, and the last pieces of us, of who we'd been, of who we were, clicked into place.

"Yes. You used to make me so crazy for you." He pushed a lock of my hair behind my ear.

"And now?" I teased.

The lids of his eyes lowered and that smoke, that unbridled darkness that was purely Declan filled his irises as his gaze fell to my mouth.

He kissed me until my knees felt weak.

He held my waist as he pulled away. "If anything, it's worse now. You taste... different, and I can't explain it, I've tried to reconcile it to a color, but it doesn't exist. I want to stay here instead of going to work, indulge in it... in you."

I laced my fingers through his and tugged. "You feel different... I love that your hands are strong and calloused in a way that scratches at the very root of what I need. You're a man, Declan, and as much as I've lingered in the past, wishing for the boy, I'd rather have you... just like this."

He leaned down and the whisper of *I love you* sent a shiver along my neck and arms.

"Are you hungry?" he asked.

"I am."

"Come on, I'll make us some breakfast," he said as he led me to his bedroom door.

Breakfast turned out to be cereal and coffee. I laughed when he pulled out a box of Cap'n Crunch.

"What?" He smirked.

I shrugged and bit the inside of my cheek holding in my full-fledged smile. That cereal had always been his favorite. "It's nice to see not everything has changed."

He poured milk into the bowl and looked at me without contrition. "It's a staple... Liam tried to buy the generic, bagged shit once... it wasn't the same." His lips tipped down as, I assumed, he thought about the horrors of eating off-brand Cap'n Crunch.

I laughed and I felt it in my stomach.

He trailed his thumb along my cheek. "I love that sound, and this..." He pulled his thumb along my lower lip tracing my smile before he bent down and kissed me, leaving me wanting more.

Our time was too short. After a night, a morning like we'd had, I wanted to stay in, catch up, laugh some more, eat five hundred pounds of sweet cereal as we remembered things about our history that had made us happy. As I'd watched him sip his coffee, I'd pretended that this was just like any other day. This was our place and, when we both returned home from our long day, we'd lavish each other in touch, lose ourselves in the sounds of the other, and eat dinner naked on the floor of our bedroom, with paints and pencils strewn around us. It was the life we should've had, but I was content knowing that it could possibly, hopefully, one day, become our reality.

I'd texted Lana while we were eating. Declan had told me I could wait in the shop until she arrived, but I hadn't needed to. She had shown up right as we started walking down the back stairs. Lana pulled in and parked behind the shop, next to a mean looking motorcycle.

"I'll see you tonight." Declan pressed his lips to mine and instead of letting him pull away, I wrapped my fingers in his hair and kissed him harder. A frantic feeling flooded my chest and anxiety pooled in my stomach. After everything, after last night, I wasn't ready to just let him go.

He pulled away and placed his hands on either side of my neck, his thumbs just above my pulse points. "I know." His voice was heavy. "I feel it, too. But, I'm right here, and I'm not going anywhere." He leaned in closer, his eyes serious. "I love you, Paige."

A lump formed in my throat and it was hard to speak around its sharp edges. This was painful. It actually physically hurt to leave him. He'd saved me last night, after I'd suffered for years in a bleak, hollow, pallid state, he'd been able to revive me. Declan took me from a blank page to a panoramic canvas filled with an assortment of brilliant shades.

"I love you, too." My voice almost cracked, and I inhaled trying to stave off my overreaction to this departure.

He squeezed my hand when he said, "Goodbye." Untying each finger as slowly as he could, kissing me one last time before he turned toward the backdoor of the shop.

I'd see him tonight, it was only a few short hours. I was being ridiculous... then why did my heart still hurt, and why the heck did I have tears in my eyes as I took a seat in the passenger side of Lana's car.

"Shit... are you okay?"

"How do I do this?" I asked.

"Do what, honey?"

"How can I survive giving myself over to it, breathe again, feel so much, and then walk away?" I sniffled.

She laughed lightly. "Awe."

I narrowed my eyes. "I'm serious."

"I can tell." She smiled, and I sat up straighter wiping under my eyes. "You've gone a long time without real love, and it's about time you're getting what you need. Would it help if I told you, beyond the snot and tears, you're actually glowing?"

My lip twitched fighting my smile. "I am?"

She nodded and shifted the car into reverse. "Yes, ma'am, you are. Maybe I slept with the wrong brother."

I gasped, "You didn't?"

"I did."

"Where?" I was floored.

"Our place."

I giggled like a freaking teenager. "Lana!"

"What? He's hot and—"

"Nope, stop right there, I don't want know." I shook my head and laughed.

"See, all better, we're all smiles again." She lifted her right eyebrow and grinned as she started to back out of the lot.

My lungs filled with a deep breath as I raised my sleeves to my nose.

Declan.

I closed my eyes and let my head fall back against the headrest of the seat. I could feel his lips on mine, his hands on my hips, my stomach—my face. I felt his heavy weight along the length of my body. He'd released all the feelings I'd stowed away, and I wanted to catalogue each one, keep it safe inside me. I didn't want to just survive it, I wanted to live it. If that meant when I left him, each time, I'd be reduced to a puddle of tears, then so be it.

I'd rather drown in a blue sea of longing than fade into the white noise of nothing.

DECLAN

Quotes, skulls, and a few anchors... I'd lost track of what I'd done all day. My head was full of Paige. Her voice, her mouth, her skin, the very feel of her under my fingertips. Halfway through the day I realized I could still taste her on my tongue. By day's end, her scent started to crowd my thoughts; clean waves of soap, something inherently female, deep purple, and sexy. The buzz of my tattoo machine hadn't provided a distraction, and my inner voice had gone missing entirely. This was how it had once been, not silence, but me. I was the only one haunting my skull. Visions of Paige beneath me, above me, my mouth on her stomach, on her thighs–everywhere, it was a welcome change from the macabre, the self-loathing, and the intruding thoughts of occasional death.

Everyone had left for the night, except for Liam, and as I locked up my supplies, I heard him laugh.

I raised my eyes. "Something funny?"

He leaned against the wall of my station and watched me for a moment as I turned to fully face him. "No, not really, you have a silly ass grin on your face."

He didn't give me his usual scowl, and I waited for his bullshit about Paige, but he said nothing.

"She makes me happy."

"It's dangerous, Dex, letting one person rule you like that." He pushed off the wall and stood at his full height. His hard, brown eyes met mine and the crease between his brows deepened as he surveyed me.

I ran my hand through my hair and held his stare. "Maybe it is... some people, Liam... some people are worth the danger."

I waited for him to roll his eyes, but he never did. Instead, the muscle in his jaw ticked before he said, "And you think Paige... is back for good? After what, one night with her? It doesn't fucking work like that." He shook his head.

"For you, Liam, it doesn't work like that for you." I pointed to my temple. "It's quiet. It's silent and I can see things, hear things, I'm back. She's always been able to do that for me. She gets me, always has, this isn't a bright and fucking shiny fresh start. It's a continuation." Liam's shoulders fell as I pointed to my chest. "She never left, man, she never left." My throat started to close off and I clenched my jaw.

Liam walked up to me, his eyes almost wet as he gripped the back of my head and pulled our foreheads together like he used to do when we were kids. He spoke in a low voice as he said, "I'm glad your back, little brother, I'm fucking glad, but I won't lose you again, so be careful."

I grasped his shoulder. "I will, but someday... you're going to have to start taking care of you."

He dropped his hold on me and leaned away, his eyes clouding over. "I'm fine."

I increased the pressure of my grip. "You're not, and if you can't see that... that pride... it'll make you just like him, just like Pop."

He stepped back and shrugged out of my hold. "I'm..." His jaw flexed and he closed his eyes. "Shit, Dex, I don't know what the fuck I'm doing." His eyes opened again and he nodded his chin to the back door. "It's getting late, don't make her wait."

The line of his jaw relaxed, and his features softened, but his eyes, they still held a stubborn edge. "Will you be okay?" I asked.

He nodded. "Of course. I got no other choice."

Every light in The Gallery was on as I walked toward the back of the store. Paige's music played through the open studio door, and I thought for a minute I'd heard her singing along. My lips curled up at the corners as my view came into focus. She was kneeling on the ground, wearing jeans and an oversized, white button up with the sleeves rolled heavily at her elbows. Her hair was piled at the top of her head, and the light caught a few of the strands that had escaped around the nape of her neck. The golden color was warm and invited me in as I stepped farther through the threshold of the studio.

Her hand stilled above one of the canvases she was working on as I sucked in a ragged breath. There were at least twenty of them on the floor. Each canvas was a different size. Some of them were covered in different shades of gray, blue, some had warmer tones, and from where I was standing, if you looked at them as a whole they created an almost pixelated collage.

"Paige?" Her name was a winded surprise.

She stood seamlessly, stepping back and lacing her fingers with mine.

"This... this is fucking incredible." My eyes scanned the ground, soaking in the massive piece of art in front of me. Every canvas was unique in its own right, but when you looked at them all together, as one big picture, they formed a pair of eyes.

My eyes.

The creases were deep on either side of the oval shapes, the slope of the nose, it was me... the dark blond hair of my brow... it was all here in this multicolored assortment of paint. My eyes stared back at me from the canvases, and even without the expression of a smile, I could tell the eyes watching me were happy. They were clear, open, and alive.

"I didn't sleep," she whispered. "I went home, changed, and then came straight here. I've been here all day." As she said it she rubbed the back of her neck with the paint-stained fingers of her free hand.

We both stood there, hand in hand, silent, in awe, as the expanse of talent spread out before us.

"It's yours," she said and turned her head to look at me. There were blotches of blue paint on her pink cheeks. "I wanted to show you. I wanted you to see what I see when I look at you." She raised her gaze and searched mine. "I wanted to recreate the moment... that moment when your eyes find mine... and you see me, you really see *me,* Declan. Everything else disappears and all I want to do is fall into you." She laughed softly and licked her lips. "I sound crazy." She laughed again and shook her head. "Crazy, right?"

I kissed her instead of answering.

I dropped our linked hands and framed her face. My thumbs tilted her head back, and my fingers pushed into the mess of her hair. Her arms wound around my neck, and her body pressed against me. I had no words, only emotion. I didn't close my eyes as I kissed Paige. My eyes were mirrored in hers and it was then I saw her inspiration, I saw that *moment* when my eyes sparked and cleared and filled with just her. I saw it and as our kiss intensified, and my eyes finally closed, I let her fall into me.

She sighed as she lazily kissed my lips, then my jaw before she asked, "So you like it?"

I chuckled and trailed my nose to the crook of her neck. "This belongs in a gallery not my apartment."

"It belongs with you." She leaned back and her lips parted with a shy smile. "If you want it, it's yours."

"I love it, Paige." My hands fell to her waist as I pulled her closer. "I'll have one of my brothers help me move it to my place when you're ready." I lowered my chin, bringing my lips to hers again. I brushed them across her top lip and then her bottom as her eyes fluttered close. "You have no idea how talented you are." I kissed her cheek as my hands slid under the thin fabric of her shirt. My palms melted against her skin, and softly caged her in place. "How talented you've always been..." I raised one hand and trailed my thumb along her jaw lifting her chin as her eyes opened and found mine. "Even after everything, after what you've been through, you still own the brush."

The color in her irises seemed to swirl, the illusion set by the tears that filled her eyes. I kissed a drop that escaped before our mouths collided. She moaned, and the music heated the room as the bass matched the beat of my pulse. I wanted to show her how unbelievable she was. Show her what I couldn't formulate into sentences, smother her in feeling and flame, let it lick and burn her like she did me.

It wasn't long before I had her tangled on the floor, a mixture of sound, paint, and limbs. My pants pushed down, our discarded clothes shoved to the side, my body inside hers, my palms bracing her head, the cement floor of the studio cold beneath my knuckles. My teeth on her jaw, her neck, her shoulder, each wave of her hips below me clouded my control. Her small hands, her nails, her lips pressed against my skin as I sank deeply inside her. My fingers fisted in her hair as I slipped past that line of reality and reason. The tender side of me lost to the beast as I moved above her with rough strokes. The muscles in my stomach coiled as I came. She cried out, her nails digging into my neck as her entire body tightened around me. I consumed the sound as I brought my mouth to hers. Her lips were salted and sweet as we both descended with each breath in and each breath out.

I shuddered, despite the sticky sweat that beaded on my brow as she painted patterns along the line of my neck and shoulders. The movement made her tremble as well, and I groaned as I moved my weight onto my forearms. I kissed her mouth, the wet heat grounding me. She licked my lips as I pulled away and then settled onto my back beside her.

She snuggled against my chest and audibly winced.

"Shit, did I hurt you?" My brows knotted, but her giggle untied them immediately.

"No. The floor, that's another story... but it was worth it."

My hand moved under her shirt and trailed up and down her spine a few times with a firm pressure. The hem barely covered her ass, and I rested my hand just below it. The soft curve had always been my favorite spot. I didn't care that my pants were still on, pushed well past my hips allowing the cold of the solid cement to sink into my bones, I just wanted to enjoy this, enjoy her. All I ever wanted to hear was that giggle, that sound she made when she came, and that light whispered *I love you* just after. No more voices, no feelings of hopelessness, or worthlessness, only Paige.

She shivered against me, and I said, "I don't think I completely thought this through."

"I'm glad you didn't." She shifted, kissed the cross in the center of my chest and then sat up. The reverent way her lips touched the ink, it spread warmth through my limbs every time.

"Since we're being spontaneous..." She lifted her left eyebrow and grinned.

"Yeah?"

"I want to get that tattoo, that quote we talked about." Her grin pulled into a wide smile.

I sat up, adjusted my jeans and then zipped them up as I asked, "Are you sure?"

"I've been thinking about it." She stood and I watched her with a hidden smile before I stood as well. Paige's shirt moved with the sway of her hips exposing every curve. "And I think... I think I want this. I don't want to wait." She grabbed her pants and underwear, slipping them on quickly to my disappointment.

I pulled my own shirt over my head and pushed the sleeves up to my elbows. "You want this," I repeated.

She nodded and cast her gaze to her hands. She fidgeted as she spoke, "I started thinking about this specific idea in the Bible, in Genesis it says God took a rib from Adam to create Eve. I used to always think that scripture was so patriarchal, but I think, in reality, it's actually really romantic. Adam gave Eve life, I know Plath is talking about her heartbeat when she says *I am, I am, I am*, but you've given me life again, Declan, because of you, I can breathe." I stepped toward her, my hands sliding under her shirt and encasing her small rib cage on either side. She inhaled and exhaled, proving her point. "I want the quote along one of my left ribs a few inches down from my heart."

I moved my thumb along the bone. "Here?"

She nodded.

I kissed her forehead and spoke, my lips smiling against her skin, "I can do that." The steady tone of my voice hid the true excitement. She had no idea how much I wanted to mark her skin with my own hand. My handwriting inked into her flesh... forever... she was wrong, she was why *I* breathed again. Why I even existed beyond mist and hallucinations.

Her lips pulled into a slow, broad smile. "Let's get out of here."

Paige was lying on her back, her shirt was off, and her arms rested comfortably above her head. Her white skin looked like porcelain against the blood-red vinyl of my work table, the only thing that interrupted the smooth line of alabaster was her nude-colored lace bra. The hard curve of it just two inches above where I planned to place the quote. If this was like any other day, Liam would swear at me, or Kemper would make some crude comment and the picture before me would've rippled like the flat surface of a lake just as it began to rain. But, it wasn't any other day, it was right now, just past one in the morning, and I was all alone in Avenues with Paige.

She gave me a shaky smile. "Are you nervous?"

The humor in her voice steadied my own trembling fingertip as I traced the pad of my forefinger along the rib that would bear my mark for life. "I've never been nervous before, but I am now." Self-doubt crept in and I heard the whispers of shadows prickle inside my brain.

She lowered her arm and placed her hand on my cheek. "I want this."

You'll stain her.

The familiar voice was slippery and moved easily through the wall I'd created to keep it out, the wall Paige had always made stronger, the wall that would always have holes in its armor no matter what I did.

"Come back to me," she whispered, and I lifted my blank stare to hers. The twisted voice in my head faded. "There you are." Her smile was kind, filled with love, and it abated the pain growing behind my temples.

She trusts you. She loves you.

She moved her arm back above her head and I turned on my machine. The initial buzz made her jump and she laughed.

I held my machine in my right hand and used my foot to roll the stool that held my ink a little closer. I took a deep breath and ran the fingers of my left hand along the rib one last time. I chose not to wear gloves. What was the point? I wanted to feel the ink and her blood on my skin. I wanted it to set under my fingernails, and tint the hard surface of my knuckles.

"This is going to hurt," I said and her lips began to quiver, but her eyes stayed locked on mine. It was only ink in flesh, but this meant more to me than sex, than any words of affirmation ever would.

"I know." The corners of her lips twitched with a smile as her nose wrinkled and her eyes clamped shut.

Paige was giving me her body, I would always be present below the cells, inside her skin, thriving with words that gave meaning to us. I leaned over and kissed the spot just as reverently as she'd kissed me earlier back at the studio. I asked quietly, "Are you ready?"

She nodded her head and I brought the needle to her skin as she cringed. The pain was creased along her features and her skin was goose flesh; raised, and welted pink along the edges of where I worked. The words took form along her rib in my own sloping script. She didn't speak, just breathed through it. I was bringing her to the brink, almost to the edge of her limit, but she never broke.

The vibration stopped and all I could hear was her heavy breathing. I set my machine down and wiped away the excess ink. She flinched, but as I brought my lips to hers, her body relaxed, unwound, and finally she opened her eyes. I pulled away with a smile.

"You survived."

"Barely."

I chuckled.

"Do you want see it?" I asked, as my eyes devoured the ink, and a feral pride coursed through me.

The shadow from before was blinded by the light of her smile. "Yes."

I helped her up and stood her in front of the mirror. She leaned her back against my chest, raising her left arm and wrapping her fingers into my hairline. I held her right hip as her eyes scanned the phrase. Her lips moved as she mouthed the words, "I am, I am, I am." Her eyes met mine in the mirror. "It's perfect."

I was struck by the image that was reflected back at me. She was touching me, and I was touching her.

We were one infinite line as I brought my lips to her ear and said, "This is forever."

PAIGE

This is forever...

This is forever...

Forever, with Declan, was the only Heaven I ever wanted to go to. My tattoo was only two weeks old, and every time I caught sight of it I'd hear him say those three words in my head. *This is forever.* Today was no different as I stood fresh from the shower with my towel pooled around my feet. I ran my fingers over the ink and smiled. I'd decided, in the end, just the words were enough, I'd loved the heartbeat Declan had originally drawn, but the words, and how *he* had breathed life back into *me*—this was exactly how I'd wanted it.

I stayed with him that night, and we'd made love until the pink rays of dawn filled his room. We'd discovered each other again, and each time, he'd show me what I was capable of feeling, what I'd been deprived of, what he'd been without, for so long. Each time, our craving for the other had become more desperate instead of sated, until we'd both lie spent, saturated in the other's scent.

We'd slept the day away, neither of us working that weekend. Over the weekend we'd numbered the pieces in the studio, and Liam and Kieran had helped pick them up and hang them on the blank brick above Declan's bed. Even though Liam's reception of me had been frosty at first, by the end of the weekend he'd come around a little more. These past two weeks, every night when I was alone, I still prayed on my knees and thanked God for bringing Declan back to me. We'd spent every night together that we could, Lana was starting to tease me about maybe getting another roommate because I was never here. Tonight I was going to his mother's house for dinner, just me and him. He never finished framing the large piece he'd painted at the studio and he wanted to work on it.

Seeing his mom again, after all this time, I was nervous. Did she hate me like Liam did, or would she be happy that Declan was happy? Would she even recognize me? I inhaled and exhaled deeply, watching my ribcage expand and contract in the mirror. *This is forever...* he wanted me in his life, and his mother was part of it. I closed my eyes briefly, and when I opened them, I stared at the woman in the mirror. Her curves were minimal, but formed, and her bones less pronounced. Her face was full, and her lips were a natural shade of rose. The eyes that watched me, that scanned each nuance, were a vibrant shade of blue. I was finally starting to see myself again. I actually recognized the woman in the mirror, her reflection, it was the "me" that had been lost, and I'd found her again.

My phone vibrated against the top of my dresser startling me. I picked it up and my lips parted into an involuntary smile as Declan's name flashed on the screen.

Declan: *I'll be there in fifteen minutes, Kieran is dropping me off and then heading back to the shop.*

Are you still okay to drive?

Me: *I'm nervous.*

Me: *I don't mind driving.*

Declan: *Don't be nervous, my mom has always loved you.*

He wouldn't lie to me.

Me: *Okay. I'll see you soon, getting dressed, love you.*

Declan: *Love you, too.*

I threw my phone onto my bed next to the clothes I'd laid out before my shower. I slipped on my underwear and bra, before pulling on my pants. I was filling out my jeans again, and I grinned as I wiggled in order to pull them up all the way. I borrowed an emerald green hoodie from Lana, the color complimented the blonde of my hair and made my skin look like cream. Declan liked my hair best when I let it air dry so I left it down. I scanned the top of my dresser for a hair tie, just in case I wanted it later, and couldn't find one. I was pretty sure I had a stash of them in my bedside table. I opened the drawer and rummaged through it. I found one just as my fingers touched the cool metal of my wedding band. I gasped softly. I'd forgotten I'd thrown it in the drawer the day I moved in.

My hand trembled as I picked it up, placing it in the palm of my left hand. It had been made up simple, just a plain, gold band. Clark had said Christ didn't need treasures or expensive jewels because he had the love of God, and if I truly atoned for my sins I would as well. I'd been so depressed, so far gone, I'd actually thought maybe he was right. I'd thought maybe Clark was a good man, and maybe, eventually, I'd be worthy of God's forgiveness.

I dropped the band back into the side table drawer and slammed it shut. My eyes closed as I tried to push back the memory. I didn't want or need Clark's version of God. I'd found my peace again, I'd come clean and was moving on, but he still lingered. I'd gotten so wrapped up in Declan, I'd never called again about the papers. It was easy to pretend Clark didn't exist when I was with Declan.

There was a light knock on my door and my eyes opened. "Yes?"

"Hey, I'm leaving, will you be back later or are you staying with Declan?" Lana sounded muffled through the wood of the door.

"I'm not sure yet. I'll let you know." I raised my voice so she could hear me and to mask the shiver in my tone. That ring... *I was still married.* Clark was a reality I couldn't hide from. Not anymore, and not if I wanted to really be finished with him and move forward with Declan.

"Alright, I'll be back late, just send me a text." She knocked on the door twice. "Have fun."

"You too."

There was no reply, so I assumed she'd left or hadn't heard me. My heartbeat became rapid as I thought about what I had to do next, what I should've done weeks ago. I lifted my phone from the bed with clammy hands, and dialed his number.

It rang twice before he picked up. "Paige?" Clark's deep voice vibrated through the phone. He was probably standing in our kitchen... his kitchen, still dressed in his work button down and tie, his dark hair perfectly parted, and his jaw tight with annoyance.

"When are you sending the papers?" I was surprised how even my tone was, it was almost cold... strong.

This is forever.

"Are you in a hurry to head to Hell?" The cruel smile I'd grown accustomed laced every syllable.

"I just want to be done with it." Silence. "Don't you?" I cringed. The question came out sounding like a plea.

"Maybe I'm not."

I exhaled into the phone and I swore I heard him laugh.

"Stop, this isn't a game, Clark. Let's just be done."

"Paige, you know how I—"

"I don't have time for this," I interrupted as I looked at my bedside alarm clock, "Declan—" I stopped mid-sentence realizing my mistake.

"Declan?" He almost growled the name and all the warmth in my body evaporated. "You went back to him... after all the work we did, to help you overcome your sin, you went straight back to the Devil."

Anger boiled in my belly, and my eyes pricked with resentment, but I wouldn't let a tear fall, I wouldn't let him know how much he'd hurt me. "You have no room to talk, you had an affair. You're probably still with her. I bet the church counsel loves that."

"They excommunicated her for breaking up our marriage." He was smug.

"You just threw her away like me." I was indignant.

"No, she's still around. She's useful on the nights I need her."

Bile crept up my throat. "You're a horrible person."

He laughed.

"And you're still married to me in the eyes of God, tell me, Paige, does one sin beget another. I cheated, but, now, so have you... you went straight from my bed to his, don't—"

I pulled the phone from my ear and squeezed it with every bit of strength I had in my grip as I screamed under my breath.

I hate him.

I hate him.

I hate him.

"We're even," he said as I brought the phone back to my ear.

"Then give me a divorce."

Silence again. His breathing was all I could hear and it increased with each second that ticked by, I'd gotten to him.

"I'll bring the papers on Wednesday. I don't need a whore for a wife."

The line went dead. He'd thought his last barb would injure me, but as I lowered my phone from my ear I smiled. He was giving me a divorce. He was done toying with me.

I won.

Before I pocketed my phone, I sent Clark a final text, giving him the address of The Gallery and telling him I'd be there all day on Wednesday. I dropped my arms to my side and raised my chin. My eyes on the heavens, I whispered, "Thank you."

Declan's mother's house was exactly the same. That warmth, that steadfast, deep brown, the dingy walls, the worn carpet... I was home.

He squeezed my hand with his as we walked into the family room. "She's gotten frail since Pop died, be prepared," he spoke quietly under his breath, and I met his eyes with a nod.

I hadn't brought up my phone call with Clark on the ride over, Declan was too excited to be bringing me home again. I wanted to just live in the moment. I'd tell him after.

"Declan, is that you? Did you bring her, honey?" His mom's voice was the same, but was edged with that certain breathlessness that came with age.

Declan chuckled as she came out of the hallway and smiled. I gathered myself as her appearance hit me in the chest. I let my mouth mirror hers as she approached me. Her shoulders had rounded so severely she seemed to have shrunk in stature, as if she was bearing a great weight all this time. Her hair was white and short, her skin thin, like vellum, and her blue eyes seemed almost milky in the light. She'd had the boys late in life, but not that late, she'd only be seventy-two if I was remembering correctly.

"You don't look a day over seventeen, Paige." She grinned. "It's good to have you home." She took my hand in hers and her bones felt brittle. I held her hand like it was precious glass, hoping some of my warmth would fill her pulse.

"It's good to be back. It looks exactly the same," I said releasing her hand and looking around the room.

"Is that a good thing?" She laughed and Declan smiled.

"It really is." My throat contracted as she stared at me, her smile reaching her eyes. She'd always welcomed me with open arms, unlike my own parents.

My conversation with Clark had probably been reported back to them. Maybe they'd call me tomorrow so I wouldn't have to call them. My smile dimmed.

"Are you okay?" Declan whispered and his minted breath brought me back to a happier place.

"Just feeling nostalgic."

He kissed the side of my head, and I didn't miss how his mother watched us.

"You always made my Declan smile," she said.

"I'm lucky to have her." He tugged on my hand. "Always have been."

"Dinner is on the stove, settle in, and then come help me set the table. I want to hear how you've been all these years." She nodded and turned to walk into the kitchen.

"I'll be right there, Mrs. O'Connell."

"It's just Irene, honey, you know that," she said over her shoulder.

I giggled, she may have aged more than she should've, but she hadn't really changed at all.

"I told you she always loved you." Declan pulled me to his chest and covered my mouth with his. He kissed me until every knot of stress in my shoulders untied. His hands were on the small of my back, and his fingers walked along my spine until they tangled in my hair.

I pulled away before I moaned into his mouth. "How do you do that?"

"Kiss?" He raised his eyebrow and smirked.

I hit his chest. "No." I shook my head and laughed. "You kiss me like that and I forget the world."

"You're stressed, I can feel it."

"What happened to your mom, Declan? She looks ten years older than she should."

He took a step back and linked our hands. "She was married to a drunk, she suffered through his death, and it doesn't help she never tells us anything. She finally admitted to Liam a few weeks ago that she's been having some heart issues. That's why Kieran won't move out, he helps her around the house. She can't do much." The color in Declan's irises went dark, his pupils narrowed, and he squinted just enough that the creases around his eyes deepened. He was hearing them, it was the face he made when the voices began to speak. Guilt being his biggest trigger it seemed.

"Hey, you *all* do a lot for your mom."

It took him a moment to answer as he sifted through his thoughts. "I know."

"Come on, let's go help her with dinner." I gave him a small smile.

His lips spread into a grin. "I had her make your favorite."

"Beef stew?" My eyes widened—I died for her stew.

234

He nodded. "Kieran went out and bought the Guinness last night. He made me promise to save him some leftovers." Declan chuckled, his good mood back in place, set firmly in a brilliant smile.

"Now I'm even more excited." I laughed as he pulled me into the kitchen.

Over dinner Declan was quiet as his mother recounted his father's last days. It was like she never really got a chance to mourn, and a part of me wondered if the guys hadn't let her. They all had their issues with him, but she'd love him regardless of how he'd lived his life.

"Enough about all that depressing nonsense. Tell me about you. How've you been?"

My smile waned. My life wasn't a departure from depression, it had once been the definition.

The heat of Declan's hand found mine under the table. The stew bowls were empty, the bread she'd put out half eaten, and for some reason my eyes trained on the crusty crumbs that sat on the tablecloth as I tried to think of where to start.

"Mom, let's—"

"It's okay." I squeezed his hand.

"I got married not too long after Declan and I split. It was what my parents wanted... he wasn't a very good husband." I inhaled a shaky breath and pushed through it. His mom's attention was on me, her eyes soft and open, awaiting my confession. "And, he's not really a good man either. I got lost there for a while, but I found my way back. We're getting a divorce. He's bringing the papers on Wednesday."

"He is?" Declan turned to look at me, his brows dipping into a V.

"He is. I spoke to him today."

"Why didn't you tell me?" The words were tinted with hurt.

"I was going to."

"I think I'll clean up." Declan's mother stood and we both turned our heads to face her. "Don't stop working things out on my account. I'll just throw everything in the sink and make Kieran clean up." She grabbed our bowls.

"I can help." I made an effort to stand, but Declan tightened his grip on my hand.

"No, no. I've got it. Relax, you're the guest."

"We'll be there in a few minutes, Mom." He gave her a weak smile just before she left the room.

He let go of my hand and stood from the table.

"I didn't want to ruin dinner, Declan. I was going to tell you tonight, after we left."

He raised his hands to his temples and closed his eyes. My heart started to hammer, he'd been having more moments like this over the past few days.

"Have... have you been taking your meds like you're supposed to?"

He didn't answer and the wrinkles around his eyes multiplied the tighter he held them shut.

I stood and cupped his cheek with my palm. "What are they saying?" When his eyes opened they were filled with fog. "I'm right here." I dropped my hold on his face and leaned in, placing my cheek on his chest.

The sound of his voice rumbled in my ear as he said, "It's always the same. Some form of fucking doubt."

"I was getting ready to come over tonight and I saw my wedding band. I got so caught up in us these past few weeks... I love you and... it was time, so I called him. I told him we needed to just be done with it. He was awful, just like always. He called me a whore..."

Declan went rigid and his right hand balled into a fist. "He called you a—"

"It doesn't matter." I pulled back and let our gazes collide. "I got what I wanted. He's letting me go and I get you. I won."

The rage in his eyes simmered to a calm gray.

"You have no reason to ever doubt us, Declan."

His fist relaxed and his eyes cleared. "I'm sorry I got upset." He kissed my cheek.

When he pulled away I asked, "Have you been missing doses?"

He dropped his eyes to the floor. "I have. I don't always like how they make me feel, I've been good though, you make it easier to control."

"Declan, it scares me when I see the light leave your eyes... I love you too much." My fear for him choked me.

I could hear the loud clanging of pots and dishes from the kitchen as he pushed a few strands of my hair behind my right ear. He lifted my chin with his thumb. "I don't ever want to scare you."

"I'm not scared of you, Declan, I never have been. I'm scared I'll lose you to the void."

His eyes searched mine. "Sometimes, it's easier to forget to take them, because then I can make believe I'm like every other guy. But I'm not, am I? And I fucking hate it."

"I don't want every other guy, I want you and all your colorful crazy." I smiled and he tugged on my chin with a quiet laugh before he let go. "It's who you are, but I want you to be healthy... present... here with me."

"I promise." He was serious. "I'll take them every day."

Declan kissed me softly, sealing his promise to my lips.

DECLAN

"Hey, Dex, when are you heading to The Gallery?" Liam asked as he walked into my station.

"Getting ready to leave. Why?"

"I wanted to see if I could come with you, I bought some badass prints for the front of the shop. Chandler called, they came in today."

"I could just get them, bring them on my way home," I offered.

"I thought you were taking Paige out tonight?" Liam leaned against the wall.

"I am. That asshole ex of hers is supposed to come by this afternoon, finally give her the papers. I figured she might need to take her mind off shit, so I'm taking her to see a movie at The Broadview Theater."

"Sounds romantic." Liam smirked and rolled his eyes as he pulled a set of keys from his pocket. "Come on, Kieran gave me the keys to his truck. I gotta hurry, my next appointment is in twenty minutes."

Kemper was busy working on a detailed sleeve as we walked to the front where Kieran was talking with the new guy, Bart.

"I'll be back as soon as I can. If my client shows up before I do, let her know I'm running late. I shouldn't be too long." Liam raised the keys. "Thanks for letting me borrow the truck."

"No problem." Kieran stood and slapped Liam on the shoulder. He was the baby, but the tallest out of all of us. Liam and I were barely six foot tall on a good day, this kid was six-foot-two. "I'm taking Mom to confession tonight, is it okay if I cut out early when you get back?"

"Sure. Bart, you think you could run the desk?" Liam asked.

Bart nodded. "It's not rocket science."

I laughed as Kieran raised his hands in protest.

"It's a lot of work, somebody has to be the charming one." Kieran's mouth pulled into a lopsided grin.

"Yeah, yeah." Liam shook his head with a half-smile. "Come on, let's go, Dex, before this asshole starts spouting off about what a hard ass his boss is."

The ride over to The Gallery was only about five minutes. I texted Paige to tell her I was on my way and she responded, letting me know not to hurry. Clark hadn't stopped by yet and she was worried he wasn't going to show.

"He hasn't shown yet," I said as we pulled into the parking lot behind The Gallery.

"Shit." Liam put the car in park and shut off the engine. "You think you can handle seeing this fuck?"

"I'm worried he's not going to show more than anything. She's off work in fifteen minutes." I undid my seatbelt and exhaled a harsh breath. "I just want her to be free to do what she wants."

"She already is." Liam furrowed his brow. "That chick is at our place almost every night, she's not tied to him, Dex. It's just a piece of paper."

It was more than that, Liam didn't understand. Clark thought he owned her under the laws of God, and I hated that another man could use anything against her like that.

"I guess it's the principal then," I said, as I opened the door and exited the truck.

Liam shut the cab door as he spoke, "I get that. No other man needs to be pissing on what's yours."

I laughed, it was a simple explanation but true. "And I love her."

He exhaled. "And that."

Liam was just ahead of me as we walked around the building to the front door. The sun had just set, it was still early evening, and the fall air was chilly. We were supposed to get our first snowfall this weekend.

I wasn't paying attention. My eyes were fixed on the dull gray of the concrete, my head full of Paige when Liam swore under his breath. He stopped dead in his tracks and was staring into the store window. I followed his gaze and every muscle in my body constricted.

"Dex," Liam warned holding up his hand as if to steady me.

I could see him, Clark, he was standing too close to her, his hand clasped around her upper arm. Her face was pale, and her eyes were wide.

"What the fuck?" I pushed past Liam, ignoring him as he called after me, and swung open the door to the store.

Liam groaned, "Shit."

"Take your hand off of her!" Anger swelled in my chest, my head throbbed, and my jaw ached as I moved closer to where they were standing.

"Declan." Paige's voice shook, in panic or fear, I wasn't sure.

Clark's jaw pulsed twice before he smiled and tightened his hold on her arm pulling her closer to him. "Don't worry, I didn't hurt your whore," he said before dropping his hold.

I watched as her eyes, those beautiful blue eyes emptied into clear tears, his words splitting her open and everything in my peripheral vision blurred.

"What the fuck did you just say?"

"I said I didn't hurt her." His brow furrowed, but his smile never fell.

"Cool down, Dex." Liam's voice reverberated in my head. He sounded as if he was in a tunnel behind me, but all I could do was focus on Clark.

His lips moved but I couldn't hear what he was saying. Paige's eyes widened farther as she moved to take a step toward me, but Clark held out his arm, holding her back.

My hands curled into fists. He was taller than me, but what he had in height, I had in bulk. "Let her go." The command in my voice was coated in shadowed rage, but his smile only grew.

Trash.

Worthless Trash.

She's a whore.

Whore.

Clark's mouth continued to move, and the voices in my head mixed with his words making it hard for me to hear. I swallowed and clenched my jaw as he raised to his full height. I tried not to show my confusion, the murmurings in my brain started to roar as they fed off my adrenaline. I should've backed off. The tornado of fury in my head was wreaking havoc on what was real and what wasn't. His arm holding her back was the only piece of reality I needed.

I closed the distance between us and grabbed his forearm twisting it with all my strength. His features contorted as I spoke to Paige, "Go to Liam."

"Declan?"

"Go, he can't hold you anymore." I turned, looked Clark in the eyes, and spoke in a tight whisper. "You don't own her, and you never did." I shoved him backward as I released my grip on his arm.

Paige quickly moved behind me, and just as I was about turn to check on her, Clark shoved me with more power than I thought him capable. I stumbled back and almost lost my footing.

"Don't start something you can't finish." I cracked my knuckles.

"Come on, Dex, you don't need this guy's shit." Liam placed his hand on my shoulder from behind but I shrugged it off.

Clark's jaw set into a smug line as he inched closer to me. My spine stiffened and everything around me started to fade. His lips moved, and at first no sound emanated from them... it was like I was on a phone and the line was cutting in and out.

He spoke softly, his breath sour and polluting the space between us. "Useless... whore... sinful... on her back just like she liked to be fucked."

The demons in my head were violently hungry, bleeding red into my vision as my hand drove into Clark's sternum. I shoved him just enough, enough to push him back, but the air around me was toxic, filled with his black words, and without thinking I punched him square in the jaw. The pain rippled up my arm, the blood pooled on his lip, and the voices smothered me until everything went silent and dark.

The bones around my eyes hurt, my hand throbbed and my mouth tasted like metal. It was too quiet, and when I opened my eyes, the glaring white walls burned my retinas.

"Declan?" Paige's voice was uneasy.

I turned my head to the sound of it and groaned as the pain behind my temples pulsed. I sat up, taking in everything around me under the bright light.

"You took a hit, little brother, and blacked out. We're in the ER." Liam came into view, everything was distorted and curved as if I was looking through a fish bowl.

"I don't remember." The heat of Paige's hand covered mine, and as I turned to look at her, everything began to come into focus. Her cheeks were stained with tears, but she wasn't crying. Her eyes were bloodshot and swollen. "Are you okay?" I asked.

I tried to swing my legs over the side of the hospital bed, but she stopped me, holding her other hand on my thigh. "Don't get up, I'm fine. I was just worried about you." Paige's eyes flicked to Liam and her eyes narrowed.

"What happened? The last thing I remember was hitting Clark."

Liam stepped closer and lowered his voice. "You went ape shit, Dex. I've never seen you lose control like that." He slid his eyes to Paige and then back to me. "I had to pull you off of him, Chandler called the cops. You weren't in your right mind, you kept trying to get at him, you wouldn't listen... wouldn't look at me, so I... I knocked you on your ass."

I raised my hand to my jaw and rubbed it. "You punched me?"

He nodded. "You were taking his hits pretty good though, so I had to put a lot of force into it, I'm sorry about that." He smiled suggesting otherwise. "The doctor seems to think you're fine, they scanned you when we got here, no concussion." He swallowed. "I wasn't sure if I was going to stop you, but I was scared as fuck, Dex, you could've killed him."

"Is he hurt?"

"He'll live." Liam's brown eyes darkened.

There was a knock on the hospital door and two police officers walked in.

"Oh, good, he's awake," one of them said.

The other smiled at me and pulled out a pad from his belt. "Just a few quick questions, we need to corroborate what the other witnesses said, no need to worry." He nodded his head at Paige. He held out his hand. "I'm Officer Prouse, and this is Officer Stratton, Declan O'Connell?" he asked, as I took his hand and shook it.

I nodded.

"So can you tell me what happened today at The Gallery?" Officer Prouse asked and Stratton leaned against the wall, his eyes never leaving me.

My arm was stiff as I ran my hand through my hair. "I can't really remember."

Prouse flipped through his pad of paper. "The store manager, Chandler Wilson, reported that Clark Jensen, Paige Simon's husband, entered the property to drop off divorce papers. Mr. Wilson said he stepped into the back to give them some privacy, but heard an altercation. When he came to the store front, he said you were being attacked by her estranged spouse so he called nine-one-one." His eyes met mine. "Any of this ringing a bell."

Liam gave me a pointed glare. Chandler had covered my ass, but what had Clark told them? "Honestly, I don't remember much." I licked my cracked lip and winced.

"Do you want to press charges?" The other officer pushed off the wall as he spoke.

I shook my head. "No." I looked at Paige and she squeezed my thigh. "It's done."

She nodded and I covered her hand with mine.

"Are you sure? That's a pretty wicked shiner he gave you." Prouse placed the pad of paper in his belt.

"I'm good. Like I said, I can't really remember much."

"We'll let his attorney know. If you change your mind, here's my card." He placed it on the tray table. "Stay out of trouble."

Once they left, Paige stood from her chair and sat next to me on the bed. She placed her hands on my face and gently kissed my cheek. I tried not to, but I hissed at the pressure of it, and she pulled away.

"I'm so sorry." The wrinkle between her eyes deepened.

"It's okay." I lightly kissed her lips once. "You got me good," I said to Liam and he laughed.

"You really don't remember anything?" Paige's brows dipped and her bottom lip trembled.

"No. I blacked out, it happens every now and then." Just as I finished speaking, the doctor, or someone I assumed was the doctor, walked in holding an iPad. His face was stern and his white jacket made me nervous.

His eyes were lowered to the screen as he said my name.

"That's me."

He raised his gaze. "My name is Dr. Adams, I'm the on-call psychiatrist. I need to ask you a few questions. Would you like anyone to step out before I proceed?"

Liam's posture straightened.

"I can leave if you want," Paige whispered.

I kissed her cheek. "No, this is my family. Besides, they were there. I can't really remember much."

He hummed under his breath and tapped his finger on the iPad.

"That's what the ER doctor said." His eyes were still on the screen. "You see Dr. Han, outpatient?"

"I do."

"Do you have these blackouts often?" he asked without looking at me.

"I used to."

He raised his eyes. "I see you have a history of hallucinations? Are the medications you're on currently helping?"

"Yes."

Liar.

"You haven't been taking them like you should." Paige tried to keep her voice down, but he'd heard her and his eyes tensed.

Liam ran his hand through his hair and glared at Paige. "He takes them, he's been a lot better since his recent med change."

"When he was brought in today, you reported to the physician that he was 'out of it' and 'uncontrollable'." The doctor set the iPad down on my bedside tray and looked at Liam.

"He was just protecting Paige." Liam's irritation resonated in the room.

"My ex, he started it," Paige agreed.

"How often do you have internal stimuli?" The doctor frowned and turned his attention back to me.

"When I'm taking my meds regularly, not often, maybe once a day, sometimes, when I'm with Paige, I won't hear them for days." I laced my fingers with hers.

"But, you haven't been taking them regularly?" He raised his eyebrows.

I shook my head. "I forget, and if I'm being honest, I don't like how they make me feel at times."

He clicked his tongue. "And your depression?"

"Nonexistent," I answered.

"Because of her, I'm guessing?" He shifted his eyes to Paige and then back to me. "Here's the thing, Mr. O'Connell, according to what your brother told the ER doctor, and your long history of mental illness, I'm worried you're a danger to yourself and others until we can reestablish your medications. You snapped today, you were impulsive. I can't ethically let you leave here knowing that you're not taking medications like you should, hearing voices, and losing time, blacking out... I'm recommending an acute admission to our behavioral health unit for med stabilization."

"This is ridiculous, he's never been hospitalized!" Liam's hands balled into fists.

"I realize that, but—"

"We can take care of him, make sure he takes his medications," Paige offered, but her voice wavered.

My chest felt heavy and it became difficult to swallow past the boulder in my throat.

They're locking you up.

You're sick.

Sick.

Mentally ill.

I pinched the bridge of my nose and tried to steady my breathing.

"I'm afraid this is my decision. He can either be admitted voluntarily or I can hold him... it's up to you."

Liam swore and for a second I thought he was going to punch the wall. "You can hold him?" His tone was acidic. "Against his will?" He was unconvinced.

"Yes."

"Fuck this," Liam growled and Paige gasped.

"Enough." Paige was breaking and I had to be strong for her. "I'll do it. How long will I have to stay?"

"Maybe a week, maybe a little longer, it depends on how you do with the med changes." He picked up his iPad. "I'll get the paperwork started."

He left the room and Paige started crying. I pulled her to my chest and ignored the suffocating panic that was building in my lungs.

"Give us a minute?" I asked Liam and he nodded reluctantly.

Once he was out of the room, Paige leaned back and said, "This is all my fault. I shouldn't have told you to come. I should've met you at Avenues once I was off work."

"My mental illness is not your fault. I should've taken my meds like I was supposed to. Maybe I wouldn't have reacted like I had. Maybe I could've kept my cool. Don't blame yourself, this is all me and my fucked-up brain."

You're her burden.

She pities you.

She saw the monster, she saw him.

She saw what you really are.

"They're getting worse, I can tell, you zone out." Paige dropped her eyes. "Like today. Your eyes went totally blank, Declan... I was so scared for you."

"Maybe this is a good thing."

I was terrified.

"Maybe." She sniffled and wiped under her eyes. "I hope they let me visit."

The thought of her seeing me in a place like that made me sick.

"I don't want you to visit me in there." Her face fell and I cupped her cheek. "I don't want you to see me like that. I have no idea what's going to happen, and the last thing I want is for you to pity me, I can do this... I need to get better, get my head straight... for us."

"I don't pity you, Declan, I love you."

"Paige, I can't."

"Will you at least call me?" One tear escaped the corner of her eye and I wiped it with my thumb before I lowered my hand.

"If I can."

The door opened again and Liam came through with two staff members.

"They're gonna move you now."

Paige sucked in a deep breath and my heart plummeted into my stomach. It felt as if the acid from my gut was shredding it to pieces as they asked her and my brother to leave.

"We can't go with him?" Liam was reaching his limit.

"They allow visiting once a day from seven to eight in the evening." The girl in gray scrubs picked at her nails like she was bored and his jaw compressed.

I tilted my head toward Paige's ear. "I love you."

I kissed her in front of everyone, not giving a shit, holding on to the taste. I looked into her eyes and inhaled her scent. I'd take as much of her with me as I could. My biggest fear as I watched her and Liam leave was not knowing which medications they would give me. I've always dealt with the voices, but being numb, not feeling that fucking flame in my chest for Paige, not having that need, that warmth, I'd slit open every vein before I'd let them turn me into a robot.

I'd die before I let them erase my love for her.

PAIGE

"May I please speak to Declan O'Connell, patient code four-five-two-seven?" I held the phone to my ear with my left hand, and chewed the fingernail of my right pinky as I waited for the clerk to tell me what I already knew.

Her breathing was even and I could hear her tapping on the keyboard of her computer as she most likely was searching for Declan's information. "He's not taking phone calls at this time, would you like to leave a message?"

Let him know I'm going crazy not knowing what's happening to him. Tell him I love him, tell him I'm sorry... tell him I need him here. Tell him to come back to me. "Will you let him know Paige Simon called... again?" My throat ached as I spoke around my emotion.

She exhaled an annoyed breath. "Yeah, I'll let him know."

I'd called every day, three times a day since I'd left Declan in the ER. That night had forged a steel vice around my heart. The fear in his eyes as I left the room... I'd never forget it. He watched me leave, and if the silence had spoken it would have shouted from his lips, "Please... please don't leave me alone." That was two weeks ago.

He'd spoken to me on the phone the first day. He'd told me he was fine, that he would manage, that he needed this time, for himself... for treatment. I hadn't known that he'd intended to cut me off completely. I'd gone from worried, to panicked, and moved straight to an all-out breakdown by the seventh day. I hadn't gone to work, I'd hardly eaten, and if I hadn't decided to finally stop pacing the house, I think Lana would've had me committed. It wasn't until Liam started to ignore my calls that I'd began to think maybe Declan had given up on us. Maybe he didn't need me to get through this, maybe he'd decided what I'd known all along... I was cursed, and all I ever brought us was pain.

I threw my cell phone on the bed and let the tears leak from my eyes. We'd come so far, and everything we'd built since we'd gotten back together came burning to the ground in bright cinders of red and blood. I'd never seen Declan like that before. His body had moved and thrashed as it sought out Clark's flesh for redemption. Declan's face had gone slack, as if he no longer belonged to himself, to this world, and if it hadn't been for Liam, I'd have been a widow instead of just a divorcee.

Two weeks.

Two weeks of worry.

Two weeks of fear.

Without him... there was no color.

I plopped down on the bed, wiped my cheeks with my fingertips, leaned over, grabbed my boots and slipped them on. I had to be strong... for me... for us.

There may not be an 'us' anymore, Paige.

I shook off my doubt as I prepared for what today would bring. Today was the day I had to meet with my parents. I'd tried to push it off, but they'd heard what had happened, and my mother had called me almost every day since. I wasn't naïve enough, not anymore, to think she gave a crap about me. All she wanted to do was try and manipulate me into feeling guilty. Blame me, and tell me I needed to win Clark back. Win my chance at an exclusive seat in Heaven next to my eternal partner. My only chance at deliverance. Bile rose in my throat at the thought. Declan was all I'd ever want in this life, and all I'd ever hope for in the next. My mother was delusional if she thought I'd ever fight to get back together with Clark, and I was sure he no longer wanted to *own* me either.

After the incident, his lawyer was the one to contact me. Clark had finally let go. I guess almost going to jail for an alleged assault was the wakeup call he'd needed. I was still indebted to Chandler for making sure Declan hadn't been the one implicated. It was a few days ago, when Clark's lawyer called me to tell me the divorce papers had been sent to the court, and now all we had to do was wait for it to be official. It could take up to a month. One month might've sounded like an eternity if I hadn't known what it was like to live through these past two weeks.

Lana had been gone all morning meeting with her thesis professor, and the house was too quiet as I walked out the front door. I pulled the hood of my jacket over my head once the frigid air hit my cheeks and tangled my hair. The snow was falling in fat, wet flakes, and they clumped on my jacket as I walked to my car. It seemed too early to be snowing already, and our abnormally hot summer had become an unusually cold fall. I tossed my purse onto the passenger side seat and nearly slipped as I quickly sat in my car. I turned on the engine and flipped the heat to full blast. The wipers easily removed the damp and heavy snow from my windshield.

My body was still numb by the time I got to my parents' home and it wasn't from the cold. I let the car run for a moment as I stared up at the house. It looked the same, except the trees had lost their leaves in the storm, the quaking aspens were bare and made me think of Declan and his painting. The vice squeezed my heart and my stomach tensed. I reached into my purse and grabbed my phone. I dialed Liam again. I needed something, some piece of Declan to take with me into Hell, because once I walked into that house, I was afraid I'd lose myself all over again.

It rang three times before his deep voice answered, "Hello."

"Liam," I said with severe relief. If he hadn't picked up, my next stop on my way home would've been Avenues.

Silence.

"Please," I begged.

He exhaled a long breath. "He doesn't want to talk to you."

My sternum cracked down the center. "Why?" I whispered past the pain in my throat.

Nothing.

"Liam, I'm frightened... worried... I love him, and I... I need to know if—"

"It's been rough, Paige, real fucking rough."

A silent sob shook my shoulders and I closed my eyes.

"They fucked with his head, they changed his meds, and he had a reaction to one of them, so the doctors did a med wash and—"

"A med wash?" I opened my eyes and looked up at the front windows. The curtains were still shut tight.

"Yeah, they stopped all of his meds. Weaned him off for a few days, but he..." the low timbre strangled the words as if he was fighting his own feelings. "He went into this psychotic state, and he wouldn't talk to anyone. He almost became violent with a staff member when they tried to take his journal." I couldn't help the tears that poured down my cheeks. He'd been in the dark all alone. "He's doing better now. They've put him back on his meds. A few of the old ones and this new anti-psychotic. He's looking good. Talking again, but... he doesn't want anyone to see him like this. He won't talk to my mom or Kieran. Just me."

"He's okay? He's getting better?" The tremor in my voice blurred the words.

Liam exhaled again. "Here's the thing. When we got hold of his journal... it was all crazy shit. Pages of random words, sketches of eyes ... your name. The phrase... *This is forever*, was written over and over. He refused meals, and when I was there it was like he didn't know me. He couldn't remember his own fucking name, but... he knew you."

My eyes brimmed, my heart burst from its cage and my lips trembled.

"He gets discharged in four days. I want you to be there for him."

"Yes. Of course." I had to see him.

"No, I need you to fucking listen to me. I *need* you to be there. No more running, no more bullshit. Nine years, Paige, he was a goddamn zombie and then you came back... and he got... better. Seeing Dex like that, in that hell hole, watching him become possessed by the shit in his head... it's the hardest thing I've ever seen. You were in there with him... in the chaos... you kept his spirit, and you better fucking be there for him when he gets out."

I sucked in a jagged breath. I'd been with him. He'd lost himself, but I was the tether. We were bound, we were one. "Declan is my life, he always has been, and there is nothing that will keep me from him ever again."

"You destroyed him last time, and it's hard—"

"I'm here. I'm here, Liam." I sat up straighter in the front seat. "He's my forever."

"I'll see you Tuesday."

The phone went silent and I let myself break apart. I let myself think of Declan, in a small hospital room, lost, and confused, his eyes empty, scribbling away in a journal. Busy trying to piece himself back together, flashes of who we were keeping him in the now as much as it could. I thought of all of these things, and fell into the abyss with him.

The large, open living room, clad in all white, was slowly suffocating me. My father stood, leaned against the back of the couch, his hands gripping the Italian leather, as my mom rattled on about my duties as a daughter, as a wife. I ran my sweaty palms down my jeans and he frowned.

"He's sent the paperwork. It's done. In a month's time I'll no longer be his wife. It's what I want... what he wants."

"What about in the eyes of the Lord, you've been running around with Declan, you left your husband for another man, he attacked—"

"Clark was hurting me, Declan was defending me!" My eyes raised to the ceiling as I tried to calm my temper.

"You've lost your way." My mother's self-righteous voice picked at every insecurity I had.

"Don't be ridiculous, this is crazy. Why can't you see that? Why can't you see that I was miserable with Clark, that he treated me like garbage? For God's sake, I'm your daughter."

"Watch your mouth." My mother's lips mashed into a straight line, and I rolled my eyes.

"You think you're better than us?" My father's tone was unforgiving, and his eyes narrowed.

"N-no," I stuttered as those hard eyes met mine.

"The outside world judges us every day with their dirty mouths. I can see it on you. Those clothes you wear, they can't hide what's inside you, what lurks and lives inside your heart. You've given yourself to that man again, and you'll sink even further." He laughed without humor, and my stomach dropped as he stood to his full height and rounded the sofa. "His sickness has polluted your mind. Have you forgotten the scriptures? James chapter one, verse fifteen. *'Then, after desire has conceived, it gives birth to sin; and sin, when it is full-grown, gives birth to death.'* You've let the Devil claim your soul, and you're as good as dead to me."

I waited for the tears to come as he walked toward me, but they didn't. Anger bloomed an orange flame, and it set my chest ablaze as I stood with my hands fisted at my sides.

"Sit down," my mother hissed, but I locked my eyes on hers.

"Neither of you are truly God-fearing. You don't care about your daughter's wellbeing. All you care about is status. You both have turned your back on your so-called Savior. My God, my Savior... he sees you for what you are, and believe me, you will be judged accordingly."

A searing pain erupted across my cheekbone, and the sound of my father's hand against my skin filled the open room. I raised my palm to my cheek and my eyes watered.

"Get out of this house!" he roared.

I turned to my mother as I picked up my jacket from the arm of the couch and slipped it on. Nursing my cheek with my shaking fingers, I grabbed my bag with my free hand. "The Bible also teaches acceptance, and love, and forgiveness. Even after judgement, we all still have a chance." My eyes dried as I watched my mother's fill with tears. "I can't live a life where love doesn't exist, and this house, it's filled with hate. If Heaven is what you've painted, I want no part of it."

I waited. I watched. My mother turned her face to the right, and a lone tear trickled down her cheek as her eyes fixed on the wall. My father's face was red, filled with disdain as I tried to meet his eyes.

"Get out." This time he whispered through thin lips tight with suppressed rage.

As I placed my bag on my shoulder and turned to leave, I thought about saying I love you, but what I felt for them was purely nostalgic, written in a primal blood tie that pulled at my heart as I walked out of my family home onto the snow-covered porch.

For the short time I was there, my mother pleaded with me to see her perverted reason. She'd begged me to come back to the church, to let them help me. But, unfortunately, their help involved wiping myself away with washed-out morals and half-truths. I was dead to them. I lifted my hood and took in a deep breath, and as I blew out the humid fog from my lips, I tilted my head back and let the clean air bite at my nose and cheeks. I was dead to them, but in four days, I'd rise again.

Declan had held out hope for me inside his own madness, and I'd be there for him when he returned to his realities. I'd wade through it, drown in it, swallow down the murky moments, and revel in the joyful ones. Because that was our love, and as I watched the giant white flakes twirl inside the static atmosphere, I felt it. I felt a warmth come over my body, and my lips parted with a smile as I stepped off the last step into the white void.

DECLAN

"I'm going to need you to remove all your piercings, and change into this..." The male nurse handed me a white and blue hospital gown.

"All of my piercings? I'm not trying to kill myself, I—"

"Are we going to have a problem?" The nurse rolled his large shoulders. He was a few inches taller than me, and just as muscular. His eyes narrowed on mine, begging me to fuck with him.

I wasn't scared of the physical pain he'd inflict, it was the possible drugs he could wield. "No, no problem." I removed my earrings and he held out a small plastic bag for me to drop them in. I started to remove my shirt, and paused as I looked around the small bathroom then back at him. "Are you going to watch?"

"Yup." His lips pressed together into a firm line.

I took off my shirt, "Where should I—"

"Just throw it on the floor. We'll wash it, everything you have here... we'll wash. You can call your family tomorrow to bring you more clothes. You'll need three sets. We do laundry *every night, but for right now, just take everything off, put on that gown and you'll have your clothes back in the morning when you wake up."*

My heart hammered as I flipped the button of my jeans. I dropped my eyes to the floor as I slipped out of my pants. Thousands of bugs crawled under the surface of my skin as I felt his gaze on my chest. I didn't look at him as I removed my body piercings and placed them in the small bag with the earrings.

The door to the bathroom cracked open and my spine stiffened.

"You ready for me?" another male voice spoke through the crack in the door.

"Yeah, come on in." The male nurse, I looked at his badge, Evan, gave me a small nod as the other man walked in.

The room had white tile floors with dirty looking gray grout. The walls were a faded beige, and as both of the men approached me, everything around me narrowed and closed in. I took a step backward and my calves touched the toilet.

"It's okay... I'm just here to help with the skin check." He smiled trying to reassure me, but it sat sour in my gut. "Every patient that comes in, we check their skin, make documentation of any tattoos, any significant marks, it helps us know if anything changes while you're here."

Evan grabbed a large towel from the cupboard next to the sink and handed it to me. "Remove your underwear and hold this towel in front of you as a cover."

My eyes shifted anxiously to the other nurse as he pulled a pen and pad from his pocket. I felt trapped, and each breath, each bit of air that I inhaled became harder to take. He started to scribble as he verbally counted off my tattoos and scars. My fingers gripped the towel, holding it in front of me, as the last bit of my dignity hit the floor with my boxer briefs.

"Do you think you should go home first?" Kieran asked from the back seat of my mother's car. Liam had borrowed it to pick me up from the hospital.

It took m a moment to answer, my head was still in the psych ward. " Jo, I want to see her."

I was su pposed to discharge Tuesday, but they held me, stating I needed a few more days of observation. Three weeks. Three fucking weeks without her, without life.

"Maybe she could meet you at our place, Kieran has a point. You could use the structure, Dex." Liam lifted his attention from the road to look at me briefly.

He'd aged these past three weeks, not much, but I could see the stress I'd caused him. The creases in the corner of his eyes were met by dark circles. His lips were dry, his cheeks sunken in. Liam's eyes focused back on the road.

"I'm good. I'm better." That much at least was true. These meds, the psychiatrist, he'd found a combination that actually worked. My hallucinations were barely there, and it was the first time, without Paige, that I hadn't heard a voice in over four days. The medications made me tired, but they didn't stifle me. The last week I was in the hospital, I'd drawn real pictures, not just all the fucked-up shit in my head, but actual renderings of her face, her hands... Paige... in pure form. They might have taken my dignity, but I still had my inspiration, my creative brain—my soul.

"I know, but don't you think... it would be better to be some place familiar?" Kieran's hand clasped my shoulder as he moved closer to the front seat. "I'm sure she wouldn't mind."

My brothers thought I was too fragile, but they didn't know that I'd been broken already. In treatment, I'd fallen into a fathomless darkness, something I'd feared forever, something I'd die before entering again. I'd met the monster inside my heart, the devil in my head, and they'd smiled at me, cut me, brought me down into the depths of the animal within my skin. I'd almost given myself over to it... almost.

"Can you tell me what this means, Declan?" Dr. Barra pointed at my journal.

The words on the page caught fire and disappeared, leaving behind a pair of blue eyes.

She's not real, she's forgotten and gone.

You are nothing, she is nothing.

You created her.

No.

She is forever.

She hates you.

The ghosts twisted my thoughts, lied to me, and told me things I never wanted to believe.

"Declan, tell me about Paige?" The doctor's voice taunted the devil in my head.

My jaw ached as I grit my teeth trying to remember, trying to see past the flame, and fog, and smoke. The pressure built in my knuckles as I squeezed my fists and said, "She hates me."

I'd lost myself in the past, in the memories I'd had, in the reality I'd lived for so long without her. I ran my hand through my hair and turned to face Kieran.

"I won't lose her again... that place... I almost let the shit in my head devour the last good thing... the last memory. I don't care where, I just need to see her, and if going to her place gets me there faster then that's where I'm going." My eyes fixed on his and he nodded.

"Alright," Liam said. "The doctor set up some appointments for you tomorrow. New patient intake, and med reconciliation. She gonna take you? It's at nine in the morning."

"I'm sure she would." I hadn't spoken to her in three weeks. I hadn't wanted her to hear my voice, or the vacant black that would've spilled from my lips. I hadn't wanted her to see the beast inside me.

"She's been coming to the shop every day since you missed your discharge date." Liam frowned. "I think she thinks you're hiding from her. She started crying when I called her today to tell her we were on our way to pick you up."

My stomach fell. "She cried?"

Kieran cleared his throat, and said, "I know you thought keeping her away for her own good was the right thing, but—"

"But she's been fucking nuts." Liam looked at me again. "Get your apologies ready, Dex, she's gonna want them." He gave me a lopsided smile before turning his eyes onto the road.

"I'm going to ask her to move in with me."

The car came to an abrupt stop. My eyes flicked up to the red light and then to Liam. His dark irises trained on me. "What?"

Kieran leaned forward again. "No way, Declan, you need to take care of—"

"I want her with me. We've been apart long enough. That apartment... it's mine too, and I pay half, just like Liam. I'm feeling better. I've got a doctor who knows what the fuck he's doing... I'm a goddamn man, and I'm tired of being treated like at any minute I'm going to fracture."

Liam's glare softened.

"They already broke me, Liam... and I know..." My throat threatened to close off. "I know you saw it... I know they let you see me at my worst, but seeing it isn't living it. I'll never go there again. Paige, she's the last piece... she's just as important... without her... meds don't fucking matter."

The light turned green, but he didn't move. We were stopped on a slow street, and at the moment we were the only car. "What I saw in the hospital..." Liam shook his head trying to wipe away the bad memories. "You're good, Declan, you always have been. You work hard, you create things no one ever could, and you're a badass when it comes to ink. If this is what you need, if this will keep you happy, it's your home, Dex, you do what you want."

A car honked behind us and Liam let off the brakes and moved forward.

"Thank you." I let myself smile as he nodded.

Kieran exhaled and rested his back into his seat. "Do you think she'll say yes?" he asked.

"I have no idea." But I hoped.

My hand shook as I raised it to the doorbell. About ten minutes ago, I'd texted Paige telling her that we were almost to her house. My head was turned, watching Liam drive away when the front door opened. Her scent filled my lungs as I inhaled, and the light sound of a gasp brought my gaze to her wide eyes. The plane of her cheeks were pink, and her bottom lip was trapped between her teeth. Paige's hair was wet and the blonde tendrils spilled across her shoulders. My breath captured itself into small clouds within the cold air as I struggled for something to say.

She shivered and wrapped her hands around her body. I'd like to think it was because she was cold, but as I stepped closer to the doorway, she hugged herself tighter as if she was bracing herself, protecting herself from me. The acid in my stomach turned. My brothers were right, I shouldn't have kept her away as long as I had.

"You're freezing." I lifted my hand and took a piece of her hair between my thumb and finger.

"I just got out of the shower." Her words were quiet, but her voice filled me with courage. I'd missed the sound of it more than I'd thought.

She was wearing an oversized, black and red University of Utah sweatshirt and yoga pants.

"Can I—"

She stepped to the side and her hair fell from my fingers. She shook her head and gave me a shy smile. "Sorry, you're probably freezing, too, come in."

The warmth of her house embraced me as I walked over the threshold. The door clicked shut behind me as I moved farther into the small house. There was music coming from down the hall to my right.

"Is Lana home?" I asked, as Paige fell into place at my side and led me to her room.

"No, she's at school, she'll be back in a little while," Paige spoke as she shut her bedroom door. The music played from the docking station on her dresser as I turned to face her. She looked up at me with giant eyes, and the color, a thick azure, speckled with bits of green and amber, set my pulse to a sprint. "I've been crazy, these past few weeks, the days, they've blended together, and the nights, I haven't slept... Declan, I—"

"I'm sorry." I held her face with my hands. "I didn't want—"

"I know, you didn't want me to see you in there, but—"

"No." I grazed my thumbs gently under her eyes and wiped away the tears. "I didn't want to hurt you, and yes... I didn't want you to see me in there, and I knew if you saw what I was like, what they boiled me down to, you'd never look at me the same."

She raised her hands to my shoulders. "Liam told me... he said... he said you were gone for a while?"

I nodded.

"He said... he'd never seen you that blank... like you were lost, but..." She exhaled a shaky breath. "He said that I was there... in your head and that you still drew my eyes?"

Shadows flickered through my thoughts. I dropped my hold, stepping away, her arms fell to her sides, and I laced her hand with mine. "I was in an eternal state of night. It was starless, void of light, and filled with hate and rage... and lies. All I could focus on was the bad. Once all the meds were out of my system, and I faded to the background of my own mind... you were the only fragment of myself I had to hold on to. The night I gave you the tattoo, that memory... it was rooted inside me. And once they started the new meds, it grew, and each branch, each piece of us... they became the steps I'd use to rise from the hole I'd fallen into."

She let go of my hand, and draped her arms around my waist. Her cheek pressed to the center of my chest as she breathed deeply. "I missed you," she whispered.

"I should've called you when I didn't discharge like I was supposed to." The guilt bared down on me.

She nodded and I pulled her as close as I could. My arms swallowed her small body. "You should've called." She leaned back, but kept the heat of her hands at my waist. Her eyes were vibrant, no more tears to blur the pristine blue as they met mine. "But, I get it. I understand that you needed to go through this on your own, and that you were trying to protect me, but you know I've always loved your dark, even that pitch black night... because at some point it gives way to the light of day. It's scary, and I will never fully understand what it's like for you, but it's beautiful, and it's perfect... because it's you."

I shook my head in disbelief. "They took my pride, Paige. They stripped me down, they took away my reason, they stopped my meds, and they showed me what I was really like. I was nothing more than my illness."

"That experience taught you what *could* happen, Declan. The *illness*, the voices, the depression, it's too much to contain all on your own. You'll burst if you try to keep it from me. You have to take care of yourself, and I want to help you. Let me help you... let me want you, let me see it all."

She raised up on her tiptoes and I tilted my head down enough that our lips almost touched as I spoke, "The past three weeks... it was a nightmare I didn't think I could escape. I've never felt so empty." She briefly brushed her lips against mine and it lit my spine and sent a shuddering heat through my limbs. "I didn't know who I was anymore." I lowered my nose to the crook in her neck and she leaned her head to the side as I inhaled. I raised my lips to her ear and whispered, "Show me I'm still human, that I'm still a man."

Our mouths crashed together as my hands slid into her hair. The wet strands cooled the fever in my fingertips and slowed my over-eager lips. I'd spent the past three weeks in the circles of Hell, but all it took was one taste of her, and every miserable fucking minute dissipated into her soft gasp as I pressed my body against hers.

My name parted her lips as I pulled away. Paige blushed, and as I lifted her sweatshirt, she raised her arms for me. Her stare penetrated mine, and I began to breathe again. Deep, real breaths filled with the warmth of orange and gold. My heartbeat thundered as she unclasped her bra and let it fall to the floor. The teardrop shape of her breasts, the dusted pink of her nipples, I licked my lips and felt the color of life fill each beat of my heart. I laid her down on the stark white of her comforter and she moved herself to the middle of the bed, watching me as I pulled my sweater over my head. Her eyes scanned my chest as I kicked off my shoes, unbuttoned my jeans, and removed them along with my boxer-briefs.

I moved to the foot of the bed and crawled over her body, taking her breast into my mouth. My hands were braced on the mattress as I tasted her, letting the feeling surge through me. That death I'd suffered had almost been cured. My mouth created a path past her tattoo to the top of her pants, and as I peeled them down, my lips followed. I kissed her thighs and her calves as I slowly undressed her, leaving the rest of her clothes on the floor. Her scent revived me as my mouth moved along the length of her inner thigh. Her fingers knotted in my hair, and she gasped as I brought my mouth between her legs.

Paige tasted like the color of champagne, the shade of strawberries stained her chest and cheeks as she came in my mouth. Her legs trembled as I moved my body over hers and pushed inside her. She worshipped my name as our bodies collided, and the heat of her skin, the way she dug her nails into the flesh of my back, the way we fit together, the way her lips savored mine... I'd never last. Her cries were whispered along the bow of my bottom lip, as she moved in pace with my rhythm, letting me have the control, letting me be a man, letting me live... through her I had everything.

The muscles in my stomach coiled, my hand fisted in her hair and my tongue licked the seam of her lips, dipping into her mouth as I growled out my release. Paige wrapped her arms around my neck, letting her fingers run through my hairline, pulling me closer as she melted below me.

Out of breath and content, we stared at each other. The corner of her lips curled into a smile as I smoothed my thumbs over her cheeks. I watched the electric blue of her eyes dim as she fell back to Earth with me, and without any hesitation I said, "I want you to move in with me."

PAIGE

His eyes were clear, open windows, no shade clouding his soul, no reluctance or anxiety, just pure and honest anticipation. The weight of his body shifted as the seconds ticked by. He rested onto his side and, with his finger, he moved a strand of my hair off my forehead.

"Are you sure?" I'd seen the answer already in his eyes, but the girl in me needed that reassurance. The wounded parts of me needed to hear it, needed to finally heal over for good.

His lips spread into a soft smile and he nodded. "If you're worried about Liam... don't be. He's okay with it."

My heartbeat fluttered as I rolled onto my side. We were eye to eye on the pillow as I said, "Move in?" It wasn't really a question, the way it whispered across my tongue... I was playing with the notion.

Declan raised his hand and trailed his thumb along the ink on my ribcage. "Yes," he said. "Move in. Your face, these eyes, your mouth, Paige, I need to see it all every day. In the morning, and before I close my eyes. I need it as much as I need to take my damn medications." His smile curled and creased around his eyes. "You're good for my mental health."

A quiet laugh parted my lips. "When?"

"Whenever you're ready." He lifted his weight onto his elbow.

"I'm ready."

Declan's smile met mine and our lips broke against one another's with a delicate sweetness. It was tender and hungry and it pooled inside my stomach with a delicious heat. Declan's mouth didn't leave mine as he leaned back. His hands on my waist pulled my weight above him. A deep, rumbling groan vibrated within his chest below my palms, as I moved my legs, positioning them, one on each side of his hips. His body was hard and the pressure, the ache he stirred in my core felt a partial relief as he pressed himself against me.

"I'm ready," I whispered again and he took my breath away, filling me, as he connected my pulse with his.

We hadn't left my bed since he'd shown up, and when I'd heard Lana come home about ten minutes ago, the sound of the front door had roused me from my sleep. Declan's arm was wrapped around me, his hand on my belly keeping me close. The position made it easy for me to explore the smooth surface of his muscles. My fingers created serpentine lines down Declan's chest. His breathing was even as he slept, his face without any tension, his lips slightly separated as he inhaled and exhaled in peace. A loud grumble erupted in my belly and my mouth watered with nausea. I was starting to get hungry.

When my thumb dusted against his nipple, it was the first time I noticed he'd taken out his piercings, and it distracted me from my empty stomach. I'd grown used to the way the metal had felt under my fingertips.

"I had to take out all of my piercings." His groggy voice startled me, and he chuckled.

He moved his arm and I sat up. My gaze lifted to his ears, where his earrings were secured in place.

"The ear piercings didn't close." He lifted his hand and the pads of his fingers ran along the silver jewelry in his ear.

"Will you pierce them again?" I asked and felt my cheeks heat.

He grinned. "Do you want me to?"

"I think I do." It fit him, and it was kind of sexy. "Does it hurt?"

"Like hell." He laughed when my stomach growled again. "You sound hungry."

"I am. Lana just got home, and on the nights she meets with her professor she brings home take out." I leaned across his body to my nightstand to grab my hair tie. His firm hands gripped my waist, and I squealed as he gently tossed me onto my back before I could reach it. His smile was full and his stare landed on my mouth. "Declan, Lana is *here*." I giggled as he buried his nose in my neck. The hairs of his beard scratched and tickled my overheated skin.

"I don't care," he mumbled as his teeth nipped my earlobe.

I wiggled under the heavy muscles of his chest. "This house has thinner walls than your apartment." He hummed in agreement and the heat of his breath spread down my arms, chest, and legs. I laughed as I said, "I'm serious." I playfully shoved him and he groaned as he sat up on his knees. I pressed my lips together and admired his body. Everything between Declan and I felt normal... things felt better, easy.

He smiled down at me when he caught me staring. "You don't look serious."

"I'm starving... and don't you want me to tell Lana I'm moving out?" I brought my triumphant gaze to his.

Declan's eyes brightened as he said, "Let's get dressed."

We quickly threw on our clothes, and I brushed out my hair and pulled it up into a knot. Declan watched me in the mirror as I secured the mess on the top of my head. My cheeks were flushed and my skin tingled all the places where his mouth had been.

I met his stare in the mirror. "This feels different."

I turned to look at him face-to-face when he asked, "How?"

I smiled as his brows furrowed and said, "It's a good thing. Now that Clark agreed to the divorce..." Declan's eyes narrowed just enough I noticed. "Even though everything isn't final... I feel free. I'm free." His shoulders relaxed. "And, I can tell you feel better. When was the last time the voices spoke to you?"

He ran his hand through his hair and his smile reached his eyes. "It's been almost five days."

"Declan, that's—"

"A fucking miracle." He moved toward me and took my hand in his. "I'm happy, Paige." Those crystal blue windows opened wide again as he leaned down to kiss me on the cheek. "Come on."

He opened the door to my bedroom and the smell of Chinese food hit me like a brick. My head swam and all the acid in my stomach churned.

"Declan—"

"Paige, I got the Jade Dragon, I ordered your favorite..." Lana paused when she noticed Declan at my side. "Well, hello there." Her teasing smile fell as she turned her eyes to me. "You alright?"

I tried to swallow down the sick feeling but that smell...

"I'm going to be sick." I dropped Declan's hand and ran to the bathroom.

My knees hit the cool floor and my shoulders burned as I dry heaved over and over again. My stomach was empty, and I prayed for relief as the room began to spin. My fingers gripped the bowl of the toilet as I tried desperately to expel the bile from my throat. Declan kneeled down behind me, his hand on my lower back moving in comforting circles as I spit into the bowl.

"Shit, Paige, are you okay?" Lana's voice filtered through the small bathroom.

I shook my head.

"What can I do?" Declan asked, his tone even and soothing.

I cleared my throat. "Maybe some water?"

"On it!" Lana volunteered.

I leaned over and flushed the toilet, already feeling a little less nauseated.

Declan stood, grabbed the hand towel that was hanging on the side of the sink, wet it under the faucet and wrung it out before he handed it to me. "Here."

"Thank you," my throat hurt as I spoke. The cold towel felt like heaven against my forehead.

"Your color is coming back." Declan gave me a small smile.

"I didn't realize I was that hungry." It wasn't normal for me to get that sick. I mean, I'd barely eaten at all after I'd left Clark and I'd been fine.

"Maybe it's a stomach bug? Either way, I should go home tonight, let you rest." He offered his hand and I took it standing on wobbly legs.

Declan placed his palm on my forehead as I wiped my mouth with the towel. "I think I just need to eat." The thought of food made my stomach twist.

"I don't know, you just got pale again." Worry furrowed his brow.

I took a deep breath, leaning against the counter as I handed him the towel. "Will you throw this in the hamper in my room?"

He lingered in the doorway for a second before he turned to leave. I closed my eyes as I heard ice clink into a glass from the kitchen. I exhaled and opened my eyes before I reached down and opened the cabinet to grab another towel. I rummaged through a few toiletries and lifted a towel from the back of the cupboard. Just as I was about to shut the cabinet door my eyes fell onto a box of unopened tampons. The butterflies in my stomach took flight.

It wasn't possible.

I counted in my head... I never paid attention to dates anymore. After Clark and I had tried for so long... with no results...

I was two weeks late.

There was no way.

I couldn't conceive.

But you have before.

Clark and I had never been tested. He'd blamed me, said I'd been damned, that God would never grant me another child because of my sin.

I dropped my hand to my stomach, kneeled on the floor, and squeezed my eyes shut.

Please.

It was crazy to want this. Declan and I had finally begun to find our way... he was getting better.

Dear Heavenly Father, I beg you.

"Paige?" Declan's anxious tone opened my eyes. "Are you feeling sick again?"

I want this, I want this. Dear God, I want this.

"I'm late, Declan. Two weeks." Tears pricked my eyes but I wouldn't let them fall. I wouldn't let him think this was a bad thing.

I felt the heat of his body as he kneeled down next to me again and my eyes opened.

"I thought you couldn't get pregnant?"

"Pregnant?" Lana gasped and I turned to face her. She handed me the water and the glass shook in my hand.

Declan held it steady for me as I raised it to my lips. The water was a blessing as it poured down my throat. No one spoke as I drank the entirety of the glass and set it on the floor. I'd expected Lana to leave, giving Declan and I some space, but she just stared at me as I kept my eyes to the tile. I was too afraid to look at Declan, too afraid of what I'd see in those eyes.

He lifted my chin with two fingers forcing my attention. The blue color of his irises hadn't faded, the shadows hadn't returned, if anything they were illuminated. "I thought you said—"

"We weren't able to conceive, Declan, and I'd thought it was my fault. He'd said it was my fault."

"Asshole," Lana whispered under her breath and Declan's jaw ticked.

"Lana, I love you but maybe some privacy?" I raised my eyebrows as I looked back at her.

"Oh, my God, I'm sorry. Yes, I'll... um... be in the kitchen." She made a move to leave, but an idea lit her features. "Back left corner, under the sink, pregnancy test..." She shrugged her shoulders. "Had a little scare last month, all is well, no fetus for this girl." She gave me a sideways grin and turned to leave.

Declan's eyes were on the cabinet, his face flat and unreadable.

"Are you angry?" I asked around the lump in my throat.

He tilted his head to the right and palmed my cheek. "Why would I be angry?"

"You can't possibly want this, not now, when you—"

"Don't do that," he interrupted me, dropped his hand, and stood, leaving me cold without his body heat. I rose and my knees felt weak as I met his hard glare. "I feel like I'm seventeen all over again, and you're going to tell me—"

"I want this, Declan." I laced his fingers through mine as I spoke with trembling lips.

"You do?" he asked and his breathing increased.

I nodded.

"You're not worried, about..." He raised our linked hands and pointed to his head, "My illness?"

"No." I shook my head and exhaled a shaky breath in an attempt to stave off the tears. My heart felt unburdened as it all finally clicked into place. "I never conceived with Clark, not because I was beyond redemption, but because I wasn't supposed to. If we've been given the chance... if I'm pregnant, I hope the baby is just like you."

His eyes filled with tears and the muscle in his jaw pulsed as he struggled to speak, "Don't ever say that, don't wish for that."

I released his grip and raised onto my toes, placing my hands on his cheeks. His nostrils flared as he fought back his emotion. "I wish for it, Declan, I do, because then I'd know this child could see it all, see the world just like you."

He leaned his forehead against mine as a few of his tears wet the flesh of my thumbs.

"I want this, too." He breathed the words and, as I closed my eyes, I almost felt hope give way to truth.

I pulled back and said, "Should we check?"

He nodded as his lips pulled up at the corners.

He gave me a moment and left the bathroom. I found the test, opened it, and read the information provided. I did exactly as instructed and left the purple and white stick sitting on the back of the toilet. Declan wasn't pacing the hall like I thought he'd be, he was leaning against the wall, his face without stress, his eyes on mine.

"Three minutes," I said as I wrapped my arms around his waist, placed my ear to his chest, and listened to his heart. His pulse wasn't fast, or apprehensive, it was steady and strong.

He set his hand on the small of my back. "Three minutes," he repeated.

One hundred ninety-five heartbeats later we both entered the bathroom, hand in hand, and smiled at the bold plus sign... at our future.

DECLAN

"I think that's everything," Kieran said as he set one large suitcase onto the floor of my bedroom.

"Thank you." Paige raised to her feet, she'd been kneeling, looking through a box, and gave Kieran a smile. "I could've carried that up the stairs, it's not that heavy." She shifted her gaze to me and narrowed her eyes with a smirk.

"I don't want you to overexert yourself, not until we confirm everything with the doctor." What if she really wasn't supposed to conceive and this was some fluke? She was holding the most precious gift I'd ever receive, and I couldn't help it if I'd become a little overprotective.

Kieran laughed when Paige rolled her eyes at me. "I'm pretty sure I'll be the same way when I have a kid."

"You'll have to actually have sex at some point... you know... to have a baby." Liam's sarcasm came with a lopsided grin as he walked into the room.

Paige blushed and Kieran's smile dropped as he said, "You're a dick."

"Tell me something I don't know." Liam laughed and Kieran shook his head.

"Taking Mom to church, let us know how it goes tomorrow." Kieran gave both Paige and I a hug before he turned to leave. "Go easy on them." He punched Liam in the shoulder just as he walked out of the bedroom door.

"You think that kid could get laid? Twenty-six-year-old virgin... it's not right." Liam eyed me. "And you two... you think you could use a condom, for fuck's sake?"

Paige's eyes went wide with shock and I laughed without humor. "Don't worry, we'll get our own place soon."

Paige had gone pale and I wanted to punch my asshole of a brother.

"Thank you for letting me stay here." Paige's voice was too timid and it pissed me off.

"Don't thank him... he doesn't deserve it."

Liam wouldn't talk to me after I told him Paige was pregnant. He'd finally come around at the shop a few days ago and asked me how I'd felt about everything. I told him the truth... that I was scared, that I wanted this, that I loved her and wanted to do everything right... for her... for my child.

It'd been a little over a week since we'd first found out, and tomorrow we had an appointment with her doctor. The last time I went with her to that clinic it had been to end a life. The past few days the voices stirred, just a few here and there. Paige worried for me, but I'd told her that I was fine, that it was bound to happen every now and then. I wasn't cured, but functioning. And Liam worried about me, too, worried that this baby could ruin my progress, set me back again... but he just didn't have faith. Not in God, not in himself, and certainly not in me. I wrapped my fingers through Paige's and she looked up at me. The panic I'd seen in her eyes faded to a soft powder blue and her cream cheeks stained with pink.

"I actually came in here to tell you guys something." The corner of Liam's mouth twitched. "Ronnie's girlfriend's boss, he's selling the loft above his antique store, just a few blocks down, I put in a bid and they accepted my offer."

A small sound of surprise parted Paige's lips and my stomach turned. "You don't have to move out, you own Avenues, Liam. If it's that big of a burden we'll—"

"I'm not moving out, you guys are, in a month. It will be ready then. The place is huge, three bedrooms, studio space... I thought you guys would like it better without my ass around."

"We can't afford that." My brows furrowed as his smile spread to his eyes.

"I know, but I can."

"Liam?" Paige was breathless. "You don't need to—"

"It's already taken care of. When you guys get on your feet, you can take over the payments. It was dirt cheap, considering the square footage, but it needs a lot of work, Kieran and I can help make it livable."

The pain in my throat was impossible to speak around.

Can't take care of her, not on your own.

"Liam, I..." I shook my head, warding off the voices. I felt that guilt threefold. "I'm not your problem anymore... I can do this, you didn't have to—"

He held up his hand and swallowed. "Our dad was a piece of shit. We didn't get the childhood we should have... I tried... but I'm no father figure, and fuck, I struggle, too, but I want to do this. I have the money. The shop has taken off, you're a partner, so is Kieran, it's *our* money." He stepped toward me and clasped my shoulder. "I know you can take care of your own... but so do I."

I pressed my lips together in order to keep myself in check. Maybe he had faith in me after all. This was too much, but goddammit, I was grateful. Paige squeezed my hand, and

I lowered my gaze from Liam to her. Her irises were sapphire, filled with a hundred facets of unshed tears. "Thank you," she whispered and Liam nodded.

I raised my free hand to his shoulder and gripped it as I said, "I'd be dead without you. I only hope to be as good of a father to this child, as you were for me."

His jaw clenched. "You'll be better." The strain in his voice was evident as I released my hold.

Paige moved quicker than Liam was prepared for. She dropped my hand and wrapped both of her arms around his waist. He stood stiff for a few seconds and then pulled her into a hug. I laughed quietly at the awkward posture of his shoulders. Once she let go, the room went quiet for a moment. The weight on my heart lifted as Liam gave Paige a sideways smile.

"I'm staying at a friend's tonight. Give you guys some privacy, get settled in." He clapped me on the shoulder and turned to leave.

"Liam," I called and he paused. "Thank you."

"Don't thank me yet... you haven't seen the place." He chuckled as he left the room and shut the door.

Paige weaved her arm around my waist. "Our own place," she spoke with reverence.

"I can't believe he did that for us."

"I can't believe he doesn't hate me." She giggled at first, but it was one of those nervous giggles, the kind that eventually breaks into that stomach aching, uncontrollable laughter, and the sound of it, of her... happy, it broke the mood into something different, some brilliant shade of yellow, and it chased the voices from my head as I laughed, too.

The waiting room hadn't changed much, maybe new paint over the years, but the tables were covered in the same types of women's magazines, and the place was still just as packed. The old memory stayed in the recess of my mind as the excitement built in my chest. The couple sitting next to us was talking about baby names, and the older woman across the way smiled as she listened in on their conversation. My hand practically crushed Paige's and she smiled at me when I brought my eyes to hers.

"You need to breathe," she said and raised her right brow.

"What if the test was wrong?" I'd never wanted anything like this... and there was still some small part of me that didn't think I deserved it... deserved her.

"We took three." She bit her bottom lip to subdue her growing grin.

"I know, but—"

"Paige?" The nurse in pink scrubs called her name, and the heat in my chest set fire to the surrounding tissue.

I swore under my breath as she stood with a giggle. "You coming?" she asked and held out her hand.

As I stood, I took her hand in mine, and we walked in silence through the door. The nurse spoke to Paige only, asking her about her last menstrual period, and if she'd had a positive test at home. She penned Paige's answers into the chart and then handed her a cup directing her to the bathroom.

"You can follow me." The nurse held out her arm showing me the way, her pink scrubs were the only welcoming thing about her.

She brought me to a room with an exam table and a large machine with a monitor. She pulled out a paper square and unfolded it setting it on the table. "Have her take everything off from the waist down." She pointed at the paper blanket reciting it as if she'd done this a million times already today. "She can use that to cover up. Dr. Carmichael will be in shortly to start the ultrasound."

She left with a tight professional smile on her face, but not even a minute later Paige came into the room. She scanned my face and her smile pulled wide.

"You look terrified." She laughed as she unbuttoned her jeans and slipped them off along with her underwear handing them to me. Any other time, I would have loved that she was half-naked in front of me, but right now, the excitement had turned to anxiety, and my stomach felt hollow. I rolled up her clothes and stuffed them next to me on the chair.

"I thought I was supposed to tell you to undress from the waist down?"

"The nurse caught me in the hallway," she said as she lifted the cover up and sat on the exam table. She maneuvered the thin, fragile looking material over her legs.

"She was pleasant." My tone fell flat.

"Are you okay?" Her smile dimmed a little as she observed me, looking for that piece of night.

I nodded and the muscle in my jaw pulsed. "I'm nervous."

"Me too."

"What if I screw this up?" I asked.

"You won't." She grinned. "We both know what it's like to have horrible parents."

"I have all this feeling... pent up in my chest, this love for a person I don't even know, an idea... a chance... I want to give this child everything. And that's impossible."

"Give our child all that love, Declan. That feeling in your chest... it's enough... it's everything." She smiled as I let what she said soak into my spine, and I relaxed.

The door opened, and a tall, blonde woman walked in wearing green scrubs. Her smile was genuine as it pulled into a dimple on her left cheek, "I'm Dr. Carmichael, and you must be Paige?"

She shook Paige's hand and then mine. I introduced myself and she explained what was going to happen next. She was going to do an exam first and then the ultrasound. She offered me the opportunity to step out for the exam and I declined as I rose from the chair. I chose to stand next to Paige on her right and wound my hand with hers as she lay back onto the table. The exam was quick, but I assumed not painless for Paige, since she winced a few times. I hated that I was pretty much useless, but at least this time I was there for her.

The doctor lowered the lights and my heart began to hammer.

"I'm guessing from the dates you provided, you're most likely around seven to eight weeks along." Dr. Carmichael smiled at us and I looked at Paige. "I'm hoping you'll get to hear the heartbeat today."

Paige had created a miracle.

"I love you," I whispered as I leaned down and kissed her forehead.

The doctor began the ultrasound and Paige's eyes locked on mine. The room filled with the static of white noise. I kept my eyes on her, the blank buzz squeezed the walls of my heart as I waited... for something... for anything. Paige's lower lip was pinned between her teeth, her blue eyes colored in hope. A soft gallop echoed in the room. Its rhythm was disjointed, fast and irregular, but Paige and I both exhaled, and our lips spread across our faces into huge fucking grins.

Her smile was unending and it fed the beat of my heart, bleeding out the uncertainty. I'd never felt such a clean and clear happiness like this. That smile, it would forever be all I needed to steady my feet on the unleveled ground I walked on every day.

"Huh," Dr. Carmichael murmured to herself.

"Does everything look okay?" Paige asked me and I turned my head to look at the screen.

"I can't tell."

"Can you hear it?" the doctor asked and I shook my head. "There are two heartbeats."

"T-two?" Paige stuttered.

Two...

The air in the room was thin, and made me work for each breath.

"See?" She pointed to the screen. "There are two separate sacs. Each baby will have its own placenta. This is good. We'll have to watch you more carefully, but don't worry too much, this is actually more common than people think."

Paige and I stared at the monitor. Two distinct hearts fluttered on the screen.

"Twins." My voice cracked, and I brought my gaze to Paige's. She gave me a watery smile, and maybe it was just a hallucination, but as I leaned down to kiss her I felt hands on my shoulders. Strong hands that held me in place, kept my weak knees from crumbling, and the warmth from them seeped into my bloodstream pulsing out all of my remaining shadows.

They are yours.

My lips brushed against hers as the doctor turned up the lights in the room. I held Paige's face with my hands and the tears in hers eyes pooled onto her lashes.

They are meant for you.

"Say something." My lips feathered against hers as I spoke and then pulled away.

The perfect curve of her mouth reached higher mirroring my own smile as she said, "We were always meant to have two."

EPILOGUE

DECLAN

The light poured through the floor-to-ceiling windows inside our studio, and even though it had snowed earlier, the sun heated the room with its yellow glow. The sunlight illuminated Paige's hair into strands of gold as she sat with our son, Royal, on one side of the huge piece of white canvas we'd rolled out earlier. The length of it took up almost a quarter of the room. Royal's hands were covered in washable paint. His white blond hair was stained green, and as he squealed, his hands smacked the fabric, swirling the red and green and blue colors together in front of Paige. He sat between her legs, and Indigo sat between mine. My daughter's palette was darker. Indie picked the gray and navy blue paint from the bucket, and instead of smearing her fingers in the blots of color I'd poured for her, she dipped her fingertips into the paint carefully. Using them almost like a brush as she made tiny little dots across the canvas. She giggled, sat back onto her diaper, and turned her head. Indigo's round, pale blue eyes shimmered with flecks of amber as she gave me a toothy smile.

"I think she's the artist." Paige laughed as Royal started to paint himself instead of the cloth.

I chuckled. "He's more abstract."

Paige lifted Royal's hand with hers and placed it palm side down in the paint. Indie stopped what she was doing and watched her mother with an intent face that shouldn't belong to a one year old.

"Like this, baby." Paige took Royal's hand and pressed it gently onto the canvas, creating a perfect handprint. His lips spread into a smile and his light blue eyes widened.

Indie's fingers felt fragile under mine as I showed her how to make her own handprint. I'd never get used to how soft their skin was, or how each breath they took gave me life. Royal looked just like me, and Indie was a carbon copy of Paige. Two people, two souls born on the same day, and yet so different. Royal was a whirlwind, always laughing and smiling, and Indigo... she was more reserved. She'd spoken her first word after Royal, but excelled in other milestones. Paige joked about how she was like me, stuck in her own world, and at times I could see myself in Indie's eyes and instead of fear I felt pride.

My children, our children were gifted to us, and even though each day was different, at any moment shit could fall out from under me. My meds were still working, my head was as clear as it was going to get, and I had my family.

"Da-Da." Royal rose to his feet, and wobbled as he caught his balance.

He walked on unsure legs, stepping in his paint and leaving footprints in his wake as he moved toward me. I held out my arms and he fell into me, smudging Indie's paints, making her cry.

Paige laughed and stood, wiping her hands on her overalls. "Awe, come here, my sad little girl."

Royal traced his fingers across the ink on my chest leaving a trail of paint on my bare skin. "I think we should shower before we head over to Liam's," I suggested and Paige nodded and leaned down to pick up Indie.

I settled Royal onto my left hip and he ran his hands through my hair.

"You're a mess." Paige's eyes creased as she laughed and wiped what I assumed was paint from my forehead.

"This is nothing new." I gave her a lopsided grin and I leaned in and kissed Indie on the nose before raising my gaze to Paige.

Paige's lips naturally parted for me, the rose in her cheeks still burned to a crimson when I gave her my full attention.

I cupped her face with my right hand, my thumb dusting along the length of her cheek, and I kissed her, softly at first, but she tasted like candy canes, and I gave myself over to her control. She kissed me until I groaned, capturing the sound and then pulled away.

I kissed her cheek and brought my lips to her ear and she shivered as I whispered, "Merry Christmas, Paige."

THE END

A LETTER TO THE READER

First, thank you for reading. As always I am grateful for you, and I hope you enjoyed Declan and Paige's story.

I knew when I wrote this book, I'd be riding, for some people, a precarious line of morality. Whether you're pro-choice or pro-life, religious or atheist... it doesn't matter. That's not what this book is about. I wanted to write a story about a mental illness that has affected me, in some ways, personally. I work as a psychiatric nurse, and I see these things. I wanted to give two characters a real life, have them make tough choices, and explore how I could, in the end, have their happiness blot out all of their dark.

Possession has no agenda, has no real stance... it's a fictional story written from my heart.

Depression is real, psychosis is real... if you suffer from anything in this story, I encourage you to seek help. I have such low moments, but then there are brilliant moments, too. I know what it's like to be in *The Bell Jar* and writing this story as much as I enjoyed it, it was an act of therapy, as well.

"You can only come to the morning through the shadows."
J. R. R. Tolkien

If you are in emotional distress or struggling to cope, and are affected by any of the issues covered in this book, please contact:

National Suicide Crisis Line: Call 1-800-2738255

The Samaritans USA 1(800) 273-TALK

The Samaritans UK 08457 90 90 90

ACKNOWLEDGEMENTS

As always, thank you to my readers... You are the support and the very legs I stand on.

My family, you guys are my rock, my foundation, my metaphor for solid things... Love you, Wolverine, and our little cubs.

To my beta team, um, yeah... you rock:

Anna, Laurie, Kelly, Melissa, Marissa, Cornelia, Karlee, Christy, Lucy, Taylor, Hayley, Emma, Lisa, Stephanie A., Mg, Sarah, Michelle, Crystal, Gio, and Simmy. Whether you have to deal with chapter to chapter reads, or second rounds or proofs, you ladies make my work shine, help me emotionally, and keep me sane... even when dieting and I can't have fucking Oreos...

To AJ's Crew (Jo, Jellie, Lisa, Anna, Michelle, Narine, Lacey, Mg, and Lucy) and my IG family, I'd be passed out, covered in tater tots and chewed up Oreo crumbs if it wasn't for you. Big, HUGE... side hugs.

To my editing team, thank you for finding all my errors and making sure my ducks were in a row, and for dealing with my whining.

To Kathleen, your comments keep me sane.

To Sassy Savvy Fabulous, Kristi, thank you for having faith in me and for making me feel relevant.

To my friends... I can't even begin... I don't have the words. You know who you are and you know I love you more than peanut butter M&Ms.

Special Thanks to Hayley Stumbo, Ace Gray, M. Andrews, Danielle Rocco, Linda Oaks, A. Wilding Wells, A. Cramton, Steph Alba, Tali Alexander, Jaci Wheeler, and Jodi Drake, you ladies show true kindness, you give without expectation, and you deserve all the success.

I've probably forgotten someone and will feel like a dick later about it, but please know I love your freaking faces.

As always, if you are in my life, you know I love you. My heart is your heart. A~

PLAYLIST

"Get Hurt" by The Gaslight Anthem
"I Of The Storm" by Of Monsters and Men
"Runaway" by Aurora
"Have Yourself A Merry Little Christmas" by She & Him
"Get On The Road" by Tired Pony
"Sleep" by Azure Ray
"Superstar" by Broods
"Letters From The Sky" by Civil Twilight
"'Till I Collapse" by Eminem
"Jet Black Heart" by 5 Seconds of Summer
"Phenomenal" by Eminem
"i hate u, i love u" by gnash, Olivia O'Brien
"Never Forget You" by Zara Larsson, MNEK
"Clarity" by Andy Lange, Andrew Garcia
"Evergreen" by Broods
"Hate Me" by Blue October
"Just Say Yes" by Snow Patrol
"Don't Deserve You" by Plumb
"Gasoline" by Halsey
"Jesus Christ" by Brand New
"The Resolution" by Jack's Mannequin

"Brick" by Ben Folds Five

"True Colors" by Ane Brun

"Windows" by AWOLNATION

"Love Story" by Yelawolf

"I See Fire" by Jasmine Thompson

"This Love" by Craig Armstrong

"Everybody Hurts" by Jasmine Thompson

"Till The End of Time" by A Boy and His Kite

"Condemnation" by Depeche Mode

"Unsteady" by X Ambassadors

"Silent All These Years" by Tori Amos

"Paralyzed" by NF

"Sane" by Fear of Men

"No Light, No Light" by Florence + The Machine

"Over The Ocean" by Low

"What I've Done" by Marie Digby

"Rescue Me" by Unions

"Pretty Thoughts" by Galmatias, Alina Baraz

"Ocean Eyes" by Billie Eilish

"Crystals" by Of Monsters and Men

"Turning Page" by Noah Guthrie

"Paint" by The Paper Kites

"You Got Me" By The Roots, Erykah Badu

ABOUT THE AUTHOR

A.M. Johnson lives in Utah with her family where she works as a full-time nurse. If she's not busy with her three munchkins, you'll find her buried in a book or behind the keyboard. She loves romance and all things passionate. Amanda enjoys exploring all genres and bringing life to the human experience.

MORE TITLES

Still Life (Forever Still #1)
Still Water (Forever Still #2)
Still Surviving (Forever Still #3)
Now and Forever Still Novella
Sacred Hart

Coming Soon
Kingdom (Avenues Ink #2)

A.M. Johnson writing as
Lillian Bryant
Beneath the Vine

amjohnsonauthor.com

Instagram
@am_johnson_author
www.instagram.com/am_johnson_author
@author_lillian_bryant
www.instagram.com/author_lillian_bryant

Email
a.m.johnson713@gmail.com

Facebook
https://www.facebook.com/AMJOHNSONBOOKS/?fref=ts

Goodreads
https://www.goodreads.com/author/show/1013748.A_M_
Johnson

4621

Made in the USA
San Bernardino, CA
15 June 2017